D0200567

THE PERFECT STAR

THE PERFECT STAR

ROB BUYEA

DELACORTE PRESS

Text copyright © 2019 by Rob Buyea
Jacket art copyright © 2019 by Will Staehle
Interior illustrations copyright © 2019 by Penguin Random House LLC

Visit us on the Web! rhcbooks.com

Educators and librarians, for a variety of teaching tools, visit us at RHTeachersLibrarians.com

Library of Congress Cataloging-in-Publication Data
Name: Buyea, Rob, author.
Title: The perfect star / Rob Buyea.
Description: [New York] : Delacorte Press, [2019] | Summary: "Told from different viewpoints, five eighth-graders who have challenges at home and at school also experience a sad loss as a group and welcome a new addition to their extended family"—Provided by publisher.
Identifiers: LCCN 2018052744 (print) | LCCN 2018057381 (ebook) |
ISBN 978-1-5247-6465-4 (ebook) | ISBN 978-1-5247-6463-0 (trade hc) |
ISBN 978-1-5247-6464-7 (library binding)
Subjects: CYAC: Interpersonal relations—Fiction. | Middle schools—Fiction. |
Schools—Fiction. | Loss (Psychology)—Fiction.
Classification: LCC PZ7.B98316 (ebook) | LCC PZ7.B98316 Pex 2019 (print) |
DDC [Fic]—dc23

The text of this book is set in 11-point Amassis.
Interior design by Trish Parcell
Interior illustrations created by Leslie Mechanic

Printed in the United States of America
10 9 8 7 6 5 4 3 2 1
First Edition

For Wendy—

the first person I ever remember

talking to me about books

1

SUMMERTIME BLUES

GAVIN

I'd said it before and I would say it again, babies popped out looking uglier than a linebacker, but for some, that ugliness turned into cuteness by the time the toddler phase rolled around. It was a fact. Once you got 'em past the poopy diapers stage, the baby started looking and smelling better. What made me the expert on this stuff? My little sister, Meggie.

Megs was good and ugly in the beginning, but nowadays it didn't matter where we were: as soon as people saw her, the "oohs" and "awws" would start. And that was always followed by, "She's so cute." I would just laugh. If these people only knew that my precious little sister was the same cutie-pie who'd tried to eat cigarette butts off the ground in the Foodland parking lot—granted, that was when she was three, but still. And it wasn't long ago that Megs needed help wiping her butt and a reminder to wash her hands after using the bathroom. She was also the same peanut who shared her bed with our very large and slobbery bullmastiff, Otis. By morning she would have a mouth full of Otis hair and a soaking wet pillowcase, but she didn't care, and neither did the rest of the world, 'cause here was the other thing about Megs: she was a little person with a great big vocabulary. She was only going into first grade, but she liked using grown-up words when she talked, and that just made her cute card even stronger. It was her whole package that gave her the superpower ability to melt hearts—and we were gonna need all of that to save our family this time around.

I was firing another pass through my trusty tire target when Meggie yelled, "Gavvy, Daddy needs your assistance!" *Assistance?* See what I mean? She scared me pretty good by yelling like that when I wasn't ready for it, so my throw sailed high. It was the first pass I'd missed all afternoon. Blockhead Otis ran and snatched my football and raced around with it in his mouth.

"Drop it!" I shouted. Fat chance. I had to go and grab one of his tennis balls from near the porch, and then he came bounding over and dropped my football. The stupid dog was smart enough to know I'd throw his tennis ball for him all day long if he captured my football first, so who was the dumb one? I chucked his ball across the yard, and he tore after it. Then I turned to Megs, ready to yell at her for scaring me like that, but instead I burst out laughing. She had grease and dirt smeared across her upper lip.

"What?" she whined.

"Nothing." I wasn't gonna tell her. Cute or not, she was still my little sister. "What's Dad need help with?" I asked.

She shrugged. "He didn't say."

I picked up my football and wiped it clean on my quarterbacking towel. "Let's go see."

We walked around the side of the house, and I saw that Dad had the jack slid under the front of Mom's car. "You're gonna be drivin' before we know it," he said. "Figure it's time you learned how to change a flat. Not everything can be about football, you know."

"I know," I said, even though football was all I could think about these days. Preseason would be starting soon—I hoped. The school still hadn't hired a new coach.

Dad got down and showed me where he'd positioned the jack under the car and how he'd stuck a block of wood behind the back tire to keep it from rolling. "Safety first," he emphasized. "Always, safety first."

I nodded.

He handed me a screwdriver and the lug wrench. "Pop the hubcap and loosen the lug nuts," he said. "Then jack her up and take the wheel off."

It took all the horsepower I could muster to loosen a few of those nuts, but I got it. Then I raised the car, pulled the flat off, and slid the new tire on. Dad showed me how to give everything a final tightening after we had the car back on the ground, 'cause that kept the wheel from spinning when you

cranked on the wrench, same reason why he'd had me loosen the lug nuts before jacking it up.

"Margaret," Dad said. "You see this?" He pointed to a small puddle by the side of the car. "You want to make sure Otis doesn't go drinkin' puddles that are near vehicles, like this is. If it's the wrong stuff, it could kill him."

"Okay, Daddy," Meggie said, her eyes big.

"I do a good job of makin' sure there's nothin' bad out here, 'cause I don't want any accidents, but it's good for you to be payin' attention, too."

She nodded some more. Too bad that wasn't the only thing we had to be careful of when it came to Otis and accidents.

"*Mija,* can you come inside for a minute?" Mom called from the front porch.

"Coming," Meggie yelled. "C'mon, Otis. Mommy requests our company."

Me and Dad chuckled as the partners in crime ran off. Then Dad turned and tossed me the keys. "Time to take her for a test drive, don'tcha think?"

He hopped in on the passenger's side, and I stood there. He rolled down his window. "Let's go."

"You're serious?"

"Yes! My old man had me drivin' when I was your age. Now c'mon, 'fore your mother stops us."

My mother had gotten in trouble for driving without a license, and now Dad was telling me to do it. My eyes popped in disbelief, but I didn't waste another second. I hopped in behind the wheel and stuck the key he'd handed to me in the ignition— but that was as far as I got. I couldn't get the key to turn.

4

Dad started cracking up. I felt my face growing red. I tried again. Nothing.

"This car can be finicky," he said. "Give the steering wheel a yank and try her again."

I'm so stupid, I thought. I did what he said and turned the key, and the engine came to life.

"Now push the brake in and put the car in drive," Dad coached.

I did.

"Ease off the brake."

I did, and we crept forward.

"Give it some gas, big shot," he encouraged.

I gave it too much, and we shot forward like a lineman firing out of his stance. That startled me, so I mashed the brakes, and we slammed to a stop.

"You tryin' to make me a human milkshake?" Dad said. "Go easy with the pedals. You don't need to stomp on them." He chuckled.

I took a deep breath like before a big play and tried again, and this time I did better. Dad had me drive around the hills. We stuck to the back roads, so we didn't see any other cars, which was good 'cause I didn't know what I'd do if that happened. I woulda driven by Randi's house so I could show off, but she was busy training for gymnastics. She had a big event coming up, so she was putting in extra time.

I did a pretty good job driving for my first time behind the wheel—until we got back home. I forgot to slow down before pulling into our driveway. I took the turn so fast, Mom's car came up on two wheels. I yanked the steering wheel and mashed the brakes again, and we slammed to another instant stop. I put the car in park and sat there shaking, but Dad burst out laughing, which made me feel better.

"Well, you've got some improvin' to do, but not bad," he said.

I turned the engine off and handed him the keys. That was enough for one day. Little did I know how important this early training would be for later.

Randi

The way seventh grade had ended had been terrific. I really couldn't have asked for anything more. We had Mrs. Woods and Mrs. Magenta together again, Mrs. Davids was home, and then I finished the year off by winning the gymnastics all-around title at Regionals.

The hug Mom and I shared when I met her on my way into the awards area was one of extreme happiness mixed with relief. After years of hard work, I was finally regional champ. "I'm so proud of you, honey," she said into my ear, squeezing me tighter. "You were amazing today."

"Thanks, Mom."

Coach Andrea and Mom hugged next. Then a man I hadn't noticed before stepped forward. "Congratulations, Andrea."

"Thank you, Jacob," she replied.

Jacob? Wait. What?

The man turned to face me. "Randi, this is Jacob," Mom said.

This is Jacob, I repeated in my head. *The man Mom has been talking to since Coach Andrea introduced them last year, and the man she went to see during April break. This is Jacob? The man Mom has feelings for?* He offered me his hand, and I shook it. He was tall—and good-looking.

"Congratulations, Randi. You were wonderful out there. Your floor routine was beautiful," he said.

"Thank you."

"Next up is the USA Summer Showcase," Coach Andrea said. "You qualified with your scores today."

I smiled. I'd had no idea.

"I'd love to have you come and spend time training at my gym," Jacob said. "We have a group of top-notch athletes getting ready for the event, and I know you'd thrive in that atmosphere."

"That sounds great," I said, because I didn't know what else to say. He'd caught me off guard. From what Mom had told me, I knew that Jacob owned a big gym, and I had loved training with other serious gymnasts at camp last year, but deep down I wasn't sure I liked his idea. I didn't like the way Mom was looking at him, either. Was she falling for this man?

Mom beamed. She grasped Jacob's hand, and he kissed her on the cheek. Then the four of us stood there, staring at each other.

"C'mon, Randi. We'd better get you to the athlete area," Coach Andrea said, saving me from an uncomfortable situation. She gave me a gentle nudge in the small of my back, and we started walking.

"See you after, honey," Mom said.

"Nice meeting you, Randi," Jacob said.

"You too," I replied.

But had it been nice? "Concerning" was more like it.

Fast forward just a few weeks, and all of a sudden I was inside Jacob's gym—Svetlana's. Mom had really wanted us to come, and Coach Andrea had agreed that it would be good for me. I wasn't sure I believed that, but I hadn't put up a fight.

Svetlana's was a gorgeous gym. There was way more space and equipment than in my home gym. Coach Barbara and Coach Linda introduced themselves as soon as I got there and said they were happy to have me joining them. The other gymnasts were all very nice, too. We were competing in different divisions at the showcase, so it was a friendly and supportive environment. Coach Linda put some music on, and we got started warming up—and all was good.

After stretching, we began working on floor. We drilled cartwheels and roundoffs, front and back handsprings, and front and back tucks to loosen up, and then we took turns running through our tumbling passes. I watched a couple of girls hit high-flying and acrobatic passes and felt myself getting excited. The energy in the gym was incredible. My competitive juices were flowing. When it was my turn, I soared. I nailed my pass. And I did it again. And again. I felt great.

"Randi, that's got a perfect ten written all over it," Coach Linda said.

I smiled and high-fived with a couple of girls.

Next up, the coaches had us rehearsing our dance and leap passes. I hit a few routine straddle jumps. Then I did a sissonne and ran into my switch full.

Pop!

The moment my lead leg came down onto the mat, I felt it. My knee disappeared from under me, and I crumbled. I lay in a heap on the mat, clutching at the burning and throbbing pain shooting through my body.

It hurt—but I was more scared than I was in pain. I knew it was bad.

Natalie Kurtsman
ASPIRING LAWYER
Kurtsman Law Offices

BRIEF #1
Summer:A Case of Things Coming in Threes:
A Letter, a Talk, a Text

Unlike the big-announcement letters that had arrived closer
to the start of school the previous two summers, this one
came early. It was addressed to Mother and Father, but I was
allowed to open it, since it was from Lake View Middle; that
was our rule. I waited until I was at the law office, and then I
found a chair in the conference room and began reading.

Dear Eighth-Grade Parents & Guardians:

*I hope this letter finds you well and that you've been able
to enjoy the beautiful weather and time with your children.
I don't want to rush away the summer, but I have news
to share.*

The eighth-grade teachers and administration have been in search of something special for our students, and we believe we've found it. We'd like to send our eighth graders to Nature's Learning Lab this fall. Nature's Learning Lab is an overnight, outdoor-education experience roughly two hours northwest of here. This opportunity would enrich our curriculum and provide a wonderful community-building component. Students would live and learn together and gain a new appreciation for and perspective on our world and their place in it. We would leave school on a Monday morning and return the following Friday afternoon. You can read more about the facility and the experience on their website, www.natureslearninglab.org.

We are in the early stages of the planning process, but before getting too far into the details, we'd first like to gather your feedback. We ask that by the end of next week you kindly complete the short survey that can be found on our school website. Essentially, we need to know how many of our students would like to participate in this adventure.

Thank you for your time and your continued support of our children's education.

Go Warriors!
Albert Allen (principal)
and the eighth-grade team

An overnight outdoor learning experience? What did that mean? Was I supposed to sleep in a tent? Preposterous!

Completely out of the question. If that were the case, Mother could inform Mr. Allen that I would not be attending.

I grabbed the letter and marched directly into her office. I could see that she was busy, buried in work behind her computer, but there was no time to waste. "Mother, I'm sorry to interrupt, but something came from school that I need you to read."

"Is it about Nature's Learning Lab?"

My brow furrowed. "Yes," I replied. "How did you know?"

"The letter was sent electronically as well."

"And you didn't tell me?"

"I meant to, but then I got busy and forgot. I'm sorry."

"What about the survey? Did you complete that?" I asked.

"Already taken care of."

"Mother! Without consulting me! How did you respond?"

"I said you'd go."

"Mother! How could you? I might have to sleep in a tent!"

Finally, she stopped what she was doing and looked at me. "So?"

"So!" I shrieked.

"It will be good for you."

"Good for me! I'm not talking to you for the rest of the day. I can't believe you didn't consider asking me first. Now you can send Mr. Allen an email explaining your mistake, because I'm. Not. Going." I spun around and stamped out her door.

I heard Mother sigh, but she didn't try to stop me; she knew not to mess with me when I got into one of my moods—and I was in a mood.

Needless to say, I left the office with much on my mind that

afternoon. I hated to bother Randi when she was away training, but I sent her a quick text: Need to talk.

It wasn't surprising that I struggled to fall asleep that night.
I had the dread of Nature's Learning Lab haunting me, and as
if that weren't enough, I received a text just before bed that
put me over the edge—and it wasn't from Randi.

Trevor

My summer was a catch-22. What the heck did that mean? For one, it meant I was glad to be done with early mornings and homework and classes, but without school, I didn't get to see my friends. For two, it meant Mrs. Magenta was spending all her time with her mom and dad and husband now that we had helped fix their family feud—and I couldn't blame her for that—so her community service program wasn't happening. And for three, it meant Mark was around in the beginning, but then he took off on this month-long family vacation seeing relatives, leaving me with nothing to do. I wanted to hang out with everyone—especially Natalie—but I didn't know how to make that happen. How was Natalie supposed to be my girlfriend if I never got to see her? Basically, the catch-22 was, it was great that it was summer, but my summer sucked.

To tell you the truth, I don't know if any of the junk I just mentioned really qualified as a catch-22. You'd have to ask my brother, Brian. He was the one I'd heard use the phrase.

He was reading a book with that title, so he'd started saying it. According to him, *Catch-22* was on some list of the greatest one hundred books of all time, and reading those books had become one of his new goals. His girlfriend, Madison, had encouraged it. Brian and Madison had only been together a few months, but my brother was way better with her in his life. She was a definite keeper, even though the book thing was stupid, but I didn't care—until Brian tried talking to me about the crap he was reading.

"You wasting your time reading that garbage is the catch-22, because it sounds really dumb," I said.

"That's not a catch-22, it's irony," he corrected me.

"It's a catch-22 because you're dumb, then."

Brian laughed.

Thanks to my pathetic summer, I was in no mood to hear him babble about any of his stupid books. Simple as that. But he got my attention when he popped over on his way to work one night and mentioned the beach.

"I'm taking Madison to the beach next Friday. You want to come along with your girlfriend?"

With those few words my summer instantly went from sucky and boring to scary and exciting. Here was my chance, the perk of having an older brother, but what came out of my mouth was, "I don't know."

"You don't know? What do you mean? Natalie's your girlfriend, right?"

"Yeah."

"Then what don't you know?"

"I don't know if she'll come," I admitted.

"Ask her," Brian said, making it sound that easy when it wasn't.

"But we haven't ever gone anywhere as a couple."

"So here's your chance, Romeo. Call and ask her. But don't text her. Got it?"

I nodded.

"Good. I've gotta run. See you later."

"Later."

Brian left, and I stared at my phone. Here was the real catch-22. I finally understood. If I didn't call, I was an idiot. But if I did call, I was still an idiot, because Natalie had made it clear that we were taking our relationship slow, which meant we only talked on the phone on Tuesdays and Thursdays, and it was Wednesday. So I could wait and call her later, but if I did that, I was an idiot, because the longer I waited, the greater the chance was that she'd make plans to do something else. And knowing Natalie, she'd probably want the extra time to prepare. No matter which way you sliced it, I was an idiot. It was an impossible situation—a catch-22.

I wished I had somebody to talk to about this stuff, but Mark was gone, and besides, he was the last person I could talk to about Natalie. I was on my own. After considerable stressing out, I finally decided to suck it up and go for it.

I'll call on three, I told myself. *One. Two. Three.* Nothing. I counted again. Then again. It didn't matter how many times I tried, I wasn't calling. I was too chicken, and that was all there was to it, so I settled for the safer approach—against Brian's advice. I sent her a text. Two texts.

want 2 go 2 the beach w/me next friday

my brother and his gf are going 2

And then I waited for her reply.
The waiting was the hardest part.

Randi

If you train and compete at a high level, injuries are bound to happen. It's almost inevitable. Some would say it's part of the sport. But was it part of my destiny? Or was it a warning?

SCOTT

My little brother, Mickey, needed to get a physical before starting school this year. I didn't want to get dragged along to his appointment, because that would be worse than clothes shopping, so I made a deal with Mom that she would drop me off at the Senior Center to spend the afternoon with Grandpa while she took Mickey. I got Gavin to come with me because we weren't in Mrs. Magenta's program this summer and I was super-bored and missing the Recruits—and also because I knew Gavin would want to see Coach.

"Hi, Gavin," Mom said, greeting him when he got into our van.

"Hi, Mrs. Mason. Hi, Mickey. Hi, Scott," Gavin replied.

Mickey waved, but Gavin and I did a fist bump.

"How's summer going?" Mom asked.

"Pretty good. Just waiting for the school to hire a football coach."

"Yes, I've heard. I'm sure they'll find somebody soon," Mom said.

It didn't take us long to get to the Senior Center from Gavin's house, and that was good because I was starting to have a hard time sitting still. When Mom pulled into the parking lot, I unbuckled my seat belt before she even stopped.

"Have fun at the doctor's," I said.

Mickey stuck his tongue out at us and scowled.

"Gavin, I'm counting on you to keep Scott and his grandfather out of trouble," Mom said.

Gavin chuckled. "Sure thing, Mrs. Mason."

I pulled open the sliding door, and we hopped out and ran inside. We found Grandpa and Coach hanging out in Coach's room just like we'd expected. Mrs. Woods was there, too, which was an extra bonus.

"Hi, everybody," I sang when we walked in.

"Well, hello, gentlemen," Mrs. Woods replied in a cheery voice. "What a nice surprise to see you here."

"Hi, boys," Grandpa said.

Coach didn't bother saying anything. He was busy studying some kind of book.

"What're you doing, Grandpa?" I asked.

"Oh, nothing really. Just sitting here with my cat, farting around with this crossword puzzle until Coach decides it's time for our chess match."

I walked over and gave Smoky a scratch behind the ears, and his purring motor fired up. He loved a scratch behind the ears almost as much as he loved Grandpa's lap.

"What's Coach looking at?" Gavin asked Grandpa.

"Pearl brought him an old scrapbook today to exercise his memory."

"How's he doing?" Gavin whispered.

Grandpa shrugged and tried smiling, but it was a smile that said, *Not the greatest.* We watched Coach. Mrs. Woods was sitting next to him so that she could remind his memory when he needed it. I wondered if she'd been helping him a lot.

"Go have a peek," Grandpa said.

Gavin and I crept closer and saw the newspaper clippings, photographs, ticket stubs, and other things stuck on those pages.

"What's this?" Coach asked.

Mrs. Woods looked. "That's from a long time ago when you took me to a concert at the beach," she reminded him.

Coach flipped the page over. His face scrunched. "Who's that?" he asked, pointing to an old snapshot.

"That's you with your first football captains."

"Wow, that's Coach?" I shouted. "He's so young. Look at all that hair!"

Coach glanced up at Gavin and me and then turned back to his book.

Mrs. Woods chuckled. "Any word from the school about a new football coach yet?" she asked us.

"No, not yet," Gavin mumbled. "If we don't hire someone soon, we're gonna be in danger of missing preseason camp."

"We did get a letter about the eighth grade maybe going to a sleepaway camp!" I exclaimed. "An outdoor-education place. I hope we go."

"Sleepaway camp?" Grandpa repeated. "You let me know about that, because I've got a few tricks I can show you ahead of time."

"Mom said not to tell you because you'd say that."

"You didn't tell me. You told Mrs. Woods. I just happened to hear."

I grinned.

"You boys don't need to keep standing there," Mrs. Woods said. "Pull up a chair."

Gavin did, but I decided to get the chessboard and challenge Grandpa to a match since Coach wasn't playing. It was fun trying to outwit Grandpa, and it was also fun listening to Mrs. Woods talk about the different pictures and clippings even when I couldn't see them. I just wished Coach were the one doing more of the talking. I liked when he told his stories.

"How are the rest of the Recruits?" Mrs. Woods asked after they'd finished with the scrapbook.

"Mark's gone on some sorta family vacation, and I haven't heard much from Trevor or Kurtsman," Gavin said. "And Randi's away training for a big summer showcase at some guy's gym her mom knows."

"I didn't know that," I exclaimed.

"That's exciting," Mrs. Woods said. She patted Gavin's knee. "You boys hang in there. You'll have a coach soon. You mark my words."

Mrs. Woods got up then and walked over to her bag. "Now, one more thing," she said. "I've been waiting to give you these." She handed each of us a book.

Gavin got *From the Mixed-Up Files of Mrs. Basil E. Frankweiler*. Mrs. Woods told him it would be a good one to read with Meggie, and I agreed. I'd read it and loved it. It was about a brother and sister running away together. My book was called *Chasing Space*. It was an autobiography by Leland

Melvin, a football player turned astronaut. That seemed like a good combination, so I knew it was going to be a good book.

"Thank you," we said.

I sure liked leaving with presents that afternoon, but I would've felt better if Coach had at least talked to us a little. Gavin said the same thing.

Randi

Jacob did everything he could to make it better—but making it better was impossible. Still, he tried—and I noticed, even if I didn't say anything. He helped me onto a bench in their training room and grabbed me some ice.

"How bad is it?" Mom kept asking.

Jacob continued to reassure her, so I didn't have to answer. He got Mom a coffee and calmed her down, and then he made a phone call to his sports doctor friend. Because it was Jacob, they pulled some strings at the office and got me in that afternoon, so I didn't have to go to the emergency room.

Dr. Pierce was nice but not overly sympathetic, and that was good, because I wanted answers, not condolences. Mom was the one who needed the shoulder to cry on, and lucky for her, Jacob was there. Dr. Pierce ordered X-rays so that he could rule out the possibility of a fracture—there wasn't one—and then he fit me with a knee brace and gave me a pair of crutches.

"I was able to get you scheduled for an MRI tomorrow," he said. "After I get the results, we'll make a plan."

"Thank you," Mom said.

Jacob shook Dr. Pierce's hand. "Thanks, buddy."

Dr. Pierce nodded. "I'll be in touch soon."

I grabbed my stupid crutches and hobbled out of the room.

The results came back two days later. As expected, the MRI showed that I had torn my anterior cruciate ligament—the ACL. I remembered Gav talking about an ACL injury after some famous football player had hurt his knee. I'd never thought I'd be the one dealing with the same thing.

My ligament had snapped when I'd landed my switch full—a landing I'd done hundreds of times, maybe even thousands. Just when I'd been coming into my own, gymnastics—the only thing I was really good at—had been taken from me.

Why?

Why?

2

BICEPS AND
BUTT CHEEKS

GAVIN

I was out back throwing passes when a car pulled into our driveway. The instant Otis heard it, he tore around the side of our house, barking like a maniac. That was how he greeted guests. He did it every time. Dad called him a built-in security system.

I fired one last bullet through my tire target, then scooped up my football and jogged out front to see who it was. The barking stopped before I got out there. I knew then that something was wrong, 'cause Otis never stopped like that. I broke into a sprint. When I came around the corner, I saw Otis lying on his belly near Randi's side of the car. He looked at me and whimpered.

Ms. Cunningham got out and walked around to the passenger's side. She opened the door and took the crutches from Randi. I watched my best friend climb out of the car. Her right leg was wrapped in a big black brace. I'd seen enough football injuries to know it was her knee.

Randi grasped the crutches and stood. Otis got up then and

crept closer and sniffed her leg. He gave her brace a couple of slobbery kisses, and that made Randi chuckle. She patted his head and looked up at me.

I didn't bother asking her what had happened or if she was okay. I asked what mattered most to her right then. "How long are you out?"

"For the season." Her voice cracked. "I have surgery in two weeks."

I dropped the football, stepped closer, and hugged her. Randi broke down, sobbing into my shoulder. No one's strong enough to hold that kind of hurt and disappointment inside forever. "I'm sorry," I whispered. I really was.

"It's okay," she lied. "I'm having the procedure done in New York City with a specialist. Jacob's sports doctor friend got me hooked up with her. She's supposed to be the best, so hopefully that means I'll recover faster."

I saw Ms. Cunningham wiping her eyes, but I didn't see my

sister. I didn't even realize Megs was out there until she spoke. "You'll come back stronger than ever, Randi. You're the best," Meggie said.

Right on cue, Otis let out one of his thunder barks to show his agreement, and we jumped. His bark could wake the dead.

"Thanks, Meggie," Randi said. "And thanks, Otis." She rubbed his head.

"What do you have there?" Ms. Cunningham asked Megs, noticing the craft project she was holding.

"I'm working on a thank-you card for Mrs. Woods. She gave Gavvy a splendid book for us to read, but first we need to finish *James and the Giant Peach*. Right, Gavvy?"

I smiled and nodded.

"That's sweet," Ms. Cunningham said.

"When did you see Mrs. Woods?" Randi asked.

"Me and Scott saw her at the Senior Center."

"She told Gavvy to mark her words, he'd have a football coach soon," Megs said.

"Still no coach? Gav, I'm sorry," Randi said. "Here I am crying about my knee and gymnastics and—"

"You don't need to apologize for being upset about your injury," I said. "You know I understand."

"Don't worry, Randi. Everything will be okay," Megs said.

Otis let out another one of his thunder barks, and everyone jumped again.

Meggie giggled. "C'mon, Otis. We need to go and finish our card." She gave Randi a hug and skipped off with her dog.

"She's the cutest thing in the world," Ms. Cunningham said, watching my little sister go.

Melting hearts, I thought.

"You should call Kurtsman," I told Randi. "She'll want to know about your knee."

"I know. She texted me last week, and I never replied. Wasn't feeling up to it."

"I'm going to the Senior Center with Scott on Wednesday. You two should come with us. Mrs. Woods was asking about you."

Randi shrugged. "Maybe."

I wasn't gonna push it, but I hoped she would decide to come. Sitting around was only gonna make her sadder.

After she left, I went back to throwing passes. Knowing that my best friend couldn't compete made me want to train even harder. The only thing that could slow me down now was not having a coach.

BRIEF #2
Summer: Shortcomings

The instant I saw Randi's name pop up on my phone, I felt anger coursing through my veins. It was a good thing I was an expert at maintaining my composure. Otherwise, I might've said some things I would have been certain to regret—and there was plenty I wanted to say, like, *Nice of you to finally call.* I hadn't heard boo from her since I'd sent my text, but maybe there was an explanation for her shortcomings as a friend. It wasn't easy, but I was able to remind myself that she was innocent until proven guilty.

I answered her call. "Hello."

I waited. The guilty always blabber—Randi didn't.

"Hello," I said again. "Randi?"

"Hi," she croaked, her voice fragile and barely above a whisper.

"What's wrong?"

She filled me in. I felt terrible—for her, but also because I suddenly realized that I was the one who'd come up short as a friend. Never once had I stopped to consider the possibility that something had gone wrong. I had assumed that her no response was because gymnastics was more important than me, which would've been fair, since the sport had been a part of her life for much longer than I had, but it had still hurt. I'd let jealously play tricks on me and fool my better judgment. The one piece of good news was that Randi actually sounded okay—or at least as okay as one could be in her position. I imagined she had already spilled a lot of tears by the time we talked.

"I'm sorry I haven't texted you back," she said after explaining everything.

"It's okay." I meant that.

"What did you need to talk to me about?"

I tensed. "Oh, nothing. Never mind." I couldn't bring myself to say it. Not when my problems paled in comparison to hers.

"Okay. Well, I guess I'll let you go, then."

"Randi, was there something else?" I asked. Not only was I skilled at reading body language, but I could also pick up on clues in a person's voice—and there was something else.

"No, not really," she said. "Just . . . I saw Gav, and he mentioned going to the Senior Center with Scott on Wednesday. He asked if we'd join them. I guess Mrs. Woods was asking about us. He said Mrs. Mason can give us a ride."

"Let's go."

"I don't know if I'm up for it, but you should go," she mumbled.

"No, we're going," I insisted. "It'll be fun." I was beginning to hear the sadness in Randi's voice, and I wanted to do something to cheer her up. Eddie and Agnes always made us smile.

"Okay." She sighed.

"Great. I'll let Mrs. Mason know. See you soon," I said. I ended our call and sat there thinking about how I wished that accepting Trevor's invitation to the beach could be that easy, but it wasn't. Intellectually, I understood I was being silly, but I couldn't get my nerves to comprehend that. I was agonizing over the whole situation. I still hadn't responded to his text from the previous week, and I had ignored his phone call the following day. I was such a hypocrite. I resolved to send him a message after I got back from the Senior Center. I hoped by then I'd know what to say.

Randi

Gav and Scott ran off to Coach's room while Natalie and I set out to find Agnes and Eddie. Surprisingly, they weren't in the Community Hall. It took us a few minutes because I wasn't very fast on crutches, but we finally tracked them down in the Community Theater.

"Randi! Good heavens!" Agnes exclaimed. "What happened, child? Are you okay?"

I hobbled to a nearby chair. "I tore my ACL at gymnastics," I explained.

"That sport is too dangerous. That's all there is to it," Agnes complained. "Jumping and flipping on skinny boards, and all that flying and twisting through the air that you do. It's no wonder you hurt yourself."

"Oh, Agnes. Don't go getting your panties in a bunch," Eddie countered. "Randi is plenty tough for that sport."

"I know she's tough," Agnes snapped. "But 'that sport' is dangerous."

"She's going to heal. Isn't that right?" Eddie said, turning to me.

"Of course she is," Agnes agreed. "I have no doubt about that."

"I'm going to try," I said.

"You just take your time and make sure you're all better before you go back to that flipping-and-flying-through-the-air business," Agnes ordered.

I blinked my eyes shut so that they wouldn't see me rolling them.

"She's right about that," Eddie agreed. "Don't rush it, or you'll get hurt again."

I let out a quiet sigh and nodded. I never knew you inherited so many coaches by getting injured.

Being the pro that she was at picking up on body language, Natalie jumped in and changed the subject from gymnastics. "We were surprised to find the two of you in here and not out in the Community Hall," she said.

"Agnes and I just got done watching *Days of Our Lives*."

"You watch that stuff?" Natalie asked, incredulous.

"You betcha," Eddie replied. "It's our daily soap opera. The smut keeps us young."

Agnes huffed. "The girls don't need to hear that, Edna."

Eddie mimicked her in a high-pitched voice, and I almost laughed. Poor Agnes. Natalie couldn't keep from giggling.

"Ever since your boyfriend and his buddy revamped this joint, it's been getting more and more use," Eddie told Natalie. "Matter of fact, Mrs. Woods and the old boys will be joining us soon so that we can watch *Judge Judy* together."

"*Judge Judy*!" Natalie shrieked.

"Yes," Agnes replied. "A lawyer girl like yourself oughta watch it. Might help you in your training."

"That show is more outrageous than your soap opera," Natalie said.

Agnes and Eddie laughed. "You're probably right about that," Agnes agreed.

"So how is that boyfriend of yours, anyway?" Eddie pressed Natalie.

"Trevor's not my boyfriend," she responded.

Whatever, I wanted to say. Not even the best lawyer could've made us believe that.

"What does that even mean anyway, 'boyfriend'?" Natalie said. "Does that mean I'm obligated to go places with him? Does that mean I have to act a certain way? Because that's not happening."

"Uh-oh," Eddie said. "We've struck a nerve. You'd better tell us what's wrong so the old pro here"—she pointed to herself—"can give you some advice."

Natalie hesitated, then looked at me.

I shrugged.

"You can tell us," Agnes encouraged her. "Girls need to be able to talk about this stuff with each other."

Natalie sighed. "Maybe it's time to spill my case so the jury can deliberate and give me a decision. Who knows, perhaps you can help me with my conundrum."

"Stop trying to convince yourself and just tell us," Eddie said.

Natalie took a deep breath and spit it out. "Trevor has invited me to go to the beach."

"Just the two of you?" Eddie asked.

"No, we'd go with his brother and his girlfriend." She sank down in her chair.

"That's it? That's what's got you in a tizzy?" Eddie said, which was exactly what I was thinking. "He's asked you to the beach, and you don't know what to do?"

"Yes!" Natalie cried. "It'd be the first time Trevor and I would be together without the rest of the Recruits. And if we're with his brother and his girlfriend, then there's going to be all kinds of pressure to be all boyfriendy-girlfriendy, and I'm not ready for that."

"So say no," Agnes said.

"I can't," Natalie confessed. "I don't want to hurt Trevor's feelings, and . . . I want to go."

"There's a simple solution here," Eddie declared. "You need to have a couple of friends go with you. That'll solve everything."

"That's a great idea, except I can't invite others because that would be rude."

"Well, there's got to be a way around that," Agnes said. "That's silly."

"Well, if there is, I'd like to hear it," Natalie snapped, growing frustrated.

What we heard just then instead of a solution to Natalie's problem was a commotion right outside the room. We looked toward the door, and Scott and Gav came racing in.

"I win!" Scott exclaimed.

"You got lucky," Gav teased.

"You ladies ready for our show?" Scott's grandpa hollered, entering the theater next. Coach and Mrs. Woods were right behind him.

"That a football injury?" Coach asked the instant he saw my brace.

"Girls can't play football!" Scott squawked.

"Wrong," Mrs. Woods thundered. "A girl can do anything she puts her mind to, Mr. Mason. And that includes playing football or coaching football."

Scott froze. I wasn't sure if it was Mrs. Woods's tone or her words that had scared him stiff, but he didn't make another peep. It looked like he was holding his breath.

"It's a gymnastics injury," I said, answering Coach's question.

"ACL?" he asked.

I nodded.

"Injury like that, and your recovery is all about attitude. I've seen it. Athletes who've come back even better, and others who never make it back. Valentine and Junior tell me you're the best, so keep fighting. Don't let this get you down."

I swallowed and nodded. Yes, I was sick and tired of everyone trying to give me advice, but it didn't feel that way with Coach. I understood why Gav and Scott loved when he talked to them like they were his players. I glanced at Gav, and he looked so happy. Coach was having one of his better days.

"As I was saying," Eddie said, loud enough for everyone to hear. "I'm sure others will want to go with you, Natalie."

"Go where?" Scott asked.

"To the beach," I was quick to say.

"I want to go," Scott said. "You want to go, Gavin?"

Gav shrugged. "Sure. I'll go."

"Me too," I chimed in.

"Looks like you've got some friends who want to join you,

Natalie, and you didn't even have to ask them," Eddie said. She winked at me, and I smiled—my first real smile since I'd gotten hurt.

"It's time for *Judge Judy*. Quiet now," Agnes barked, shushing us.

That was an important afternoon—for many reasons.

NATALIE KURTSMAN
ASPIRING LAWYER
Kurtsman Law Offices

BRIEF #3
Summer: Case Solved

When I returned home that evening, I responded to Trevor's text like I had promised myself I would, and it wasn't even difficult. I knew what to say.

> Me: Hi. I'd love to go, but Randi and Gavin and Scott want to come, too. Is that okay?

After hitting send, I waited to see if tiny bubbles appeared— and they did. He was replying. Suddenly I got nervous. *Should I have told him that I didn't invite them? What's he going to think? Is he going to be mad at me?*

> Trev: OK gr8t

I let out the breath I'd been holding. *Now what?* I wondered. *Should I say more?*

> Trev: does that mean ur not mad at me

Mad at him? Is that what he'd thought? True, his lack of punctuation and attention to spelling and mechanics when texting irritated me no end, but I wasn't mad at him.

> Me: I was never mad at you.

> Trev: phew 😆

> Me: Sorry I didn't respond sooner.

> Trev: no worries

> Trev: after I talk to my brother I'll text you details about pickup time and stuff

> Trev: sound good

Punctuation! I wanted to scream.

> Me: Sounds good.

I would've underlined the period in my text if I knew how.

Our conversation ended, but the thought of our day at the beach left me feeling giddy. I kept my phone nearby; my nervousness was mixed with excitement—and this was a new kind of excitement for me.

Trevor

I was ready for Brian to get mad when I told him more of my friends wanted to come to the beach, but he didn't, because that meant Dad had to let him borrow the Highlander, and the Highlander was way nicer than his car. We packed our gear in the cargo carrier on the roof, and that left us with seven seats inside the SUV—just enough for Brian and Madison sitting up front, and Natalie, Randi, Gavin, Scott, and me in the back. So what was the problem? Mark. He'd gotten back early from vacation and had texted me, wanting to hang out. I felt bad about ditching him, but I never mentioned the beach. I was nervous enough about being with Natalie. I didn't need him there busting on me . . . so I lied. I told him my mom had made plans for school shopping and I couldn't get out of it. I didn't like lying to him, but if he never found out, it wouldn't matter.

If you want to know the truth, I didn't spend a lot of time worrying about Mark after that. I was too freaked out about Natalie. A week before, the beach had only been an idea. Now it was really happening. How was I supposed to act with her?

The worst was that we had to pick her up, and that meant there was a good chance I was going to see her parents. How was I supposed to act with them? Luckily, they weren't around when we got to her place. It was just Natalie, and that was good, because I wasn't ready for her dad to put me through the boyfriend wringer.

"Hi," I said when she came to the front door.

"Hi."

"Ready?"

"Ready," she said.

She pulled the house door closed, and we walked to the Highlander, but we didn't hold hands or anything like that. I was just hoping we'd move past one-word sentences before the end of the day. We hopped inside the SUV, and Brian headed for Randi's house next. Madison was cool and started talking to Natalie right away. That helped, because I probably would've sat there in awkward silence. Why was this so hard?

"How did you and Brian meet?" Natalie asked.

"We met at the local soup kitchen where we volunteer."

"I didn't know we had a local soup kitchen," I said. "We have homeless people here?"

"Homelessness is a real thing everywhere," Madison said. "You guys should join us sometime."

"I'd like that," Natalie replied.

Did our next couples date just get planned? I wondered.

Natalie looked at me, and I smiled. I didn't know what else to do.

Before we got to Randi's house, Natalie gave us the low-down so that we wouldn't be surprised to see Randi in a knee brace and using crutches, and so we wouldn't bombard her with a million questions. "If Randi brings it up, fine," Natalie said, "but you shouldn't, because she needs a break from everyone interrogating her."

We were cool with that. Madison did more small talk after we had Randi in the car, and then we made our last stop at Scott's. Gavin was there, too, because Meggie was spending the day with Mickey. Once we had everyone, it was on to the beach.

Brian got us there early, so it wasn't crazy-crowded and we were able to claim a good spot. We spread out a blanket and our towels, set up the few chairs we had brought, positioned the coolers and other supplies where we wanted, and got some tunes playing. Brian stuck our umbrella into the sand—and then it was beach time. This was the part I had been worrying about, but I should've known Scott would take care of everything.

He yanked off his T-shirt and threw it on the ground. "Can you put sunscreen on my back?" he asked, handing me his squeeze tube.

Gavin snickered. *Are you kidding me?* I thought. This was the sort of thing I should've been doing for Natalie—not Scott! I squirted a blob onto his shoulder and did a couple of quick circles with my hand to rub it in. Then I glanced around to see if anyone had seen me. What I saw was Madison lying on her towel. I'd never seen my brother's girlfriend like that. In a bikini, I mean. She was smoking hot.

"You guys can put your eyes back into your heads now," Randi whispered.

Gavin and I jerked around. Maybe I didn't know what to do or how to act with Natalie at the beach, but I knew that staring at other girls had to be at the top of the list of what *not* to do.

"Oh my gosh!" Scott cried. "That girl's butt cheeks are showing!"

"Don't point," Gavin hissed, knocking Scott's arm down. "Next thing you know, her boyfriend will be over here wanting to beat us up."

"You should see if she needs help putting sunscreen on those," Brian teased.

Madison punched him in the arm for that comment, and my brother laughed.

"If you get to stand out here showing off your muscles, then she has the same right to flaunt her parts," Natalie said, "though you'll never catch me wearing something like that."

"My biceps and her butt cheeks aren't the same," Scott said, flexing his arms. "See?"

Everyone laughed, including Natalie, because we did see. Nothing on Scott resembled muscles. He had a point.

"Last one in's a rotten egg!" biceps boy yelled, racing toward the water.

Gavin and I looked at each other and bolted after him. Scott beat us, so we dunked him. When he came back up, we dunked him again for good measure. Tough love. We stayed in the water swimming and horsing around while the girls stuck to reading and tanning on the sand. I kept stealing glances at Natalie because she was rocking it in her swimsuit.

"I'm hungry," Scott announced after he'd had enough fun in the water.

Gavin and I didn't care, so we followed him and rejoined the others. Brian helped me pull out the fruit and chips, and we hung out chilling and snacking. When Scott had had his fill, he decided it was time for a game of beanbag toss. All the worrying I'd done about what to do at the beach had been for nothing. I had Scott to show me the way.

Beanbag toss turned out to be a great idea because that put me standing next to Natalie, just the two of us by our end.

"Sorry I didn't go swimming," she said. "I didn't want to leave Randi sitting all alone."

"It's okay. I'm just glad you came."

"Me too. Thanks for letting everyone else tag along."

"You kidding? I was happy they wanted to come. I was nervous about it being just the two of us."

"You were?"

"I'm not very good at this boyfriend stuff," I admitted.

"You're doing great," she said.

I had never wanted to kiss her more than I did right then, but I didn't dare. No way was I trying that in front of everyone. Did she even want me to kiss her? How are you supposed to know?

"Is it time for s'mores yet?" Scott yelled.

Natalie and I chuckled.

"We've got to build a fire first," Brian said. "We need rocks for the outside and wood to burn. Start collecting."

So that's what we did. Natalie went back with Randi, and I got busy helping Gavin and Scott find rocks and sticks and logs. Brian built a solid fire, and we roasted hot dogs, and marshmallows for s'mores. It was great.

We stayed at the beach until the sun went down, and we might've stayed even longer if the bugs hadn't started snacking on us. It was as close to perfect as you could get—except I was starting to feel bad that Mark wasn't there.

SCOTT

Our day at the beach was some of the most fun I'd ever had with my friends. I did so much swimming and playing games and snacking. All the chips and soda I had were great, but the best was when Trevor's brother made us a bonfire. I ate three hot dogs and four s'mores! My belly was ready to explode, but I felt terrific.

I was so whupped when I finally got home, I fell asleep as soon as my head touched the pillow. I woke up the next morning with sand in my bed and my back killing me from sunburn, but better my back than my butt cheeks. Mom rubbed aloe all over me, and that helped. I scarfed down a bowl of Cocoa Puffs and let Mickey have the prize inside the box, because after a day of fun in the sun I didn't have time for foolishness. I had to get back to work.

Football preseason was right around the corner, and we still didn't have a coach, but I wasn't panicking. Mr. Allen would find someone. In the meantime, I was doing double the studying and preparing so that I could help our new hire make as smooth a transition as possible. I was reviewing our play-book, tweaking plays, deleting others, and adding a few new wrinkles. I even began researching our opponents so that I could get cracking on scouting reports. The more we knew about our competition, the better off we'd be. I scoured school websites and local papers, looking for any news. You'd be surprised how much you can learn from a simple article. Coaches often mention key players and even tip their hand about team strengths and game plans. So far I hadn't come across anything big, but that changed when I fired up the computer and hopped onto the Internet that morning.

The Titans of North Lake were determined to get revenge after we'd spoiled their season last Thanksgiving. They knew we had a skilled quarterback in Gavin Davids, but they felt they had the answer. His name was Brutus Stonebreaker.

Brutus was their new star middle linebacker. He was a transfer, which was something I'd read about earlier in the summer, because it was becoming a hot topic with parents. Some people griped that these transfers were unethical. They said kids were moving to new schools just so they could re-peat eighth grade and delay starting high school. Supporters argued it was so the kids got an extra year of academic ma-turity, but critics claimed it was an evil scheme to make kids bigger, faster, and stronger than their peers so that teams had a better chance at winning and the transfers had a better chance of earning an athletic scholarship.

Judging by Stonebreaker's picture, the bigger, faster, stron-ger thing was definitely true. You could even throw in "uglier." The guy had a full beard, and muscles like the Rock. If he got his hands on Gavin, he might crush him.

"Houston, this is Mother Ship," Mom suddenly announced behind me. "I have news. Over."

I spun around. "Copy that, Mother Ship. What's the news? Over."

Mom stopped pretending. "This came yesterday," she said, handing me the letter. It was from school.

GAVIN

It'd been a long, hot, and tiring day at the beach, but none of that mattered to Megs. We had to read before she could go to sleep. I woulda put up a fight, except we'd finished *James and the Giant Peach* and were moving on to the book Woods had given me. Like always, I was curious why she'd picked it. I wanted to see what the mixed-up files were all about, so even though I was dog-tired, we got into Meggie's bed, and I started reading. We didn't get very far before our eyes closed, but little did we know, we'd begun one of the most important books we would read together.

As much fun as the beach had been, it was double bad when I woke up the next morning. I had a stiff neck and dog hair all over me from spending the night with Megs and Otis, but that was nothing. While I'd been gone having a good time with my friends, one of those fancy-shmanzy letters from school had arrived. I found it on the kitchen counter when I went to get breakfast. I opened it right away.

Dear Gavin,

We regret to inform you that preseason camp has been canceled . . .

There was more after that, about how the school was still hoping to save the season, but it was all a bunch of bull. After everything that had gone down with my family and Coach Holmes last year, nobody wanted anything to do with our football program. The school wasn't gonna find a coach.

My dreams had been dashed again. Me and Randi—in the same boat.

SCOTT

I called Gavin as soon as I got done reading it. "Did you see the letter?"

"Just read it," he said.

"I've got a plan."

"Oh yeah? What?"

"We're going to hire Coach."

"That won't work," he grumbled. "We can't do that."

I wasn't listening. "Don't tell me we can't. My mom's driving us to the Senior Center. We'll pick you up in fifteen minutes." I hung up and went to get dressed. We'd hired Coach once before, and we were going to do it again.

Gavin and I didn't swing by Grandpa's room when we got there. We went straight to Coach's. That's how important this was. But Grandpa was still the first person we saw, because he was hanging out with Coach like he usually did.

"Holy mackerel!" he hollered when he saw me. "You're looking mighty dapper today, Scott. What's the occasion?"

I straightened my bow tie. "We're here on official business," I said. "We need to meet with Coach. Where is he?"

"Mrs. Woods is with him in the bedroom," Grandpa said. "You'd better have a seat."

"How long will they be?"

"I don't know. Grab us the chessboard, and we'll play while you wait."

Patience wasn't my strength, and Grandpa knew that, but there wasn't anything I could do, so I grabbed the board and sat down across from him. Gavin spotted Coach's scrapbook and spent the time thumbing through it again.

Grandpa and I were getting close to finishing our match when Mrs. Woods finally came out.

"How's Coach?" I asked as soon as I saw her.

"Taking a nap," she said.

"Can you wake him up? This is important."

Mrs. Woods shook her head. "No. I'm sorry, Mr. Mason. Coach is not feeling his best, so we need to let him sleep. But maybe I can help you with whatever you need?"

I thought about it for a second, and then I let it out. Even my best hold-your-breath technique wasn't keeping this inside. "We just learned our preseason has been canceled and the school still hasn't found anyone to lead our team. We're here to hire Coach for the position."

Mrs. Woods glanced at Grandpa and Gavin and back at me. "I'm sorry, Mr. Mason, but Coach isn't your guy. You're smart enough to understand why I have to say that, so I'm not going to argue with you about it. That being said, I do have somebody in mind who might be able to help you out. And don't worry, this person would be Coach's pick for the job, too. Let me see what I can do."

"Who is it?" I asked.

"Never mind about that. You just keep studying, Junior. And you keep throwing, Valentine. That's what Coach would tell you." She walked over to the end table and grabbed her purse and car keys.

"Henry, I have a couple of quick errands to run while Coach is napping. Olivia is on her way over, but are you okay to stay here till she arrives or I get back?"

"Sure thing," Grandpa said.

"Thank you."

Mrs. Woods left, and I turned to Gavin. "Who do you think it is?"

He shrugged. I glanced at Grandpa, and he shrugged, too.

"Well, anybody is better than nobody," I said.

"After last season, I don't know if I'd say that," Gavin warned.

I nodded. He was right.

"If this person is someone Coach would pick, then I'm sure they'll be good," Grandpa said.

I nodded harder. That had to be true.

"Mr. Mason, where's Smoky today?" Gavin asked Grandpa.

I'd been so distracted with hiring Coach that I hadn't even noticed that Smoky wasn't on Grandpa's lap.

"He's in with Coach," Grandpa said. "He's been spending more time with him lately."

There couldn't have been a bigger sign, but somehow I missed it.

3

MONKEY
WRENCHES

NATALIE KURTSMAN
ASPIRING LAWYER
Kurtsman Law Offices

BRIEF #4
September: Welcome Back to School

> **monkey wrench** (noun): obstacle; something that
> interferes with plans, schedules

"Monkey wrench" was not a term in my everyday repertoire, though Father had used it a few times in my presence. He maintained it was important that a lawyer be equipped to effectively communicate with all people, which meant that the more flexibility and versatility I had with language, especially slang, the better off I'd be. I was relieved when we didn't encounter any monkey wrenches at the beach. I had a lovely time, and with that adventure safely behind me, I was able to focus my energy on the start of eighth grade.

By now I trust that you know my position: day one of a school year is all about first impressions. However, to be honest, I actually contemplated not arriving extra early this year, because somehow—I hoped by mistake—I'd been assigned to

Mr. Murdoch's homeroom. Mr. Murdoch was our big-bellied and rather smelly PE teacher who only ever wore sweatpants. I'd first met him during sixth grade; he wasn't my favorite, nor was his class, but I decided to give him a chance. I reported early so that he would see I treated homeroom seriously and that I expected the same from him.

"Here's to a great year, Mr. Murdoch," I said, handing him an apple, despite being quite certain he would've preferred a doughnut. Too bad. It was the gesture that mattered—and his cholesterol; I was not about to contribute to his health risks.

"Thank you, Natalie," he replied, whether out of sincerity or obligation, I couldn't be sure, but either way it helped us get off on the right foot, which was another point Father had taught me was important.

I'm pleased to report that Mr. Murdoch's homeroom performance was satisfactory that day. He successfully took attendance, asked about our summers, told a lame joke, and then shared announcements—thereby introducing the monkey wrench. Instead of marching off to our first-period class, we were told to report to the auditorium for a surprise assembly with Mr. Allen. This was atypical and unexpected to say the least, and definitely disrupted my schedule—the exact definition of a monkey wrench.

"What for?" one of the boys asked.

"I don't know, kid. I don't ask questions. I just do what I'm told."

I had hoped to link up with Randi in the hallway; she was one week removed from surgery, and though everything had gone well with her procedure, she was certain to need help. But it was Scott who found me instead. "Natalie," he called, running up and tapping me on the shoulder.

"Hi," I said.

"Any idea what Mr. Allen's got up his sleeve?"

"No," I replied.

"Me neither, but whatever it is, I bet it's great!" Scott loved surprises—not me. I was leery.

We filed into the auditorium and took seats. I glanced around and spotted Randi sitting up front with Gavin. I felt better knowing she wasn't alone. Trevor found Scott and me and joined us.

"Where's Mark?" Scott wanted to know.

Trevor shrugged. I didn't think much of that until Mark walked in and I saw his dejected expression when he spotted Trevor sitting with me and not looking for his best buddy. I knew right then and there that this spelled trouble, but I didn't act on my suspicions.

Once Mr. Allen had the entire eighth grade gathered, he got our attention by speaking into his microphone. "Good morning, eighth graders, and welcome back. I hope you had a fun-filled summer and that you're ready for a terrific school year."

His remarks were met by the predictable mix of cheers and moans and groans, but Mr. Allen didn't let that slow him down. "I've brought you together this morning because I have exciting news to share. News too good to wait on."

"I knew it," Scott whisper-shouted, bouncing in his seat and clapping. "I knew it."

He didn't know anything, but I sensed what was coming.

Mr. Allen waited, and a hush fell over the room. I braced myself.

"Number one," Mr. Allen said. "I'm thrilled to say we received an overwhelming response from your parents in favor of sending you to Nature's Learning Lab this fall. We've already moved ahead and reserved dates. You will be going next month."

The auditorium erupted in cheers and high fives. Scott was on his feet, jumping up and down. I sank down in my chair. Just as I'd feared.

"You okay?" Trevor asked.

I shrugged.

"It's wonderful to see such enthusiasm," Mr. Allen said. "I suspect you'll be even more excited after watching this highlight video about Nature's Learning Lab that we've prepared for you. Sit back and enjoy."

The lights dimmed, and the video commenced. I sat up. *Best to know what I'm getting myself into,* I thought.

I was pleased when I didn't see tents, but bunking in a cabin filled with girls didn't exactly thrill me, either. The scenery was pretty; the mess hall was not, but then again, neither was our cafeteria. All in all, it was good to get a feel for where I'd be going, though I can't say it did much to calm my nerves.

At the conclusion of the video, the auditorium filled with excited whispers. "Your teachers will be sharing additional information with you in the near future," Mr. Allen explained, "but you can start looking forward to this amazing experience."

Continued whispering. I focused on slow, even breaths.

"And now for my second big announcement," Mr. Allen

continued. "After an extensive search, it is with extreme happiness that I can introduce our new head football coach." Immediate silence blanketed the room. "Please put your hands together for our very own Mrs. Magenta."

There was thunderous applause for approximately three claps, and then it abruptly stopped. The room sat paralyzed. *Mrs. Magenta is our new football coach?* I thought, delighted but taken by surprise. Everyone else must've been equally shocked. Everyone except for the one person who was on his feet and still clapping.

"Woo-hoo!" Scott cheered. "Woo-hoo!"

Thanks to Scott, I snapped out of my temporary paralysis and clapped along with him, and soon half of the class had joined us, but their applause was lukewarm at best. Unlike Scott and me, their clapping was out of pity, not genuine excitement.

Mrs. Magenta stepped up beside Mr. Allen, and he handed her the microphone. Perhaps she sensed the less-than-enthusiastic response, or perhaps she was already wearing her coach hat. Whatever the reason, she didn't attempt to make a glorified speech. "Practice today at three o'clock sharp. If you want to play, I'll see you on the field. Don't be late." She passed the microphone back to Mr. Allen and walked off the stage.

I'm not certain if Mr. Allen had planned to end the assembly at that point or if this was an impromptu decision, but that was how he played it. "I wish you all a great year," he said. "You may now report to your second-period classes. Thank you."

The auditorium instantly transformed into a mob pushing

its way toward the exit doors. I held Scott back so that he didn't get trampled.

"A girl football coach. What a joke," I overheard a boy saying.

"We're going to be the laughingstock of the league," another commented.

"This is Mr. Allen's worst idea ever," said a third.

"We're going to get killed," a fourth added.

Scott heard it all. "It's going to be okay," I reassured him.

He spun around. "Of course it is!" he exclaimed. "Mrs. Magenta is Coach's daughter. It doesn't matter that she's a girl. She's got more football knowledge in her pinky than most people have in their whole bodies."

I smiled. Mrs. Woods would have been proud to hear that.

"Too bad not everyone sees it that way," Trevor said, raining on our parade.

"That's okay," Scott said. "I've been studying. I'm ready to help her. We'll show them."

"Natalie," Mr. Allen called, beckoning me to the stage.

"What's he want?" Trevor asked.

"I don't know, but I'd better go and see. I'll talk to you guys later." I walked up to the front of the auditorium. "Hi, Mr. Allen."

"Natalie, I probably don't need to explain this to you, but since Mrs. Magenta will be coaching football, her after-school program won't be running."

"Oh." My posture sagged. "I hadn't stopped to think about that, but yes, that makes sense."

"And I almost forgot. I received a call from Mrs. Woods early this morning. She said to tell you she'll be here immediately after school to meet and get the newspaper up and running. She said the news doesn't wait. You've got to strike while the iron's hot."

I smiled. Of course Mrs. Woods knew there'd be a story to report, since her daughter was taking the football coaching job. "Thanks, Mr. Allen. I'll let the others know."

"I'll swing by. There's something I want to show you," he said.

"Okay. That sounds great."

"Have a good day, Natalie."

"You too."

By "others," I meant Randi. It was clear the boys were going to be busy with Mrs. Magenta—correction: Coach Magenta—so it was only going to be Randi and me, but that was fine because Randi needed something to keep her busy so that she didn't get too depressed. I'm no doctor, but I was acutely aware of what her body language was telling me.

GAVIN

I wanted Magenta to do a good job 'cause I liked her. I wanted her to do a good job 'cause I'd spent all summer throwing passes so we could win. And I really wanted her to do a good job 'cause I was afraid of what people would say and how I would feel if she didn't.

Let me tell you, Coach Magenta put my worrying to bed at our first practice. We were all there when she stepped onto the field and blew her whistle at three o'clock sharp. She pulled the team together and told us to take a knee. Then she got down to business. We listened to her first talk, and it wasn't classroom teacher talk—it was coach talk.

"Gentlemen, we're behind the eight ball. Other teams have already started scrimmaging, and we won't even be in pads for another week. We can spend time whining about that or we can get to work. We're getting to work. If we practice hard and smart—and that's the key, gentlemen, hard and smart—then we'll be ready in time for our first game."

She paused and slowly gazed over us. No one said a word. Her seriousness gave me goose bumps.

"I can stand up here and try to convince you by talking, or I can show you. Get up and give me two laps around the field," she barked. "I'm going to show you."

That was when I realized that Mrs. Magenta and Coach Magenta weren't exactly the same person—and I liked it.

"Let's go, men!" Scott cheered, hopping to his feet.

"Let's go," I echoed, jumping up and taking off. Time to be a leader.

We jogged those two laps, and I swear we never stopped moving after that. Magenta put us through a fast-paced warm-up, and then we went right into agility stations. Scott was running in circles, arranging cones for all the different drills. When Magenta said we were behind and she was going to catch us up, she wasn't kidding. We even worked during our water break.

"Listen up. We need to start putting in plays," she announced. "There's no time to waste. If you were on the team last year, go to the position you played. You can bring the water bottles with you. If you're new to the team this year, then go to the position you'd like to play. Hustle!"

We hurried to our spots.

"Stats Man, we need a depth chart," Magenta instructed.

"On it," Scott replied.

"Make sure Scott gets your name. First and last," Magenta told us. "None of this is permanent or finalized," she explained. "I will be evaluating your play over the course of this week and all season long. If I think you'd be better in a different position or you'd help the team more from a different position, then I'll move you, but in order for us to start putting in plays, we'll go with this for today."

First we learned a new cadence for hiking the ball, and then we put in five plays—three running and two passing. The schemes were simple, which some people mighta thought meant not effective, but I wasn't one of them. I still remembered Coach telling Scott that it wasn't how many plays we had in the arsenal, but how well we executed the ones we did have.

Magenta had us rehearse the five plays over and over, and she had us change up the snap count so that the ball was hiked on one sometimes, on two sometimes, and even on the first sound out of my mouth sometimes. That meant the offense had to be very disciplined not to jump offside, but if we got good at this, then we'd have an advantage over the opposing defenses. They'd never know when we were going to start, and we might be able to trick them into jumping offside in some key situations. This was just what Magenta had been getting at when she'd said we were going to be smart.

Day one with Coach Magenta was the best-run practice I'd ever had. I couldn't wait to get home and tell Mom and Dad and Meggie all about it—and that was something I'd never wanted to do last year. Barring any injuries or major disasters, we were gonna have a great season. I was already a believer in Coach Magenta—but not everyone was.

Trevor

It wasn't until our first water break that I finally got a chance to talk to Mark. I'd missed him at the morning assembly, and he wasn't in any of my classes this trimester, not even lunch, and I hadn't seen him after school because I'd been with Natalie. I'd looked for him before practice but hadn't been able to find him, and then Mrs. Magenta had gotten things going right away. It was weird. It was almost like he was trying to avoid me. But that was crazy. Why would he do that?

"Hey, bro," I said when I finally caught up to him.

"Hey."

That was it. Nothing more, just "hey."

"Haven't seen you all day."

"That's because you're always with your girlfriend. It's been like that ever since I got back from vacation. Even when we hang out, she's all you ever want to talk about."

I was searching for a comeback, but Stats Man didn't give me the chance to say anything.

"Hey, guys!" Scott cheered. "Better drink up. Coach Magenta means business." He handed each of us a cold water bottle. "Not every day can be fun in the sun like we had at the beach, you know," he said, trying to break my chops.

As hot as I was, I felt my blood go cold. Scott smiled his goofy grin and moved on, passing out water to the other guys.

Mark looked at me. Glared at me, was more like it. He tossed his water bottle on the ground and jogged back out to the field. He wasn't supposed to find out about the beach.

I turned to look for Scott. He was scurrying around, picking up the empty bottles and refilling them. He'd only been trying to be funny, but nothing was funny about what had just happened. Scott had no idea how he'd just messed things up for me. I couldn't get mad at him, but I *was* mad— at myself.

Coach Magenta blew her whistle. There was nothing I could do to fix it now. I had to try to make it better after practice. But it only got worse.

When practice was over, I hurried and changed into my regular clothes, and then I waited for Mark just outside the locker room. I didn't want to have this talk in front of the guys, so I was going to stop him when he came out the door. He would have to listen to what I had to say. I needed to explain things. He'd be ripped, but he'd get over it. It wasn't that big a deal.

That was my plan, but before any of that happened, Natalie came around the corner and spotted me. "Hey," she said.

"Hey," I replied.

"So how was your first practice?"

"Good," I said. "Real good. Mrs. Magenta's going to be a great coach."

"Of course she is!" Natalie exclaimed. "I could've told you that, and I don't know anything about football."

I laughed. "What're you still doing here, anyway?"

"I was with Randi and Mrs. Woods. We were getting things organized and ready to go for our newspaper, but we came up with a new idea. Well, Mr. Allen approached us with the idea, actually, but I'm thrilled about it."

"Yeah? What's that?"

"Walk with me to my locker and I'll tell you."

I glanced at the door. Mark had taken too long. I couldn't tell Natalie no. "Okay," I said.

We set off in the direction of her locker, and she began filling me in. "Instead of the newspaper, we're going to launch a broadcast," she said.

"A what?"

"We're going to put together a morning news show and broadcast it over the classroom TVs. We have a space and all of the equipment for it already. Can you believe it?" She wasn't slowing down. She didn't even give me a chance to respond. "Apparently there was a teacher here years ago who purchased everything with plans to use it, but that teacher ended up leaving. The stuff has just been lying around ever since. Some of it was still in boxes. It's never been touched. Mr. Allen happened to find all of it buried in the faculty supply closet a couple of weeks ago when he was rummaging through things, looking for something else."

"A miracle," I teased.

She punched me in the arm. "Don't make fun. I don't care if it was a miracle or dumb luck. I just know we're going to use it."

We stopped at her locker.

"Cool," I said.

Natalie fumbled with her combination, and I peered down the long hall. I caught sight of Mark just as he was turning around. He'd seen us. I watched him shaking his head as he walked away, straight out the exit doors. We always got a ride home together. He left without saying anything. Just ditched me—like I'd done to him on beach day.

"Ready?" Natalie asked, closing her locker and shouldering her backpack.

"Ready," I said—but deep down, I knew I wasn't ready for any of it.

Randi

"How was your first day?" Mom asked when I got into the car.

"Fine," I said, keeping my eyes on the floor.

She stared at me and sighed. "Randi, I know—"

"It was fine, Mom. Everything's fine. Can we go now?"

She put the car in drive. "Fine," she said.

But nothing was fine—and we both knew it. How could it be when I couldn't do anything? I was exhausted from putting on a fake face and fake act for everyone at school, and Mom was paying the price. I felt bad about that—but I felt worse about me and my lousy situation.

I didn't need a football coach or any fancy broadcast show. I needed a new leg.

SCOTT

Natalie and Mrs. Woods had had two great ideas. The first was about our brand-new morning TV show, and the second was about not starting the broadcast until the following week. Natalie had said that she and Randi and Mrs. Woods needed time to get things organized and set up because if we tried meeting now, it'd just be a case of too many cooks in the kitchen. She promised that we'd meet soon to sort out parts and roles and expectations. I was super-excited to start the show because it was going to be awesome, but waiting was a good plan because it gave Coach Magenta and the guys and me a chance to focus on football—which was easier said than done.

The team had just started stretching, and I was reviewing our depth chart when Mr. Allen came jogging out onto the field. It had to be urgent because he didn't even stop to say hi to me. He went straight to Coach Magenta. I slid closer and did my best eavesdropping.

"Olivia, we have people going directly to the superintendent, calling for your resignation. There are fathers claiming it isn't safe because you can't teach proper techniques, and mothers are concerned the boys won't listen to you. The Lake View High coach is among the protesters. He fears that having you as the middle-school coach will deter kids from playing and ultimately kill his varsity program."

"That's not true!" I blurted. "We haven't lost a single player. Everyone who signed up is still here."

"Scott! I didn't realize you were listening," Mr. Allen said.

"I was listening, and it's not fair. They haven't even given Coach Magenta a chance," I argued.

"Mr. Allen, I wasn't looking to do this," Mrs. Magenta said. "You came to me after my mother went to see you, remember? Nobody wanted this job after last year. As a matter of fact, I seem to recall that I turned down your offer, but you begged me. I told you there would be backlash, and you said you'd stand by me."

"I know. I am. I will," Mr. Allen sputtered.

"Good. Because I'm not stepping down. If I do, then you'll have no choice but to cancel the season, and I'm not going to let that happen. It's not fair to these boys."

"That's right," I said. "We're going to show—"

"Oh my God," Mr. Allen said, gazing beyond me into the distance. "What now?"

I turned and looked. Walking toward us from across the field were reporters and cameramen from WGBTV Channel 13 News, ARDTV Channel 5 News, BSZTV Channel 7 News, and NESTV Channel 3 News. It said so on all their jackets and video cameras. We were going to be famous!

"I'd better go see what these people want," Mr. Allen said.

"You can tell them I'd be happy to talk after practice, but not until then," Coach Magenta said. "The boys and I have work to do." She blew her whistle and got things under way.

Same as day one, Coach Magenta kept the guys hustling. She put them through agility stations again, plus a few new drills, and then we ran through our plays and added four more. We finished with defensive work and schemes, and then conditioning.

We got through a lot, but it wasn't our best practice. The team was too distracted. Too many of the guys kept jockeying to get in front of the camera. Even Gavin was trying too hard on his throws, wanting to look impressive. The TV crews stayed and filmed our entire practice, but no station aired more than sixty seconds of it on their show that night. Coach Magenta was on the screen the longest. She was the story because she was the first female football coach in our state's history. I thought that was awesome, but not everyone agreed.

There was also footage of the TV reporters interviewing a few of the protesters Mr. Allen had mentioned.

"Women should coach girls' sports," some lady said.

"You can't coach something you've never played," a man argued.

"This is a perfect example of feminism going too far," another guy griped.

"Ugh!" Mom groaned.

"Don't worry, Mom. We're going to make them eat their words," I said.

"I hope you do."

It was the same thing all over again at practice on day three, except there were only two stations that came back.

Must have been they still weren't convinced there wouldn't be any trouble. Coach Magenta continued to ignore them. By day four we were down to only one TV crew—and they didn't stay long. Come day five, we were finally left alone.

There were still people complaining and making trouble, writing letters to the papers and sticking signs that said NO TO MAGENTA on their lawns, but Natalie told us not to worry about any of it. The school couldn't fire Mrs. Magenta just because a few parents were upset—or else they'd be in big legal trouble. Natalie said the only legitimate concern she'd heard voiced was about our locker room being unsupervised, so she got Mr. Murdoch to agree to be our assistant coach, and that took care of that problem. I don't know how she did that, but she did.

A lot happened that week, but I thought the team did a decent job of staying focused and ignoring those TV people. That was important because the guys didn't have a second to waste if they were going to stand any chance of being ready for Stonebreaker. I'd told Coach Magenta about the Titan's beast, but we'd agreed not to tell the team about him yet. We wouldn't see him until our Thanksgiving showdown, and we had a lot of football to learn and perfect before worrying about him. The thing I should've been worrying about was the fight brewing on our own team—but I never saw it coming.

4

RAZZLE-DAZZLE

NATALIE KURTSMAN
ASPIRING LAWYER
Kurtsman Law Offices

BRIEF #5
September: Showtime

We convened for our first official news show meeting before school on Monday of the second week. I had advertised our meeting, but not surprisingly, it was only the Recruits and Mrs. Woods and Mrs. Magenta in attendance. I hadn't expected otherwise, especially with us gathering early in the morning, but we had to schedule it for that time to avoid conflicting with football so Mrs. Magenta and the guys were able to come. The only one missing was Mark.

"Trevor, do you know where Mark is?" I asked him.

"No," he responded, shaking his head. He made no attempt at eye contact; on the contrary, he avoided it. That was textbook guilty behavior from a person on the stand, but I let it go—for the moment.

"Well, hopefully he'll show up, but we need to get started." I walked to the front of the room so I could see everyone.

"May I have your attention, please?" I waited. "Thank you. You've all heard the exciting news. We're hitting pause on the production of our school newspaper, the *Lake View Times*, so we can begin a morning news show. The goal is to broadcast us live on every classroom TV."

"What's the show called?" Scott interrupted, pulling his finger out of his nose.

I almost gagged. "It doesn't have a name yet," I answered.

"We should call it *The Razzle-Dazzle Show!*" he squealed.

I started to object. "We can't make an impulsive decision about something as important as—"

"I like it," Gavin interrupted.

"Me too," Mrs. Magenta agreed.

"It does have a nice ring to it," Mrs. Woods mused.

Trevor shrugged, and Randi didn't say anything.

I sighed. "Fine. We'll call it *The Razzle-Dazzle Show.*"

"Yay!" Scott cheered. "Can I be the weatherman?"

"Will you slow down?" I snapped. "There is no weatherman position."

"Why not? *The Razzle-Dazzle Show* needs a weatherman. Every news show has a weatherman," Scott argued.

exasperated (adjective): extremely annoyed or irritated

That was me. I was ready to scream. *Composure, Natalie,* I reminded myself. "I'll make a deal with you," I said. "I'll create a weatherman role if you agree not to interrupt our meeting from this point forward."

"Deal," Scott declared, sticking out his hand so that we could shake on it—the same hand I'd seen him using to dig for gold.

I gave him a fist bump and then immediately squirted sanitizer onto my hands. Mrs. Woods gave me a wink. You'd be surprised how much that actually helped me to calm down.

"Okay," I continued. "Here's what Mrs. Woods and Randi and I have in mind." I went on to explain how things would operate and the various roles that needed filling. In the end it was decided:

- **Cameramen:** Gavin and Trevor
- **Computer and sound technicians:** Trevor and Mark (assuming he was participating)
- **Reporters:** Scott and Randi (Note: Randi didn't have anything other than physical therapy in her schedule, so I hoped this would give her something more to do. I didn't say that to her, but that was my thinking.)
- **Weatherman:** Scott
- **Troubleshooters, overseers, and occasional idea-givers:** Mrs. Woods and Mrs. Magenta
- **Lead anchor and writer:** Me/Natalie

(Note: Mrs. Magenta would be with her students during the actual airing of our show but could meet with us before school when needed.)

"We will do a practice run tomorrow morning," I explained. "At that time I will give each of you a photocopy of the script so that you know what's happening when. I have most of it written already, just a few tweaks to make. Basically, our first show needs to be an introduction. We need to let our viewers know what they can expect. We'll include things like the day's lunch menu, any special schedule information and/or

77

announcements, a recap of events, and a preview of upcoming events. We'll start slowly, but once we get our feet wet, we'll add to it and make the broadcast longer—and better. *The Razzle-Dazzle Show* is our chance to bring real stories to Lake View Middle. We're going to tackle real issues. Things that matter."

"Don't forget to add the weatherman," Scott insisted.

I sighed. Incredible. That was all he could think to say after my impassioned speech. "Yes, I'll add the weatherman," I promised.

He grinned, and then his watch began beeping. "We gotta go!" he cried. He grabbed his bag and zigzagged his way toward the door. "Bye, Mrs. Woods," he called over his shoulder. "See you at practice, Coach Magenta."

"Bye, Scott," everyone replied in unison.

"I think that kid is part Tasmanian devil," Trevor remarked, eliciting laughs from all of us—except Randi.

"He's right, though. We do need to get a move on," Gavin said, pointing to the clock.

Indeed. It was nearly time for homeroom. We collected our belongings and said thank you and goodbye to Mrs. Woods and Mrs. Magenta. Gavin helped Randi with her stuff, and I left with Trevor. I would've offered to help her, but I couldn't risk arriving late; if that were to happen, then my agreement with Mr. Murdoch could be voided.

GAVIN

Kurtsman is about as smart as they come, and on top of that, she's a go-getter. She's not one bit afraid to take the bull by the horns. She coulda made one heckuva football player if she wasn't so . . . Kurtsmany. So I sorta felt bad for her when one of our first news shows went off the rails. It all worked out in the end, but I still can't believe she didn't think to give Scott advance warning about what she'd planned to say. Scott didn't do well with surprises. He loved them, but he couldn't ever control himself when there was one. He always freaked. Let me tell you, he put the razzle-dazzle in our show that morning.

Kurtsman made it so easy. She created a template of the broadcast, and we just had to fill in our parts and follow along. We did that before going live each morning. This serves as our homeroom period, thanks to Mrs. Woods. The girl was organized. *The Razzle-Dazzle Show* was going to kick butt 'cause she was going to make sure it did—plain and simple.

We got through the beginning and all the normal stuff just fine, and then we reached the place in our script where all it said was "Natalie's Monologue." I didn't even know what a monologue was. Turns out it was Kurtsman looking into the camera and giving a speech. This was where it got crazy. I zoomed in on her like it said to do in the script. Kurtsman sat up straight behind her desk and got serious.

"Before we sign off," she said, "there's something happening here in our community that needs to be called out, and that something is sexism."

"Natalie, you can't say that word on TV!" Scott squawked. "That's a bad word!" He ran in front of my camera and tried to block her out.

"Scott!" Natalie could be heard shouting. "The word 'sexism' is fine to say. It's what the word means that is bad. Now get out of the way." She shoved him aside.

I kid you not, I could hear laughter coming from the classrooms nearby. Everyone was laughing—everyone except Randi. The fact that not even Scott could get her to smile tells you how down in the dumps she was.

"What does it mean, then?" Scott asked.

"Sexism is discriminating against someone because of their gender," Kurtsman explained.

I adjusted my camera so that I had them both on-screen.

"Huh?" Scott's face scrunched.

"All those people claiming that Magenta can't be a football coach just because she's a woman are contributing to sexism. They are, in fact, sexist."

Scott slammed his hand on the desk, and Kurtsman jumped. "Those people are wrong!" he yelled.

"I know," Kurtsman agreed. "Why is it okay for a man to coach girls' basketball, but not for a woman to coach football?"

Scott turned and looked at me, which meant he was staring into the camera. "They're wrong, and we're going to show them they're wrong, aren't we, Gavin?"

I gave him a thumbs-up from behind my post.

"Don't worry, Natalie. We're going to show them," Scott promised. He turned and walked off the set, leaving Kurtsman sitting by herself.

"There you have it, Lake View Middle. Stats Man, Scott Mason, is leading our football team on a mission to prove that sexism doesn't belong here—or any place in the world, for that matter. I, for one, am rooting for the guys and Coach Magenta. I hope you'll join me in cheering them on.

"I'm Natalie Kurtsman, giving you something to think about. Have a razzle-dazzle day, Lake View Middle."

"And cut," I said after I'd turned the camera off. "Great recovery, Kurtsman."

"Thanks," she said, sagging in her chair and letting out a tiny chuckle.

"Bye, everyone!" Scott hollered. "Great job this morning." And out the door he spun, Tasmanian-devil style, running to get to his class.

"Perhaps that wasn't exactly what you had planned, Miss Kurtsman, but I've got a feeling you and Mr. Mason captured the school's attention during that segment," Mrs. Woods said.

"I hope so," Kurtsman replied. "And I hope you're ready, Gavin," she added, sitting up straight again. "You guys winning is the only thing that's going to get these protesters to calm down."

"We'll try our best," I said. I didn't know how convincing that sounded, but I wasn't ready to guarantee victory like Joe Namath had before Super Bowl III. The only thing I could promise was that I was gonna give it everything I had from start to finish. Believe me, I wanted to win for Magenta just as much as I did for me.

"Miss Cunningham, I'd like you to stick around for a few minutes," Woods said. "You don't want to try navigating the halls on crutches when everyone else is rushing to class anyway. I'll give you a late pass."

Randi shrugged.

I glanced at Woods, and she gave me a slight nod. I was no dummy. She was keeping Randi back for more than busy halls.

I grabbed my bag and eased my way to the door. "See you later," I said to them.

"Have a good day, Mr. Davids," Woods replied.

I stepped into the hall and saw Kurtsman and Trevor

walking up ahead. They were too busy with each other to notice Mark coming the other way—but he saw them. I watched him stop and turn around.

Just what I'd been afraid of. Mark hadn't been coming to our morning broadcasts 'cause he didn't want to be there. It wasn't 'cause of not feeling well or oversleeping or doctors' appointments or any other excuse him or Trevor had tried giving us.

This wasn't good.

Randi

Things were worse now than they had been before surgery. My leg was worthless, school was a drag, and I just wasn't excited about Natalie's morning news show. I wasn't excited about anything. I couldn't do anything! And there were all these people asking me what had happened and telling me how sorry they were or how much it stunk—like I didn't already know that. Dad and Kyle said the same stupid stuff, so I stopped calling them. Mom was the worst, though. She was so fragile. Me being injured was breaking her heart as much as it was mine. "I'd give you my leg if I could," she told me. I knew she meant that, but it didn't help.

The only person who had something different to say was Mrs. Woods. She asked me to stick around after our morning broadcast. I thought I knew what was coming, and I pretty much did, but that didn't mean I was ready for it. I was nowhere near ready for it. I got a full dose of her tough love.

"Miss Cunningham, I'm sorry you got hurt. I really am. But do you think you're the only one who's ever had to face hardship? Do you think you're the only one who's ever been disappointed or injured or worse? You know better than that. And you know I can say these things to you.

"This is where you need to write your own destiny. Are you going to pout for the rest of the year, go on feeling sorry for yourself, or are you going to pick yourself up and press forward? Are you going to see this setback as a challenge in the middle of your journey, or as the end? You must decide, but let's be clear, Miss Cunningham, this isn't destiny's call—it's yours."

Mrs. Woods got up from her chair and walked over to my side. "Here's your late pass." She dropped the pink notepaper onto my desk. Then she bent closer. "You can overcome this," she whispered. "Remember what Coach told you about atti-tude." She squeezed my shoulder and then she left, leaving me sitting there all alone.

I wish I could say that that was all it took to snap me out of my funk, but it wasn't. If you're not ready to hear something, then it doesn't matter who gives you the speech or even how good the speech is.

I cried.

Trevor

Saturday was the first I'd seen Brian in a couple of weeks because he was so busy working the night shift at his warehouse job and volunteering to meet his community service hours, and on top of that he was even starting classes to become a licensed electrician. If you asked me, Madison had whipped him into shape. Told you she was a keeper.

"Hey, Bro. How's it going?" he said when I got into his car. He was giving me a ride to practice.

"Good."

"How's the team looking?"

I buckled my seat belt. "Pretty good."

"Yeah? Even with a girl coach?"

"Dude, that's sexist."

Brian laughed. "Who told you that, your girlfriend?"

I shrugged.

He laughed harder.

"Shut up," I said.

He pulled out of the driveway, and we headed down the

road. "Madison would've smacked me for saying that. I was joking. How're things with Natalie, anyway?"

I shrugged again.

"You kiss her yet?"

"That's none of your business!" I snapped.

"That's a no, but that's okay. The first time is always the trickiest."

That was cool of him. Since he was being real and not making fun of me, I went ahead and asked him the million-dollar question. "How am I supposed to know if she wants me to?"

"You can ask her," Brian said.

"Pfft. Yeah, whatever."

"No, I'm serious. It might not sound romantic, but you don't want to go for it and find out she doesn't want that. You need to make sure it's cool with her. You got it? If it's not cool with her, then it's not cool—period."

"Did you ask Madison?"

"Yeah, and she dug me even more after that, because she knows I respect her."

Wow, I thought.

"And it's definitely not cool to brag about it if you're lucky enough to get a kiss. You might get away with telling Mark as long as he doesn't blab it all over, but don't go telling all the guys in the locker room."

That was easy. Mark and I weren't— Mark! I'd been so wrapped up in talking about kissing that I'd stopped paying attention to where Brian was driving. "Where're you going?" I asked in a panic.

"What do you mean? To Mark's. Aren't we giving him a ride, too?"

"No."

"No? Why not?"

"I don't know." I shrugged for the third time.

"What do you mean you don't know? Did you guys get in a fight or something?"

Shrug number four.

"This is about Natalie, isn't it?"

Number five.

"Trev, you need to talk to him. You can't let this go. You guys have been best friends since you were little. You can't let a girl get in the way of that."

"I'm not. I haven't," I said. "I don't know what's wrong with him. He's avoiding me."

"Call me sexist if you want, but girls play the silent-treatment game, not guys. Be a man and talk to him, you hear me?"

I nodded. "Okay, okay. I'll talk to him. But we're not picking him up."

Brian wasn't fooling around. To make sure I wasn't going to chicken out and wasn't just telling him what he wanted to hear to get him off my back, he coached me on what to say and what to expect Mark to say and how to respond—for the rest of our ride to school.

I wasn't blowing smoke when I'd said I would talk to him. I was for real going to do it. I had myself ready, but once we pulled into the parking lot, all that went up in flames.

SCOTT

It didn't matter how fast I packed my bag and ran in the halls, there was no way I could make it to practice early during the week, because I was stuck in social studies with Mrs. Carson for last period. If there was an award for talking, she'd win it. She droned on and on about the most boring stuff in the history of the world, and that's not a joke, because she was teaching us about the history of the world.

Saturdays were a different story. I could get to practice as early as I wanted, and that was important because there was lots to do. Like, at our first Saturday practice, I got all the different pads and practice pants and jerseys organized in advance, and that helped Coach Magenta hand out equipment much faster, which gave us extra time on the field. That was part of working smarter, like Coach Magenta had said we needed to do.

I got there extra early on our second Saturday because we were scrimmaging South Lake. This was our first chance to see how we measured up against another team. I had Dad get me there early because I couldn't wait but also because I had stuff to do. I wanted to get the water bottles and med kit out to the field, and I also needed to set up the yard markers and chains on the visiting sideline and the pylons in the end zones. But the first thing on my list was to check for seagulls. Coach had told Gavin and me that seagulls on the field meant good luck.

I walked out the doors in the back of the school and peered at our field in the distance. No seagulls. *I even beat* them *getting here,* I thought. *They've got time. They'll show up.*

I made the trek out to our field because a coach always visits the gridiron before the day's contest. It's customary to walk over the land that will be the site of ensuing battle. It was a good thing I did that, because I couldn't believe what I found when I got there. Spray-painted in the grass in big orange letters smack dab in the center of our field were the most hateful, hurtful words about Coach Magenta that you could imagine.

The first thing that went through my head was that I was real glad Natalie wasn't there, because she would've been screaming that word I don't want to say even though it's not a bad word, but after I got done thinking that, I kicked it into gear. Coach Magenta couldn't see this. I had to do something, and I had to do it fast. The last time I'd thought that had been when I was standing on top of the twisty slide covered in bird poop, and that hadn't turned out so well, so that should've told me something, but once I got going, I had a hard time stopping to listen—especially to that little voice in my head that Mom was always telling me to pay attention to. I didn't hear it because my wheels were already spinning.

The custodians had an office and special closet inside our

school, but their outside tools and equipment were kept in a separate garage—and I stood there staring at it. It was the first thing I saw after pulling my eyes away from the ugliness written in the grass. The garage stared back at me. It was calling me. I'd never been in it before, but during the week I saw mowers and tractors and workers with yard tools going in and out of it all day long, especially during Mrs. Carson's boring class when I was staring out the windows.

I took off sprinting faster than I'd ever run in the halls. I didn't know what I'd find, but there had to be something in there. Maybe more paint so I could color in the spot? Or a shovel so I could dig up the words? It was a big area with big letters, though, and I didn't know if I could do all that shoveling. Maybe a rake or hoe, then?

I was out of breath when I reached the garage, but I didn't slow down. There was no time to waste. I grabbed the doorknob and walked in. The smell of cigarettes almost knocked me down. I covered my nose and mouth and did a quick scan of the room. There was a desk pushed up against the wall, with a lunch box, a pack of those cancer sticks, and a smoldering ashtray sitting on top. At least one worker was already here somewhere, so I had to be extra sneaky and extra fast.

I crept deeper into the garage and spotted a rototiller. That scary machine could've dug up the ground way faster than a shovel and made those hateful words disappear, but I didn't know how to start it, and if I got lucky and got it running, there was a good chance that the thing would take off, dragging me behind it. I didn't have time for mess-ups. I needed to fix this on my first try.

The next thing I contemplated was a riding mower. I didn't

91

need to be strong to start that or drive it—I didn't think—but if I tried cutting the grass, would it cut short enough to erase the paint? If I drove over the words a bunch of times, would the mower keep clipping the grass shorter? Did a mower work that way? And what if I crashed? I'd never driven anything before. I decided that wasn't the best idea, either, but if I didn't find something soon, I'd have no choice but to try it. This was an emergency.

I turned and quickly surveyed the other side of the garage. Sitting against the far wall were three red cans. I glanced back at the desk and saw a lighter beside the pack of cigarettes. I had my plan.

I grabbed one can with both of my hands, because five gallons of gas is superheavy, but all my water lugging at practice had prepared my muscles for this. I paused to stuff the lighter in my pocket, and then I hobbled as fast as I could out to the field. The red metal can kept banging against my shins, and it hurt bad, but I didn't stop. I pushed through the pain like the guys on the team do, because no pain, no gain.

I couldn't pour the gas on just the letters, because then those hateful words would be burnt into the ground, not erased, so the first thing I did was use the gas to draw a large rectangle around all the writing. Then I poured zigzag lines back and forth inside the area.

"Hey!" a voice shouted. "Hey, kid! What're you doing?"

I peeked behind me and saw a man I didn't recognize running toward me. It had to be Smoker Man. No time to waste. I pulled the lighter from my pocket and flicked it. Nothing.

"Hey! Stop!" Smoker Man yelled. He was getting closer.

I flicked the lighter again. And again. And again. *C'mon,* I pleaded. I tried once more. Hands grabbed my shoulders and yanked me backward—but not before I touched the flame to the ground. I fell onto my butt and watched the fire grow and sweep across the football field like a running back scampering for a big play.

"Get back!" Smoker Man yelled, tugging me away from the inferno.

I scrambled to safety. Then I stopped and stared at what I'd done. I smiled. I'd fixed it.

"What're you smiling for?" Smoker Man said. "You could've got killed. You're crazy, kid."

He pulled his cell phone out and called the fire department. "We've got a large grass fire on the Lake View Middle School football field," he reported, "and it's spreading. We need you here fast, before this gets out of control."

My smile faded. Smoker Man was right. *Can you have a forest fire without a forest?* I wondered. This hadn't been part of my plan.

5

GAME DAY
THROW-UPS
AND MESS-UPS

Trevor

I'd given up thinking that Scott would never find a way to top whatever his last crazy stunt happened to be, because every time I started to think like that, he'd find a way to outdo himself. But I've got to admit, this latest one was going to be hard to beat.

Brian's big pep talk about approaching Mark went out the door as soon as we got to school. We pulled into the parking lot and saw smoke billowing into the air behind the building.

"What in the—" Brian started to say.

"Scott," I said, cutting him off. I jumped out of the car and ran into the school. I sprinted through the lobby, down the hall, and out the back. There were fire trucks and people everywhere. *What did you do this time?* I thought.

The short story is that Scott set fire to our football field. I guess he was only trying to burn a small portion of it, but things got out of his control. No surprise there. The question was, why had he wanted to torch any of it? No one knew. He wouldn't say. Whatever it was, he must've had a good reason, because it resulted in our scrimmage being canceled, and he definitely wouldn't have been trying for that. The whole situation was still being investigated, so nothing bad had happened to Scott yet, and I hoped nothing would, but this was no small mishap.

Thanks to Scott's fire fiasco, my big moment with Mark never happened before our scrimmage. And it never happened during the week, either. It wasn't my fault. When was I supposed to talk to him? It wasn't easy when he wasn't in any of my classes or lunch.

Mark started coming to our morning broadcast, but he timed things so that he never got there early, and he always left as soon as we were done. Besides, it wasn't like we could have the big talk with everyone around. So what about at practice? That didn't work because Mark practiced with the running backs and I was with the linemen. Coach Magenta had me playing tight end. I was going to be the Rob Gronkowski of Lake View Middle, and Gavin the Tom Brady.

The big talk just wasn't happening, and I'd lost my nerve. Brian had warned me that it needed to, or else things would get worse. He was right—but I didn't think things would ever get as bad as they did.

Randi

Something changed after Mrs. Woods gave me her tough love. I stopped feeling depressed and I started feeling angry. Angry at everyone and everything. Angry. All the time. Angry.

"Listen up, people," Natalie announced first thing when she walked through the door on Monday morning. She tossed her bag onto the floor and started passing out the day's script. She was all take-charge and high-and-mighty. I glanced at her plan and saw where it said something about the football field fire.

"The fire was big news on Saturday, but it's old news now," I said. "Everyone knows about it. Doing a segment on that is a dumb idea."

Even Natalie couldn't hide her shock. She looked at me like she couldn't believe what I'd just said. Like, how dare I challenge her. Like, how dare I call her plan dumb. She could blame Mrs. Woods.

"It's only a dumb idea if I don't add anything new to the existing story," she retaliated, regaining her composure and giving me her best lawyer stare.

"Whatever," I grumbled.

That almost put her over the edge. She sucked in a big breath, ready to let me have it, but then thought better of it and bit her tongue. Mrs. Woods was on her feet and approaching us, so that may have been the signal Natalie needed, telling her not to do it.

It was my signal to go. I was done. No way I was sticking around for this garbage. I grabbed my stuff and made my way across the room. I was finally off my stupid crutches, so I didn't need any help. I was outta there.

"Randi, where are you going?" Gav asked.

"Away," I snapped. I yanked open the door and was gone.

As soon as I was in the hall, I felt terrible, but I didn't turn around. I couldn't. I went to my first-period class, and even though I was way early and Mr. Nelson hadn't even had his homeroom yet, he was cool and let me sit at a desk in the back, and he didn't ask any questions.

I pulled out a book and pretended to read. Mr. Nelson's homeroom filtered in, and I felt some of the kids glancing my way. There was a lot of chatter, but nobody said anything to me.

"Shhh! Shut up!" one girl hissed at a group of dumb boys. "*The Razzle-Dazzle Show* is starting."

I looked up to the corner where Mr. Nelson had his TV. It was my first time watching our broadcast like this. I'd thought the kids in homeroom would probably be talking during the show and barely paying attention, but the truth was that everyone was watching. *The Razzle-Dazzle Show* was a hit. That was thanks to Natalie, and just in case I'd forgotten that, she showed me during her final segment.

"As most of you know by now, our football field went up in flames this past weekend," she began. "How? I trust that most of you have heard about that as well. It seems our football team's stats man, Scott Mason, was responsible. But why? That is the part that remains a mystery. Scott hasn't uttered a word to anyone—not Mr. Allen, not the fire chief, not the police, and not even his friends. Any good lawyer would tell you, sometimes it's just a matter of asking the right question.

"Scott, will you please join me?" Natalie said.

Scott hesitated but walked out and sat in the chair she had for him. What was she going to do?

"Thank you," she said. "Now, Scott, I'm not going to ask you what was on the field or in the grass or why you even started the fire. I have a different question for you."

"Are you trying to trick me?"

"No. Not at all. I'm just wondering, can you tell us why you don't want to talk about what happened? Why you don't want to answer those other questions that you've been asked too many times already?"

Finally, here were the right questions. "Sometimes it's better for people not to know, because what you don't know can't hurt you," he said.

"So you're protecting someone?"

He shrugged.

"Thank you, Scott," Natalie said.

Scott got up and hurried off the set, but Natalie wasn't done yet. She squared her shoulders and faced the camera. She lasered her eyes on all of us watching. It was enough to make a TV blink. "Let me make this clear, Lake View Middle. Scott Mason is willing to take the fall in order to protect the innocent. We should all aspire to be so good. And to be such a friend.

"After hearing this, I hope you will join me in signing a petition to save Scott from expulsion. If we gather enough signatures, we just might convince the administration to listen. You can find the petition hanging on a clipboard outside the gym. I will be collecting it at the end of the day and sharing your feelings with Mr. Allen.

"I'm Natalie Kurtsman, asking, what kind of person are you? Have a razzle-dazzle day, Lake View Middle."

It didn't matter how angry or sad I was feeling. I was signing that petition.

Looking back, I believe destiny had me watch our show from the classroom perspective so I could witness its potential, because there were much bigger things in store for *The Razzle-Dazzle Show.*

NATALIE KURTSMAN
ASPIRING LAWYER
Kurtsman Law Offices

BRIEF #6
September: Signatures Delivered

"Natalie, thank you for this," Mr. Allen said when I delivered the signatures to his office after school. I'd collected over four hundred names—from students and faculty—in support of saving Scott after putting him on *The Razzle-Dazzle Show* that morning.

"Is it enough to keep him from being expelled?" I asked.

Mr. Allen leaned back in his chair. "Natalie, can I tell you something that you'll keep just between you and me? Consider it confidential information in an open investigation."

"Of course," I said.

"I was never going to expel Scott. Don't get me wrong—there will need to be a consequence of some sort; he did almost burn down the equipment shed and football scoreboard. But it was never going to be expulsion. No matter what anyone says, believe me when I tell you, Scott Mason is one smart cookie. He only does dumb things because he has a heart the size of the Milky Way."

Mr. Allen was absolutely right about that. I smiled, recalling some of Scott's finer moments.

"I'm going to take some heat over not punishing him," Mr. Allen confessed, "especially from the people in our community who are still upset with Mrs. Magenta's hire as football coach. They're trying to say that her lack of control is responsible for Scott's reckless behavior." He waved the papers I'd given him. "But these four-hundred-plus signatures ought to keep them quiet."

I chuckled, and so did Mr. Allen.

"Thank you, Natalie," he said again.

"You don't need to thank me. I was only trying to do the right thing—and help my friend."

"I'd say you've done that and then some. You're just getting started, and already *The Razzle-Dazzle Show* is making a difference."

I smiled. There wasn't a better compliment.

Mr. Allen and I bid each other a good evening, and then our meeting adjourned. Little did we know, before we got done this year, *The Razzle-Dazzle Show* would have to help save more than just Scott.

Randi

Even after I'd given her my nasty attitude and been down-right mean, Natalie insisted I go to the guys' football game with her—and I hadn't even apologized. She insisted because she didn't want to go alone. She said that. But she also said that getting out would be good for me. So was she using me or looking out for me? It wasn't like she needed me to go, because she would've gone without me. She said that, too.

I don't know how much sense I'm making, but that's what it was like inside my head. When you go on feeling sorry for yourself, you do that sort of thing. There are a few ups and lots of downs.

"Randi, you can't—" Natalie stopped, but she didn't have to finish her sentence.

"I'll go," I said.

I agreed because I didn't like being angry and feeling sorry for myself. I didn't like who I was. Mrs. Woods was right: it was up to me. I agreed because I'd missed Gav's game last year, and I couldn't do that again. I was going because I had great friends who were always there for me. It was my turn to be there for them. I was going to support the guys and Mrs. Magenta.

SCOTT

The wait was killing me, so I got to the school extra early on the morning of our first game. There was lots to do before a weekend practice, but there was even more to do on game day. First things first: I had to check the field for seagulls. Seeing those birds was the only thing that could help settle my butterflies.

I dumped my gym bag in the locker room and hurried out the back. I stepped through the doors and gazed into the distance. Our field was bare, which was okay because we were playing on our practice field, since the grass hadn't grown back on our game field yet. There was an army of seagulls parading on the practice field. Today was going to be a good day.

I let out a giant sigh of relief and smiled big. I watched the birds strutting around as if they were running plays, and then I noticed a person standing near the far end zone. I didn't like that there was somebody here before me, trying to steal our good luck. I kicked the dirt and marched out there to see who it was.

As I got closer, I saw that the person was bent over, staring at the ground. And when I got even closer, I recognized that the person was Coach Magenta. I was happy to see our coach here early, anxious for the big game like me. If the guys were half as excited as the two of us, we were in for a special day. I made my way toward her, wondering what in the world she was looking at, because she was still bent over.

I was about twenty yards away when I got my answer, and boy, did I start worrying then. Coach Magenta had the jitters way worse than me. She wasn't looking at anything. She was throwing up! The noises coming out of her made me squirm worse than if I'd had ants in my pants. She was retching really bad, but the good thing was, I only saw some yellow slime coming out of her mouth. It wasn't anything like beef stew or sloppy joes. If I'd seen that, I probably would've yakked up my Fruity Pebbles right next to her.

"Coach Magenta, are you okay?"

She stood up straight and sucked in several deep breaths. Then she wiped her mouth on her shirt sleeve. I smiled—that was a football-player move if I'd ever seen one.

"I'm better now," she said, turning and facing me.

"Bad nerves, huh?"

"Something like that," she said.

"Don't worry. The seagulls are here," I said, and pointed.

"Yes, they are," she said. "C'mon. Let's get to the locker room and start getting ready."

GAVIN

Last year, I'd been tormented by nightmares of Coach Holmes. I would wake up on game days thinking I'd never see the field 'cause of him. And I pretty much didn't. This time around, my sleep was just as bad, but it was 'cause I was crazy excited. I worked hard to keep my emotions in check, 'cause if I got too high too soon, then I'd be feeling drained of energy before I even got to the field. I'd play it cool like Tom Brady does— until it was go time. Then I'd let it all out.

When I got to the locker room, I wasn't surprised to find Stats Man already hard at work, polishing our helmets. I chuck-led, remembering the scene that had unfolded last year, after he'd tried that. "I hope you're not using Stickum," I teased.

"Nope. Not this time," he said. He showed me his bottle of Windex and cleaning rag. "I came prepared."

"The helmets look great," I said. And I meant it, too.

Scott beamed. "Check this out," he said. He dug into his bag and pulled out a laminated play-calling sheet. The thing was legit. It looked just like the ones I'd seen NFL coaches holding on the sidelines.

"Whoa. That's serious," I said.

"Yup. I'm ready." He glanced over his shoulder. "But I'm a little worried about Coach Magenta," he whispered.

"Why?"

"Because I found her throwing up this morning. Her nerves are getting the best of her."

I sat on the bench. "Really?"

"Yup. You've got to drive the ball down the field on our opening possession and score our first touchdown. Then she'll be all better."

He went back to polishing helmets like it was that simple—and maybe it was. I unzipped my bag and turned soft inside. Resting on top of my things was a good-luck poster from Meggie. She'd drawn a picture of me throwing a pass through Larry, my tire target. Megs had named my tire Larry 'cause her new favorite picture book was *The Old Woman Who Named Things,* so now she was the little girl who named things. Larry Fitzgerald was one of the greatest wide receivers of all time, so "Larry" was a good name for my tire.

I took a piece of athletic tape and hung her poster inside my locker. Then I stood there staring at it. Scott had faith in me. Meggie had faith in me. Mom and Dad and my teammates had faith in me. Now I just needed to believe in myself—but sometimes that was the hardest part. The great competitors knew how to quiet that negative voice and stay positive, though. I'd never struggled with confidence last year, 'cause there'd never been any pressure on me. The only voice then had been the one reminding me how much I hated Holmes. Now I had everyone counting on me to win so we could prove to the world that Coach Magenta knew her stuff. Was that why she'd been throwing up? 'Cause she didn't have much faith in us—or me?

It was a good thing the rest of the team started rolling in, 'cause that helped distract my mind and kept those negative thoughts from sticking around. We got ourselves dressed and ready, and then we huddled together in the team room. Murdoch stayed with us while Scott went and got Coach Magenta. If Scott hadn't told me Magenta had been throwing up and that she was nervous, I never woulda known it, 'cause she gave us one killer pep talk.

"Gentlemen, do not focus on winning or losing. Focus on giving maximum effort each and every play. If you can do that, the rest will take care of itself. And be confident. It's true that our opponent has had more practice time, but they will not be as conditioned, smart, or disciplined. They will make mistakes, and opportunity will present itself. Be ready. Now let's play hard and let's play together. 'Team' on three. One. Two. Three."

"Team!" we shouted.

Even Murdoch got fired up after that. We lined up and jogged out to the field. The TV crews were back, eager to see if Magenta was gonna prove she belonged or if we were gonna get creamed. But it wasn't the cameras that had me concerned. I couldn't find Woods or Coach. I scanned the crowd a second time. I saw Mr. Magenta and Scott's grandpa. I saw my parents and Meggie waving to me. I saw Kurtsman and Randi. But Woods and Coach were nowhere to be found.

They weren't here. For their daughter's first game. For Scott. Or for me.

"Never mind who's in the stands, Gavin. Or who isn't," Coach Magenta said, pulling me aside. "You need your head in the game. My dad would tell you the same."

I had a million questions, but I nodded. She was right.

What time was it? Game time!

Randi

It was a great game. I would've been so mad at myself if I'd missed it. Not only would I have missed Gav's incredible performance, but I would've also missed Natalie's killer play.

It was midway through the fourth quarter, when our team seemed to have things under control and the game was kind of boring, that Trevor looked up at us. He must've been checking to see if we were still there. Why else would he look into the stands? Natalie got so excited that she waved and blew him a kiss. That's right, blew him a kiss!

"Ohmigoodness! What did I just do?" she shrieked, burying her face in her hands.

"You blew him a kiss," I said.

"I know," she moaned.

I stared at her, and then I lost it. I was cracking up, laughing my butt off. That was the first time I'd laughed since getting hurt—and I laughed hard.

Unfortunately, it didn't last long because of what happened next.

GAVIN

The game went just the way Coach Magenta had said it would—for three and a half quarters. Using a mix of runs and passes, nothing flashy, we drove the ball down the field on our opening possession. Mark scored our first touchdown when I hit him on a play-action pass out of the backfield. And just like Stats Man had promised, things settled down after that.

We played hard, smart, and together, and as a result we held a two-touchdown lead with less than seven minutes to go. But as we found out, that was still plenty of time for a team to stage a comeback.

Coach Magenta called a simple halfback toss to Mark. We'd been successful with this run all game long. It was a smart call 'cause it allowed us to keep the clock running. It was smart 'cause it was a safe play—as long as we continued to execute.

I told the guys in the huddle we were going on my first sound, which meant snapping the ball on the first noise out of my mouth. Going on a quick count every so often kept the defense off balance. We practiced this stuff all the time. This was part of what Magenta had meant about being smart and disciplined.

I couldn't explain it, but for some reason Trevor lost focus and wasn't ready. He was still in his stance when the ball was hiked. That wasn't good, 'cause he had to make the key block on the end. He had to force number fifty-eight to the inside so that Mark was free to go around the outside. He'd been doing his job all game long—but not this time. Number fifty-eight blew by Trevor and pile-drived Mark into the ground. The ball popped free, and the defense scooped and scored, which meant they picked up the fumble and ran it all the way in for a touchdown. It was a devastating play, but that wasn't the worst part. Mark got hurt. They carted him off the field on a stretcher.

"What happened?" I asked Trevor when we got to the sideline.

He sat on the bench and shook his head. "I don't know," was all he could say.

"Shake it off, Trevor," Scott said, coming over to us. "We're in a game now, and we need you."

He'd barely gotten the words out of his mouth when our guys fumbled the kickoff on the next play, and the defense pulled off another scoop and score. It was a dramatic turn of events. Suddenly we were in a tie game. Mark always received the kicks, but with him out, we'd had to put someone else back there, and that had led to the fumble. We'd prepared for everything except for one of our key players going down, and we didn't have enough depth on our team to make up for that. We weren't the New England Patriots.

Coach Magenta called time-out and gathered us around.

"Okay, boys. We have two minutes and nine seconds to win this game, but the only way we can win it is one play at a time. You must refocus and execute—one play at a time," she emphasized. "That starts with the kickoff. We have to field the kick, and then our offense can take us down the field on a game-winning drive."

We tried, but without Mark, we didn't have the same running attack. Our offense stalled at midfield. We were looking at fourth down and a long fifteen yards to go, with eleven seconds left in the game. Coach Magenta burned our final time-out. She'd called a great game up to this point, but now she decided it was Scott's turn. "What do you see out there, Junior?" she asked, putting him on the spot.

Maybe calling him Junior sparked a special part of his brain and got him to channel Coach's spirit and wisdom—or maybe not. All I can tell you is, Stats Man didn't hesitate. He grabbed his clipboard and marker and drew up the play.

"The defense is charging hard upfield, hoping for another big hit and a turnover. We need to take advantage of that," he said. "Trevor, block number fifty-eight for two seconds and then let him go. Gavin, you need to reverse pivot and fake the halfback toss to the right and then roll left and hit Trevor on a tight-end pop pass. He'll be wide open across the middle."

The great Vince Lombardi, who the Super Bowl trophy is named after, couldn't have drawn it up any better. The play went exactly as Scott had predicted. Number fifty-eight came charging in like an angry bull, but I was the matador. I faked him out of his jock strap and then rolled left and tossed a tight spiral over the middle. Trevor was wide open. My pass hit him right in the hands. He tucked the ball away and rambled

114

forty-eight yards for a game-winning touchdown as time expired.

It was a thrilling finish, worthy of ESPN's top ten plays of the week. There were lots of hugs and helmet slaps in the end zone, and when we got to the sideline, we hoisted our stats man into the air. It was a great play call, but it wouldn't be his best or his last. There were bigger tests yet to come—much bigger and scarier.

After we left the field and I got done in the locker room, I swung by Coach Magenta's office 'cause there was something I wanted to ask her. I'd done a good job of blocking it out of my mind for four quarters, but it was front and center now.

I knocked and stepped inside. "Mrs. Magenta, how come Coach didn't make it to our game today?"

"He wasn't feeling well. Just a little under the weather," she said.

That was believable, except she couldn't look me in the eye and say it.

"Can I go and see him?" I asked.

"No," she said—too quickly. "That wouldn't be a good idea. We don't want you to get sick."

Magenta was playing the same game as Scott. He was the one who'd said that sometimes what you don't know can't hurt you. I didn't like that Magenta was keeping something from me, but I didn't push it. "Nice game out there, Coach," I said.

"You too, Gavin," she replied, giving me a weak smile.

So instead of seeing Coach, me and Mom and Dad and Meggie stopped for ice cream on the way home. Megs insisted we celebrate, but we had to take our ice cream back to the house 'cause she got a dish for Otis, too. That dog wouldn't care if his was melted, but Meggie made us hurry anyway.

"Put it on PSN," she said as soon as we walked in the door. "I want to see Gavvy on TV."

I chuckled. "ESPN," I corrected her. "And I won't be on that station. They weren't there today."

"Maybe someday," Dad said.

I smiled.

We settled in with our ice creams and tuned in to the local news—but it wasn't me stealing the show. It was Megs. No surprise there.

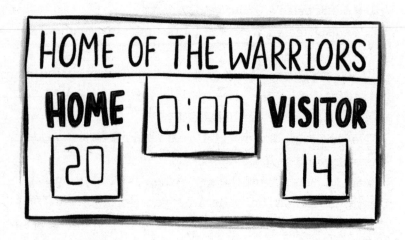

Trevor

After all those TV stations showed up at our game, after Mark got hurt, I was eager to see who and what got air-time, so I sat down with Mom and Dad to watch the local news that night. I was beginning to think they'd decided not to show anything, but all of a sudden there we were. Our team. On TV. They had saved the best story for last.

The reporter began, "After a contentious few weeks inside the Lake View Middle School community following the hiring of Olivia Magenta, the first female football coach in state history, the Warriors took to the field for their opening game this afternoon."

Coach Magenta's face appeared on the screen, and then the picture switched to us playing. They showed Gavin throwing his first touchdown pass to Mark. Then they showed the Port Johnstown defense picking up a late fumble and running it in to score.

"It was a back-and-forth battle on the gridiron," the reporter continued, "but the Warriors were able to prevail with some last-second heroics."

There I was, catching Gavin's pass and running it all the way in for the game-winning touchdown. They showed the team swarming me in the end zone. Then Gavin with his arms raised. And Scott jumping up and down, hugging Coach Magenta on the sideline.

"After today's memorable contest, it's safe to say that Olivia Magenta showed everyone she knows a thing or two about coaching football. Here at Channel Seven, we think this says it best."

The screen changed to a shot of Gavin's little sister standing in the bleachers, holding a sign high above her head. The sign read GIRLS RULE on the top, BOYS DROOL in the middle, and GO, COACH MAGENTA! across the bottom.

One look at that, and Mom and Dad burst into laughter.

"She's about the cutest thing I've ever seen," Mom said.

"I bet those ignorant anti-women people liked seeing that," Dad joked.

I laughed along with them, but my heart wasn't in it. "I've got some homework to finish," I lied, getting up from my chair.

"Okay," Mom said. "Great game today, superstar."

"Thanks."

Dad nodded.

I turned and walked down the hall and into my bedroom. Those TV crews had captured all the good stuff on their cameras. The stuff that made me look great. But they hadn't shown the one play that I couldn't stop thinking about.

Gavin had called the play and told us we were going on his first sound—twice he told us. Then we broke the huddle. Don't ask me why, but on my way to the line of scrimmage, I glanced into the bleachers. It was dumb. I told you, I don't know why I did it. I just did. Natalie saw me looking up at her, and she waved and blew me a kiss. A kiss! I shouldn't have let it, but that messed with my head. I was still smiling and thinking about her lips when I put my hand down on the ground and got into my stance. That's where my head was when number fifty-eight blew by me and massacred my best friend. Used-to-be-best friend.

When I saw that Mark wasn't getting up, when I saw that he was still down and clutching his side, I . . . It was all my fault, and no one could tell me different. My legs felt like they were in cement. It took all my strength to move them, but I walked over and kneeled next to him.

"Mark, I'm sorry," I croaked.

His face was twisted in pain, but at the sound of my voice he opened his eyes and glared at me. "You missed that block on purpose. I know you did," he hissed.

What! Was that really what he thought? Had it really looked like that? It wasn't true, but what was I supposed to say? That I'd gotten distracted by Natalie? I could never tell him that.

"Out of the way, boys," the EMTs said. "Let us in."

I got to my feet and stumbled backward. I watched as they maneuvered Mark onto a stretcher and loaded him into the back of the ambulance. He would be okay, but it felt like my best friend had just died.

The stuff they'd shown on TV had made it look like I was the hero, but I wasn't. Coach Magenta and Scott and Gavin were the heroes—not me. I was the one to blame for everything. The one who'd let his best friend get hurt. I was the loser.

Randi

"Randi, you haven't stopped smiling since that story came on the news. It must've been quite the game," Mom said.

"It was. Seeing Mark leaving in the ambulance was a buzz-kill, but only for a few minutes, because Gav got back out there and took charge and had us screaming and cheering again. It was incredible how they won on the final play. People were jumping up and down and going nuts. Natalie and I were hugging in the bleachers."

"It's so nice to see you happy," Mom said. "It's been a while."

She rubbed my leg, and my smile faded. She hadn't meant it, but that comment had reminded me why I wasn't supposed to be happy.

"I've got some news," Mom said. "You have a four-day weekend coming up, so I've made arrangements for us to go to Jacob's. Dr. Pierce will be meeting us at the gym so that he can check on you, and Jacob plans to show you a few exercises that you can add to your rehab routine to help you recover faster."

"Great," I said, and smiled—but it was a fake smile. Nothing genuine like the ones that had felt so good that afternoon. "I think I'll go up to bed now," I said. "I'm tired after all that fun today."

"Oh. Okay, honey. Good night."

I'd liked it better when I'd forgotten about my knee and gymnastics. Going to Jacob's would be a brutal reminder that I couldn't compete.

It turned out to be even more than that.

6

THE SECRET
WEAPON

Trevor

I got to school on Monday morning to do *The Razzle-Dazzle Show*, and Natalie wanted to know where Mark was and if he was okay. I was supposed to have those answers—but I didn't. I shrugged. What was I supposed to say, that he wanted nothing to do with me—or her?

"He's home resting," Scott said, saving me. "He has badly bruised ribs with some muscle strain and needs time to heal."

"Who told you that?" Natalie demanded.

"Coach Magenta. After the game she told the team not to rush to the hospital. That Mark was okay and that he was waiting to get X-rays and then he'd be going home."

"How do you know his results, then?" she pressed.

"Because I asked Coach Magenta to call me the moment she had news. I needed to know his prognosis so I can get started strategizing and game planning if we're going to be playing without our top running back."

"How long is he going to be out?" Gavin asked.

"About three to four weeks," Scott said.

"And how long will he be sidelined from our show?" Natalie followed up. She was the one thinking ahead and game planning now.

Scott shrugged. "That I don't know. But don't rush him. Proper rest is the key to healing. You'd better make a backup plan."

"Fine," she huffed. "You're the backup plan, then. We'll need you to pull double duty. You'll continue as weatherman but also fill in as our second computer and sound technician."

"Okay," Scott agreed, all excited. "I mean, aye, aye, Captain." He stamped his feet and saluted her. He also puffed out his chest, but you could barely tell.

Natalie shook her head.

Just then Mrs. Woods arrived. I hadn't even realized she was missing because I'd gotten hit by the Mark questions as soon as I'd walked through the door. "Sorry I'm late," she apologized. "I stopped and got us some doughnuts so we could celebrate the team's big win."

"Doughnuts!" Scott cried. "Mrs. Woods, you're the best!"

We stayed back while Scott went Tasmanian devil after the treats, and then the rest of us got one—even Randi, which I took as a good sign. The next sign I picked up on wasn't so good, though.

"How's Coach doing?" Gavin asked Mrs. Woods.

His question stumped her. She couldn't decide how to answer. Anyone with half a brain knew that meant there was something she didn't want to tell us—or didn't know how to tell us. I'd felt the same way when the Mark questions had started flying at me.

"When I didn't see him at our game, I asked Coach Magenta,

and she told me he was a little under the weather," Gavin said. From the way he said that, I could tell he didn't believe it, and I wasn't sure I did, either, after seeing how Mrs. Woods had reacted to his question.

"That's right," Mrs. Woods agreed. "He's still not a hundred percent, but he's doing better."

There was an awkward silence because we weren't buying it, but Scott was lost in his powdered-jelly-doughnut world and didn't notice. "These are so yummy!" he cheered. "Thank you so much, Mrs. Woods."

One look at him, and we could only chuckle and shake our heads. He had powder all over his nose and chin, and jelly on his shirt. He'd never change.

"We'd better get started," Natalie said.

Now was not the time to push Mrs. Woods. I saw the concerned look on Gavin's face, though, because when it came to Coach Woods, it had always been about time.

Natalie passed out our script, and we did our thing. *The Razzle-Dazzle Show* delivered like always, because Natalie was in charge. When we finished, we thanked Mrs. Woods for the doughnuts one more time and told her to tell Coach we hoped he felt better soon, and then we left for our first-period classes. Even though Natalie and I didn't have the same class, we always walked together because we were headed in the same direction. This was the first time I wished that wasn't the case.

"So you really haven't talked to Mark?" she asked.

"No," I said. "I'd planned on seeing him this morning."

She was quiet then, but she slipped me one of her looks.

"I need to use the bathroom," I said. "I'll see you later."

That was a desperate lie, but it got me out of there. Too bad things didn't get any better. By the end of the day, I'd been asked about Mark by almost everyone. No joke. He didn't come to school, so I got bombarded with questions. It got me understanding Mrs. Woods, and Randi, too, with people always asking how she was doing. Maybe we had answers, but we weren't interested in sharing them.

Leave me alone! I wanted to scream. But leaving things alone, ignoring the situation, was only making it worse. Sooner or later it was bound to explode.

GAVIN

Scott was the first one to tell us that Mark would be out for a few weeks, and Magenta confirmed that at practice on Monday afternoon. Getting Justin, our second-string running back, ready to go in time for our next game became a top priority. Kurtsman was right—winning our opener had quieted the protesters, but if we didn't keep winning, they were gonna be making noise again real quick.

Justin was a seventh grader and a nice kid, which didn't necessarily help when it came to football, but he was our guy. It wasn't gonna be easy, but this was where the smart part of football came into play again. Together, Magenta and Scott put in a special game plan built around helping Justin do well so that he built up some confidence—'cause believing in yourself can make a huge difference.

We spent the week working on runs to the outside, where Justin wouldn't get hit as much, and we added more quick short passes to take the place of those missing inside runs. In other words, it was up to me to pick up the slack while Mark was out, but I was ready for the challenge.

So was Scott. You shoulda seen him. We were scrimmaging at practice, running our first-team offense against a defense so we could get Justin repetitions. There was one play where I reverse-pivoted and tossed the ball to Justin, and he was supposed to take it to the sideline and then up the field. The line did a great job, and Justin sprang free just like he was supposed to. Scott went nuts. He ran down the sideline screaming and cheering. At first he was behind Justin. Then he was running side by side with him, and after ten more yards he'd left our running back and everyone else on the team in the dust.

I knew Scott was fast. He'd always been fast. But he never seemed to sprint in a straight line. He always ran zigzag style, sorta all over the place. Not this time. This time he demonstrated just how crazy-fast he was—and the best thing was, he didn't even know it.

I glanced at Coach Magenta and the guys standing around me. Everyone wore the same expression. We'd all seen the same thing.

Scott came jogging back, and Magenta made a bold coaching move. "We're suiting you up tomorrow," she told him.

"Me? I can't. My mom won't let me."

"I'll talk to her," Magenta said. "Suiting up doesn't mean playing. You'll be our secret weapon for emergency situations."

"Secret weapon?" Scott asked.

"Secret weapon," Magenta repeated.

"Secret weapon!" he cried.

She'd picked the perfect thing to tell him. She had to. You didn't keep the fastest kid in the school on your sideline.

SCOTT

Coach Magenta designated me the team's secret weapon. I was going to suit up and be at the ready for emergency situations. It was going to be awesome. Stonebreaker would never see me coming. He was no match for a secret weapon.

This new development had me more wired than if I'd eaten a box of doughnuts. I zoomed around the locker room after practice, calling a pretend play-by-play while putting equipment away.

"Davids drops back and slings one to Mason on the outside. Mason pulls it in and streaks down the sideline. He's at the forty . . . the thirty . . . the twenty . . . the ten . . . touchdown!" I yelled.

"Scott, you're bouncing around this place like a pinball," Gavin said.

"I can't help it. I can't wait to tell Grandpa I'm the secret weapon."

"Are you going to the Senior Center?"

"Yup. Mr. Allen assigned me more community service

hours there. It's part of my consequence for the fire. I get to visit Grandpa, but I also have to help Director Ruggelli with whatever she needs."

"You think I can go with you?" Gavin asked.

"Sure!" I exclaimed. "You're excited to tell Grandpa about my secret-weapon news, too, aren't you?"

"Something like that," he said. "Gimme a second to call home and I'll be ready."

"Okay." I was even more psyched to tell Grandpa my news now that Gavin was coming with me, but Gavin had a different secret-weapon plan in mind.

GAVIN

It wasn't good right off the bat. We found Scott's grandpa in his own room, not hanging out with Coach like usual.

"Grandpa, guess what! I'm the secret weapon!" Scott shouted before I even got through the doorway. The kid woulda burst if he'd had to keep that in one second longer.

"I've known that all along," Mr. Mason said, peeking at me and winking.

"Mrs. Magenta wants me to suit up because we're down a player since Mark got hurt."

Was that really what he thought? "She wants you to suit up 'cause you're the fastest kid in school," I said, setting the record straight. "You had smoke coming off the bottom of your sneakers, you burned down the sideline so fast at practice today."

"Really?" Scott said.

"Yes, really. Scott, you might be the fastest kid in the whole dang state. You made everyone else look like they were standing still."

"That's good," his grandpa said. "Run fast so you don't get hit or tackled."

"Don't worry, Mr. Mason. Coach Magenta will design the perfect secret-weapon play to make sure that doesn't happen."

"Grandpa, where's Smoky?" Scott asked out of the blue.

I hadn't noticed, but he was right. The cat was missing.

"Smoky's been staying with Coach ever since—"

Mr. Mason stopped, catching himself before the words he wasn't supposed to say had spilled out—but he'd already said too much. Grandpa and grandson weren't that different.

"Ever since what?" I asked.

"Ever since Coach got sick," he said.

"What kind of sick?" I pressed.

"Oh, he's just a little under the weather, is all."

"I'd like to go and say hi to him, then," I said.

"No," Mr. Mason was quick to say—too quick, just like Magenta.

"Grandpa, what's wrong?" Scott asked. "Is Coach okay?"

Mr. Mason sighed. "You know what, on second thought, let's go on over and pay him a visit. Seeing you boys just might help him. It always makes me feel better."

This was what I wanted. This was why I'd come. So why was I suddenly so scared?

I held my breath and didn't say a word on the walk over. When we got to Coach's place, I was both surprised and relieved to see that Coach Magenta and Mr. Magenta were there. And Mrs. Woods, too.

I spotted Coach sitting in the recliner in his living area. Smoky was curled up on his lap. One look at Coach, and I knew he wasn't just "a little under the weather." Something was wrong. The left side of his face was all droopy. He was wearing a bib, and Mrs. Woods was feeding him. She handed the bowl and spoon to Magenta and got up when she saw us.

"Don't be scared, boys," Woods said, coming over to me and Scott. "Coach had a stroke, but he'll be okay. He's had them before."

"Is that why his face looks funny?" Scott asked.

"Yes," Mrs. Woods answered. "Strokes can result in some paralysis. That's what you're seeing."

"How long will he be like this?" I asked.

Woods took a breath. "It's hard to know. That depends on the severity of the stroke. Sometimes it's a quick recovery. This one wasn't as small, so it'll take time, but he'll bounce back. He always does."

Me and Scott stood there staring at Coach in his chair.

"You can come over to him," Woods said. "He might like that."

Will he even recognize us? I wondered. We eased closer.

Coach Magenta and Mr. Magenta scooted back from Coach's chair. "Somebody's here to see you," Magenta told her dad.

Me and Scott stepped in front of Coach, and I saw his eyes lock on mine, but I couldn't tell you if he knew it was me or not. I forced down a swallow. Standing next to a person you love when they're this kinda sick is hard—but this was only practice for what was yet to come.

I swallowed again. "Hi, Coach," I croaked. "I brought you something." I reached into my pocket and pulled out a copy of our play sheet. I unfolded it and held it up for him to see. "I thought you might like to look at the Xs and Os that helped

134

us win our first game." I put the paper on the end table next to his chair. Coach followed it with his eyes. Then he glanced back at me and the unparalyzed side of his mouth lifted up some. Seeing that right then felt better than connecting on a Hail Mary pass.

"The only thing is, our game-winning play isn't on there," I continued explaining. "Junior drew that one up during our final time-out. We scored on the last play of the game."

Coach glanced at Scott, then back at me. I don't want to sound sappy, but his eyes were brighter now. I wished I knew what he was thinking, but I wasn't able to read eyes. That was Kurtsman. So I settled for telling Coach what I was thinking.

"Your game isn't over yet," I reminded him, "so you better keep fighting. I want to see you in the stands before our season is done."

He held my gaze, then put his head back and closed his eyes.

"We'd better let him rest now," Mrs. Woods said, placing one hand on my shoulder and the other on Scott's. "Thank you for coming, boys. Seeing you has given him strength. I know it has."

"Mrs. Woods, I want you to tell me the truth about how he's feeling from now on. Good or bad," I said.

She nodded. "Okay, Mr. Davids. I will. You have my word."

Me and Scott left with his grandpa. I wasn't sure how I was feeling until I noticed that Smoky was coming along with us. Believe it or not, that was the thing that gave me the most hope. That cat wouldn't have left Coach if he wasn't going to be okay.

SCOTT

Seeing Coach sick was scary. Seeing him perk up when Gavin gave him my play sheet and told him about our game wasn't scary, but it was something that made Coach Magenta's and Mrs. Woods's eyes start watering.

"Both of you boys are secret weapons," Grandpa told Gavin and me when we were getting ready to leave. "That was the most responsive I've seen Coach, so don't be strangers around here, you understand?"

We nodded.

What I understood was that Coach liked our football stories, so I was going to do my very best to keep us winning—and part of that meant perfecting my secret-weapon role.

Coach Magenta introduced my big play the next day at practice. First she diagrammed it on the whiteboard so that we could see it, and then she had us try it. I was excited because it was a sneaky wide-receiver screen pass—and I was the sneaky component.

We lined up in trips right, which meant there were three

wide receivers—I was one of them—spread out to the right of Gavin. On the snap of the ball the two bigger and taller receivers stepped forward and blocked the defensive guys covering them, while I took a step backward. Gavin did a quick one-step drop and then turned and fired a pass to me. I was supposed to take the ball and sprint down the sideline untouched because of the blocking in front of me—and because I was the fastest kid on the field. The untouched part was important, because I could suffer broken bones if I got tackled—and worse if I got hit by Stonebreaker.

It was a terrific play design. I had the running part down pat, but the catching thing was a different story. Coach Magenta was unaware that I still had cymbal hands. I'd only ever caught one pass in my life. I couldn't catch a cold in a freezer.

"I can't do this!" I yelled after dropping another one. "I'll never be ready in time!"

Coach Magenta put her arm around me. "Maybe not for this weekend," she said, "but that's okay. You and Gavin need to start playing catch before and after practice every day. Do that, and you'll be ready when the time comes. I know you will."

"Good old-fashioned hard work," I said.

"That's right. That's just what Coach would say."

"I'm going to catch that pass when the time comes," I said, "and maybe Coach will be here to see me do it."

"I hope so," she said.

The time for my secret-weapon play didn't come during our next game because Justin protected the ball and never fumbled, and Mark did a great job coaching him from the sideline and giving him pointers. Gavin played awesome, too. He and Trevor hooked up for two more touchdowns. We went on the road and beat Lewisburg without any miracles.

The Titans had another blowout win behind Stonebreaker's eight sacks, but the bigger news was that the days of wondering if a girl could coach football were long gone. The letters to the paper had stopped, the signs were disappearing from lawns, and the varsity coach wasn't complaining anymore. He liked what he saw. There were still some people who thought Mrs. Magenta should go, but there was more cheering for us. And even though Coach and Mrs. Woods didn't make it to our game again, Gavin and I knew they were cheering the loudest.

I was going to catch that pass when the time came.

NATALIE KURTSMAN
ASPIRING LAWYER
Kurtsman Law Offices

BRIEF #7
October: A Scary Idea

I asked Randi to accompany me to the Senior Center after hearing about Gavin and Scott visiting Coach. It was time we checked in on Agnes and Eddie again; plus I needed something to keep my mind busy—and the same was true for Randi.

By all standards, *The Razzle-Dazzle Show* was a hit, but if you asked me, we were falling into a rut. The show had started off making major buzz—taking on real issues and making a difference. We had tackled sexism and saved Scott from expulsion—things we could be proud of—but we had somehow fallen into the routine of doing sports recaps on Mondays and previews of upcoming matches throughout the week. Naturally, the guys liked that approach, but it wasn't enough for me. It wasn't groundbreaking—and that was the mission. I was not about to let *The Razzle-Dazzle Show* become one of those brainless sports reports that you find on that ESTN or whatever it's called. That dumb jock network.

I had already dedicated next week's shows to highlighting Nature's Learning Lab, since we were going there in two weeks, but beyond that I still didn't know what to cover. I was in search of something new. Something big and important. Whatever that turned out to be, I needed to find it soon, because this lapse had given a rather scary idea time to wake up.

Agnes and Eddie never failed to provide me with plenty to think about, so I hoped my visit with them would help lull that scary thought back to sleep. Instead, the exact opposite happened.

Randi and I found our friends in their new favorite spot, the recently renovated Community Theater. Naturally, that reminded me of Trevor, but I couldn't afford to go soft, thinking of him now, not when Eddie was certain to be teasing me about him.

"Agnes, wake up! Look who's here!" Eddie hollered.

Agnes, who'd been dozing in her chair, jumped. "You trying to give me a heart attack yelling like that?" she snapped. She wiped the drool off her chin and sat up straight. Randi and I were already giggling.

"What brings you two here today?" Eddie asked. "Need some boy advice, or are you looking for trouble? I can help you with both."

"Ugh," Agnes groaned, rolling her eyes.

Randi and I pulled two chairs over and sat down.

"Or are you checking on us because you heard about Coach?" Agnes asked, instantly changing the mood from fun to serious.

140

We didn't know how to respond.

Agnes chuckled. "Well, as you can see, Eddie is as terrible as ever. I'm still stuck dealing with her, and Coach is getting a little better every day. So I guess you could say things are good here. How're you ladies doing? How's that knee coming along, Randi?"

"It's a little better every day," Randi answered, borrowing Agnes's line.

"That's good," Eddie remarked. "You need to be able to run if you're gonna keep up with Natalie when it comes to chasing the boys."

Randi snickered, and I shook my head.

"Try dealing with this all the time," Agnes said.

"It's what keeps you young, you old biddy," Eddie jeered.

"It's gonna drive me to drink, is more like it," Agnes retorted.

They had us giggling again after that exchange.

"We've heard from Grandpa and Scott that the football team is doing well, and it sounds like that *Razzle-Dazzle Show* of yours is a hit," Agnes said, getting us back on track.

I wasn't surprised that Scott had told them about football, but the fact that he'd also mentioned our show made me smile.

"It's true," Randi said. "Natalie would never say it, but she's the mastermind behind our show. And the football team is doing better than well. They've won both of their games."

"Olivia has those boys kicking butt just like I knew she would," Eddie said.

"Hopefully all those dumbos who were complaining about her are beginning to realize what they've got," Agnes added. "Olivia's far better than that thief you kids got rid of last year."

And there it was. That scary idea was wide awake now.

"Uh-oh," Eddie said. "Natalie's got that look again. She's thinking about something."

"What is it, Natalie?" Agnes asked.

"Nothing," I lied.

"You forget who you're talking to," Eddie said. "You're thinking something. Now, spill it."

There was no use trying to hide it. "You got me thinking about Mr. Holmes," I said, coming clean. That was it. I was giving the idea life. Talking about it out loud was allowing it to breathe.

"Holmes," Agnes scoffed. "What is there to think about when it comes to that terrible man?"

I shrugged.

"Natalie?" Randi pressed. "What is it?"

"Have you ever wondered why someone does something?" I asked.

"You mean like why Mr. Holmes would've stolen all that money?"

I nodded.

"Natalie, you went down that road last year. Why in heaven's name would you want to stir the pot again?" Agnes questioned.

"Because I've been wondering about Mr. Holmes ever since I met his adorable little son, Robbie, at Kids Klub last spring. I've tried to stop thinking about him, but the question won't go away. What if Mr. Holmes did the wrong thing for the right reasons?"

"There is no right reason for the way he treated Gavin or

Gavin's mother," Eddie said, "and besides that, he's in prison. It's not like you can go and ask him."

"I know," I said. "We don't need to keep rehashing it. Let's play dominoes."

I could see that Eddie and Agnes were skeptical, but they went along with my suggestion. The remainder of our visit was full of gossip and school talk over some friendly games. But inside I never stopped pondering if there was a way for me to talk to Mr. Holmes.

If Eddie met little Robbie Holmes, she wouldn't be so quick to write off Mr. Holmes as an all-around terrible man. I was only talking about giving him the chance to explain his side of the story. That would almost certainly shake things up at Lake View Middle. That was exactly the kind of thing *The Razzle-Dazzle Show* needed to go for.

My only hesitation was out of concern for Gavin. Would pursuing this story cause him pain? That was the tricky part— but I could do some digging without him knowing.

Randi

I went with Natalie to the guys' third game. I was laughing as soon as we got there. You should've seen Scott on the sideline, dressed in all that football equipment. He's the only kid I know who could put that stuff on and somehow look smaller. He had to wrap athletic tape around his waist about a hundred times just to keep his pants from falling down. The only thing that might've been funnier—and scarier—would've been seeing him play in the game, but that never happened. Scott's best position was as Stats Man. With his help, and Coach Magenta's, the team put together another terrific performance and pushed their record to 3–0.

Gav played great again. I was happy for him because he worked really hard and deserved it, especially after all he'd been through last year. His game was a nice break from thinking about gymnastics and my upcoming trip to Jacob's, but as soon as I got home, I was right back to worrying.

It wasn't that I disliked Jacob. It was that Mom liked him too much.

NATALIE KURTSMAN
ASPIRING LAWYER
Kurtsman Law Offices

BRIEF #8
October: Research

According to my research, kids were permitted to visit prisoners as long as they were a direct relation, meaning a son or daughter of the inmate. If the child was under the age of eighteen, they had to be accompanied by a parent or legal guardian. Special visits were a possibility, but only in cases of extreme hardship or extenuating circumstances, and such requests needed to go through the security department. I didn't think my case would qualify, so I continued reading to see if I had any other options—I did.

I soon discovered the section pertaining to mail. Prisoners were allowed to receive mail, but all mail was subject to inspection before being delivered—except for that from a lawyer.

This was almost too easy.

Trevor

Mark and I still weren't talking. He came to practice every afternoon, and he stood on the sidelines during our games and did a great job helping Justin and cheering on the team, but we never talked, and he stopped coming in the mornings for *The Razzle-Dazzle Show*. His injury was the perfect excuse.

Natalie was too smart not to notice, and she was smart enough to know that I didn't want to talk about it. She stayed silent on the subject, but pretending there was nothing going on wasn't making me feel any better. I liked Natalie a lot and I wanted to hang with her, but I also didn't want to be near her, because whenever we were together, I was on edge, waiting for her to bring up Mark again.

I felt it coming one day after school when we were walking together toward the lobby. I was on my way to practice, and she was getting picked up by her mother and going to her parents' office.

"I need to ask you something," she said.

My muscles tensed. "Okay."

"Is your brother still helping out at Kids Klub? I'd like to go back."

I exhaled. *Thank goodness,* I thought. But then my eyes narrowed. What was she up to?

"What?" she said.

"Nothing."

"Then why'd you look at me like that?"

"That's not what I was expecting you to ask. That's all."

"What were you expecting?"

"Nothing," I lied.

"I thought so."

How did she do that? She could see right through me. We never said Mark's name, but we were talking about the same thing right then.

"So how about Kids Klub?" she said, letting me off the hook.

"Oh yeah. Brian still goes."

"Do you think we could go with him?"

"We?"

"Yes, 'we.' I thought you'd come with me. And maybe Meggie and Gavin, too."

I wondered if this was because Randi was going to be out of town and Natalie would be bored, but that wasn't like her. She was up to something, but I wasn't about to try questioning her. Grilling people was *her* strength, not mine.

"Friday would probably work," I said. "We have a short practice because it's the day before our game."

"Perfect. Talk to your brother, and I'll take care of Gavin and Meggie."

"Okay."

We were almost to the lobby when she stopped. Just all of

a sudden stopped. Right in the middle of the corridor. "You know what, Trev? Now that we got that out of the way, there is something else. Mark's at every practice and game, but he hasn't come back to the broadcast. I don't know what's going on with you two, but you need to fix it—or else I will."

My mouth hung open.

"Fix it," she repeated. "And don't forget to talk to your brother." She patted me on the chest and turned and walked out the door. And when I say "walked out," I mean walked out like somebody who'd just kicked some butt. And she had—mine.

I'd been worrying about her bringing up Mark and asking me more questions, but there'd been none of that. She'd skipped right over the asking and went straight to the telling.

But here was the issue. I knew what was going on with Mark, but I couldn't say it—not to her. How could Natalie be so smart but not see that she was the problem? If you're the problem, you can't also be the solution.

If she tried fixing things, it would only get worse. I was screwed. It was another catch-22.

Randi

Mom and I stopped by Gav's house on Thursday night so that I could wish him good luck on his game. The football team was 3–0, but this was going to be their first home game that I missed. I didn't want to be superstitious, but that stuff comes with the territory when you frequently ponder destiny. I left Mom in the kitchen with Mrs. Davids and went and found Gav in his bedroom. We chatted about school, and then I mentioned my concern.

"Randi, stop. I love that you've been at our games, but you're not the reason we're winning."

I was shocked when he came right out and said it like that, but he was right—and we both knew it. So then I told him the truth.

"Gav, I'm nervous about going to stay with Mom at Jacob's."

"I know, but everything is going to be okay," he said. "The bad stuff has already happened."

I nodded. I hoped he was right—but sometimes hope is not enough.

* * *

Mom and I met Jacob at the airport the next day. He was happy to see us. He gave Mom a big hug, and then he handed me a bouquet of flowers. That was really nice of him. Mom thought so, too. It was hard not to like somebody who was so thoughtful, but I had to proceed with caution. Mom's heart was on the line.

We gathered our luggage, and Jacob took us to his house. I didn't know beforehand, but we were staying at his place this time, instead of at a hotel. He had a large guest room for us. This was just as serious as I'd been fearing. "Concerning" didn't describe the situation anymore. Not only was Mom's heart on the line, but so was my destiny.

We didn't stay long when we got to his home because we had to get to the gym. Dr. Pierce was meeting us there. We dropped our bags and grabbed a quick sandwich and headed back out.

Dr. Pierce was already at Svetlana's when we pulled in.

"Hi, Randi. I don't have long because I have an afternoon appointment, but I wanted to say hi and see how you were doing."

"I'm recovering," I said.

He smiled. "That's good to hear." He took a few minutes to talk with Mom, and then he checked my scar and did a few tests on my knee to assess my range of motion and stability.

"Things look great, Randi. I'd say you're ahead of schedule."

Mom let out a sigh of relief. "That's great to hear. Thank you."

"Just keep doing what you're doing, and you'll be back before you know it."

"Thank you," Mom said again.

After Dr. Pierce left, Jacob took me into the gym and showed me some additional exercises that I could incorporate into my rehab routine. Then he put me through a modified workout, just so I could see for myself how much I could do. It wasn't anything Coach Andrea couldn't have had me do, but when we got done, Jacob kneeled next to me and said something that only he could say.

"Randi, I lost my wife much too early, and for no reason other than life not being fair. Much like it not being fair that you got hurt. But at some point you realize that you need to pick yourself up and push forward. That doesn't mean you forget—I'll never forget Svetlana, and you shouldn't forget the pain you've had to endure—but you move forward. You need to because there are other opportunities waiting. Opportunities you can't even imagine. Trust me.

"I'll always miss Svetlana and remember her, but when I met your mom, it was like I got another shot at life.

"Am I making any sense?"

"Yes," I croaked. I understood.

He leaned closer and hugged me. My eyes blurred. You could chalk that up as a very special moment—and that was why it scared me so much.

BRIEF #9
October: Kids Klub #1

I would've gone early to Kids Klub—being prompt and being first was my typical approach to matters of this sort—but I wasn't certain how Robbie would respond to seeing me after these many months, so I waited until the others could join me. Brian gave us all a ride over in the same SUV we had taken to the beach. He picked up the guys after they got out of football practice, and then he swung by and grabbed me, and last we stopped for Meggie. (FYI: When I say "the guys," I mean Trevor, Gavin, and Scott—because once Scott found out about the visit, he had to come, too. Gavin, on the other hand, was far less enthusiastic, and made a last-minute decision to get out at his house and stay behind. Understandably, he was not too keen on anything Holmes-related.)

I was pleased to have the company of friends—minus Gavin for the reasons I just stated, minus Randi because she was away at Jacob's, and minus Mark because Trevor still needed to fix that—because that made our visit feel like a sincere gesture and not something I was doing for selfish reasons. (FYI: Trevor was trying my patience with this Mark ordeal, but I had other priorities to tend to first.)

We found Robbie sitting alone at a table, reading a joke book when we arrived. "Overjoyed" might best describe how he responded to seeing us, Meggie especially; she was his good friend from class. I daresay Robbie was almost as excited as Scott gets about surprises—almost.

"Tell us a joke," Scott said upon noticing Robbie's book.

"Why does a duck have feathers?" Robbie asked.

We shrugged.

"To cover up his butt quack."

We burst into laughter, attracting stares from around the room, but we didn't care.

"Tell us another one," Scott begged.

"What's invisible and smells like bananas?" Robbie asked next.

"What?" we said.

"Monkey farts."

More raucous laughing. It went on like this for five or six more jokes before I decided to step in. "Okay, okay," I said. "How about we try something else. Would you like to play UNO?"

Robbie jumped to his feet and beelined to the games cart.

"Robbie likes his joke books because they make his daddy laugh when he visits him," Meggie whispered to me.

I nodded, even though inside, my stomach was twisting. Meggie had just answered my one question. Robbie did go to see his father. As scared as I was, that convinced me that I had to follow through with my plan. I took my coat and bag and set them off to the side—where I could easily forget them without the others noticing.

"I got it," Robbie said, dropping UNO onto the table.

Trevor took the cards and dealt the first hand. I couldn't tell you how many rounds we played, but it was a bunch. Poor Scott didn't have much luck, but Robbie and Meggie got a hoot out of watching him get all upset whenever he had to draw cards. My body flushed with warmness every time I heard Robbie giggling.

We had a fun visit, but I made certain not to lose focus. I kept my eye on the clock. Brian had driven us over, but Mother was scheduled to pick us up after one hour. It needed to be a short and sweet visit; if we overstayed our welcome, then it was possible we'd run into Robbie's older brother, Nicky—and that was on my list of don't-want-to-happen things, and I suspected was why Gavin had stayed away. But more important, if Robbie were to leave before us, then my plan would be foiled.

"Mother just texted," I said to the group. "She's here. We've got to go, Robbie."

"Oh," he said, slumping.

That was enough to soften the hardest heart. "We'll be back," I promised.

He nodded.

The guys and Meggie said bye, and we left. I waited until we were outside and getting into the car before I made my move. "I forgot my bag," I said. "I'll be right back."

"I can get it for you," Trev offered.

"It's okay. I'll go."

I hurried inside and found my belongings where I had purposely forgotten them; I'd needed a reason to go back so that I could see Robbie again—just the two of us. I walked over and sat across from him. He looked up.

"Robbie, I need to ask you a favor."

"What?" he said.

"Robbie, your father knows who I am. I'm afraid he doesn't like me very much, but I have a few questions for him, so I'm going to mail him a letter. He might not want to answer me, but I hope he does."

"I'll tell him you're nice."

I smiled. "That might help. If he chooses to respond, I'd like to tell him that the best way to get his letter to me is to give it to you. I'm afraid that if he mails it, my mother or father might find it first. Will you be my secret deliverer?"

"Okay," he agreed, eager to help.

"Thanks, Robbie. If your daddy gives you something, just hang on to it for me. I'll be back."

"Okay," he said again.

"I've got to go now. The others are waiting."

"Bye."

I waved, and then I left and joined everyone else in Mother's car, and away we went. I was there physically, but mentally I was elsewhere.

7

NATURE'S
LEARNING LAB

SCOTT

Our trip to Nature's Learning Lab was finally here. Waiting for this had been as bad as waiting to open presents on Christmas morning. I was extra excited because we weren't even there yet and the best thing had already happened: I got a phone! A phone! It was Mom's idea. She got it for me because this was my first time sleeping away from home and she was a little nervous.

I'd only had the phone for a few days, but I'd already downloaded some really cool apps. I practiced taking pictures and selfies, too, because I wanted to get some good shots of the lake and things like that when we got to the camp. When I was fooling around with the camera before morning broadcast, I discovered you could even record videos. Once I made that discovery, I got one of my best awesomest ideas. I wanted to make a documentary of our week at camp.

"Why didn't I think of that?" Natalie said when I told her. "Scott, that is a terrific idea! We can show it on *The Razzle-Dazzle Show* when we get back. I'll bring my laptop so I can download whatever you record at the end of each day; your phone will run out of room otherwise."

"Okay," I agreed. "I'm going to do a great job."

"Try to capture the place and all the important happenings and details," Natalie instructed.

"I will."

Natalie told Mr. Allen about our plan, and that was how I got special permission to keep my phone with me all day long. Everyone else only got to use their phone for thirty minutes in the morning.

I was so excited about camp and my phone and documenting the experience that I was the first one off the bus when we got there. I jumped down the steps and wiped out in the gravel, but I didn't skin my hands or knees because I fell on my sleeping bag. I bounced back to my feet.

"That's gotta be the best arrival I've ever seen," said a skinny man with a super-duper-long beard. "Is your name Kramer?"

"No, I'm Scott."

"Welcome to Nature's Learning Lab, Scott."

"Thanks," I said.

"Welcome!" the man shouted as the buses emptied behind me.

"How long have you been growing that beard?" I asked him. I'd never seen one so long.

He stroked his whiskers. "Since I was your age. I like it because I'm able to keep my leftovers in here for when I need a snack in between meals."

"Eww!" a chorus of girls whined.

"I might vomit," Natalie whispered.

I laughed. I liked this guy. Then I remembered my plan. I quickly got my phone out and started recording.

"Welcome," the man called out again, once all the students and teachers were off the buses and gathered around. "I'm Mr. Beard."

Everyone laughed.

"I wanted a name people could remember," he said.

"You've got it," I told him.

Mr. Beard chuckled. "I have a few quick announcements and house rules before I send you on your way. First, there is a second school on-site this week, but we have arranged your schedules so that you should not be overlapping or competing with them for any resources. I'm only telling you so that you're aware. Second, the boys' cabins are numbers twelve and thirteen, and the girls will be staying in numbers fourteen and fifteen." He pointed in their general direction. "The mess hall is behind you, and the bathrooms are over there." Again, he pointed to show us. "Last, you have twenty minutes to get yourselves unpacked and settled. Then we'll gather back here for official introductions and to get you started with our first activity. Questions?"

"When do we eat?" I asked.

"After," he answered.

"Do you have cookies and brownies for dessert?"

"After."

"After what?"

"After after," he said. "Now go unpack."

I wasn't sure when after after was or if there were going to be any cookies or brownies, but that was okay. I didn't have a snack in my beard, but I did have a hidden goodies stash to hold me over. I grabbed my stuff and started lugging it to my cabin. It was hard but not as hard as dragging the heavy bags at practice. I was doing good until the zipper on my suitcase broke.

NATALIE KURTSMAN
ASPIRING LAWYER
Kurtsman Law Offices

BRIEF #10
Late October: Trouble

In many ways, this excursion to Nature's Learning Lab shared similarities with the start of school. There would be new instructors, new surroundings, new routines, etc., which also meant that first impressions were on the docket. Let me just say, this supposed enrichment experience did not get off to a good start.

Upon arrival we were greeted by a skinny man with an oversize beard, outfitted in dirty jeans and a flannel shirt. Despite his presentation, I must admit, he was amiable. "Welcome!" he shouted. "Welcome! You can leave your bags off to the side and then grab a seat on one of our benches. I have a few quick announcements and house rules before I send you on your way."

I liked rules, but not the benches, which were nothing more than long dirty pieces of wood resting on top of stumps. I chose to stand. I was trying not to be judgmental, but Mr. Beard blew it when he mentioned keeping leftovers in his whiskers. Such a thought was appalling. Needless to say, I planned on keeping my distance from him.

When Mr. Beard finished with his brief introduction, I grabbed my rolling suitcase and started in the direction of cabin fourteen while the rest of my classmates shouldered duffel bags and backpacks. Gavin had his things on one arm and Randi's on the other. Unfortunately, I was in no position to assist; my roll-away was not rolling very well. In fact, I didn't make it very far before I slammed to a stop, the result of a stone getting lodged in one of my wheels. These lovely wilderness paths were made of gravel and not paved. This was a disaster from the start, and to make matters worse, I couldn't lift my suitcase because I'd packed too much.

I felt a tap on my shoulder and hoped it was Trevor coming to my rescue, but instead I found Mr. Beard standing beside me. "Need a hand?" he asked.

Of course I did, but I didn't want to admit that. I would've preferred that my boyfriend help me, much like Gavin was helping Randi, but Trevor was nowhere in sight. I sighed. Apparently Mr. Beard took that as a yes, because he hoisted my suitcase off the ground.

"Thank you," I said.

"Don't worry. You're not the first person with one of these wheeled contraptions that I've had to help out here."

He marched ahead in the direction of cabin fourteen, but I stood there, stuck in place. I'd already been worrying about spiders and bugs and other grossness, but now you could add Mr. Beard judging me to the list. As far as first impressions go, this was about my worst ever, and when I heard the snickering, I feared I'd blown it with more than just Mr. Beard.

I immediately turned and spotted a group of boys from the other school—whom we weren't supposed to interact with—patting their muscle-bound leader on the back and laughing and carrying on like a pack of hyenas. I flushed with embarrassment, but then I realized they weren't even looking at me. They were pointing at poor Scott. Don't ask me how he did it, but somehow Scott had managed to have his suitcase spill open, dumping its contents all over the ground. He was scrambling to cram everything back inside and was clearly struggling.

The laughing intensified when Scott dumped his suitcase a second time—and so did the glare I was shooting at the hyenas. Scott would encounter bullies for the rest of his life—I couldn't stop that from happening. But as long as I was around, I would do my best to help my friend. And I knew that the rest of the Recruits would be right there with me on that—and it wouldn't be necessary for us to mush our spits together to form that pact.

Bring on the bullies, I thought. I'd get to cabin fourteen soon enough. I walked over and gave Scott a hand with his things.

"Looks like you need your mommy," the muscle-head yelled. His pack cackled in response.

I flushed with anger. Clearly they did not know who they were messing with, but they would learn—the hard way.

Trevor

We were three days into camp, and I still hadn't fixed things with Mark yet—or even tried. Natalie had warned me to take care of it, to fix whatever was wrong before she did, but I didn't know how. The last time I'd tried saying anything to Mark, he'd told me to get away. I was running out of chances. Natalie was going to say something, and that was only going to make it worse. I'd end up losing my best friend and my girlfriend if she got involved.

Having both of them here was stressing me out to the point that I wasn't feeling good. I was sitting on the toilet with my fourth round of diarrhea when who showed up but Scott.

"Pee-ew!" he shouted, announcing his arrival. The kid didn't know anything about being subtle or discreet. "Is that you in there, Trevor?" he called from outside my stall.

I shook my head. "Yeah, it's me," I grumbled.

"I thought so. I recognized your sneakers under the door. Are you okay? You smell bad."

"What're you doing in here?"

"Ugh," he moaned. "I got overexcited when Mr. Beard put out the trays of brownies. I couldn't help it. They looked so big and yummy. They were chocolate frosted!"

"What happened?"

"I ran to get one and tripped and fell into the spaghetti-and-meatball platters. It's all over me. Wanna see?"

He tugged my stall door, but thankfully I had it locked. "Dude, I'm on the can!" I hollered. "Chill."

"Oh, sorry."

He had me shaking my head again. *Unbelievable,* I thought.

"I probably ruined my shirt, and Mom won't like that, but Mr. Beard gave me two brownies, so it was worth it. I need to get a selfie before I try washing the food out."

I heard him fumbling around, snapping pictures and even making a short video, and then the water turned on.

"Don't get your phone wet," I warned.

"I won't."

I chuckled. Only Scott would think to make a documentary of our experience, and only Scott would try to record something in the bathroom, but why shouldn't he? He'd recorded everything else so far.

I finished in the stall and was standing at the sink washing my hands when trouble waltzed in. Up till now we hadn't found ourselves in the same place at the same time as the kids from the other school. The counselors had done a good job of organizing our schedules. But you couldn't plan for Scott and his spaghetti mishaps or for diarrhea.

Scott's phone was propped near the sink, still recording, but he was over by the trash barrel, using wet paper towels to try to wipe the sauce off his shirt. He was singing some ridiculous song about his poor meatball and not paying attention. The stupid singing and the fact that he had his back to our sudden company made him a great target and a sitting duck.

The first loser snuck up and yanked Scott's sweatpants and underwear down to the ground. Scott dropped the towels and whipped his pants back up, but not before loser number two aimed his flashlight on Scott's privates and loser number three snapped a picture. Scott was a late bloomer, so he only had peach fuzz down there. That was all it took.

"That's not funny," Scott growled.

The group of them roared with laughter.

"What's your name, crybaby? Peachy?" the ringleader teased.

His followers laughed harder. This might sound weird, but all I could think of was my brother's old friend, that goon Chris, who'd bullied me. And that made me miss Mark.

"Stonebreaker," Scott said.

Who? I thought.

Scott looked at me with wide eyes, and then those jerks yanked his sweats and underwear down again. When he bent over to grab them this time, they shoved him from behind. Scott probably would've fallen into the urinal if I hadn't caught him first. Those idiots thought it was hilarious, but Scott sure didn't—and neither did I.

"That's enough," I said. "Get out of our way."

"Who're you," the ringleader said, "his boyfriend?"

More laughing.

"You think you're tough because you outnumber us, but you don't scare me. I've dealt with much worse than you."

166

And that was the truth—all of it. I stepped forward, closing the space between Ringleader and me. I didn't care that he had a beard and big arms. He knew I wasn't messing around. I wished Mark was with me, but I was on my own—unless you counted Scott.

"Don't make us come back with our friends," Scott warned them.

I almost smiled. The kid had guts. You could count on him to have your back. I know this might sound crazy, but that was when I knew he was going to catch that pass when we needed it. Scott might've been a wimp, but he had courage— way more than me.

"Ooo," Ringleader teased. "We're scared, Peachy. You better take your boyfriend and get out of here before we dunk you in the toilet."

Ringleader talked tough, but he stepped aside because that's all he was—talk. I grabbed Scott's phone and got us out of there.

"I need to pee," Scott said when we were walking away.

"You can go in the woods." I pointed to a spot, and he jogged off.

I stomped into our cabin, and wouldn't you know it, who was in there—Mark. "What're you doing in here?" I snapped. I didn't mean to, but I was still heated from the confrontation.

Not a word.

"Could've used your help," I said.

Still nothing.

"We had a run-in with some kids from that other school. Bunch of losers."

He shrugged.

"They pantsed Scott and took a picture of his junk. We almost got into a fight."

He looked at me. "Wow. You mean you're worried about someone other than Natalie? That's a first."

His words stung. "What did you say?" I was still on edge from the bathroom.

"You heard me. That girl is the only thing you care about."

That wasn't true—even though it maybe seemed that way. "You're just jealous," I said.

"Pfft. Dude, you're wrong. I'm not jealous."

"Oh yeah? What are you, then?"

He didn't answer.

"What are you, then?" I yelled.

"Hurt!" he shouted. "I'm hurt. And I'm not talking about my ribs. Friends don't take everyone to the beach except the person who's been their best friend for all their life."

"That wasn't what it sounds like," I said, trying to defend myself. But he wasn't done.

"Best friends don't ditch each other for a day at the beach, or at school, or after practice—or for a girl. And best friends don't miss blocks on purpose and watch their buddy get creamed."

I couldn't believe what I was hearing. At least not the last part. And I didn't mean what happened next. He was getting too close, invading my space, and he had me upset, and the bathroom bullies . . . I wasn't thinking. I shoved him—hard.

He staggered backward, clutching his side. "You're a jerk," he growled. Then, all at once, he came at me. I readied myself, expecting him to shove me back, but instead he threw a right hook that drilled me under the eye and knocked me to the ground.

"Guys!" Scott yelled, running into the cabin. "Guys! What're you doing? Stop!" He ran and kneeled over me, shielding me from Mark.

I held my cheek, staring up at my best friend—former best friend.

"Don't worry," Mark snapped. "Your girlfriend will kiss it and make it all better." He turned and stormed out of the cabin.

GAVIN

The camp thing turned out to be all right. I was bummed about missing football practice, but the good news was that it was our bye week, so we didn't have a game to worry about, and me and Scott found plenty of time to work on his catching when he wasn't doing all that documentary stuff. I didn't think he'd ever be ready for his secret-weapon play, but I wasn't telling him that. Stats Man was determined if nothing else. He had us throwing before breakfast, in between our activities, and after dinner. That's why it was weird when I found myself waiting for him on our third night. Scott was never late when it came to football. Where was he?

I was tossing my ball up in the air and catching it to kill time while I waited. I figured I'd give him a few more minutes before going to track him down. But then a funny thing happened. Instead of Scott showing up, it was Mark who came walking out to the field. I woulda started throwing with him, but his ribs still weren't a hundred percent. Man, we needed him back—and I didn't even know about Stonebreaker yet.

"Yo, did you see Scott?" I asked him.

"I think he's back in the cabin."

"Doing what?"

He hesitated, then shrugged. "It's Scott. Who knows?" He plopped down on one of the benches.

I was no expert at reading body language like Kurtsman, but the way he kept opening and closing his hand and avoiding my eyes told me that something had happened. Or maybe it was just my gut telling me. Whatever it was, I decided it was time to step up and be a leader. A true leader keeps his team together on and off the field, in the huddle and in the locker room. We needed Mark back, but we needed Trevor and Mark back together more. I walked over and sat next to him. Then I put it on the line. No beating around the bush. Woods woulda been proud of me.

"Mark, what's going on with you and Trevor?"

He turned away, but I could see his jaw shaking. He had a lot bottled up. I thought about saying more but decided against it. Sometimes you've got to give a play a chance to develop before you go running full steam ahead. So I waited, and then the hole opened up.

"It's Natalie," Mark croaked. "She's messed everything up. She's all he cares about."

"That's not true," I said. "Trevor's just as upset as you."

"Sure doesn't seem it," he snapped. "Why'd he take her and everyone else to the beach and not me, then? He goes with her everywhere, before school, after practice. He doesn't give a crap about me. That's why he missed that block."

Talk about misunderstandings. This was like what had happened with me and Randi last year. "Okay, listen," I said.

171

"Here's what happened with the beach." I explained how it all went down. How Scott had invited himself and the rest of us and Trevor hadn't planned it that way. And I told Mark that I didn't know what had happened on that play, but I did know that Trevor hadn't missed his block on purpose. And I told him if Trevor and him didn't take care of this soon, they were gonna have Kurtsman reaming them both out, 'cause Randi had told me so. "Kurtsman doesn't want to break you and Trevor up. She wants you to fix things. You guys are being stupid," I said.

He shrugged.

"You are."

"Yeah, well, I wish we'd talked sooner, because I just got in a fight with Trevor."

"What?"

"I punched him."

That explained his hand. "What the heck happened?"

I didn't know what to say after he got done telling me the story, but that was okay 'cause the play was still developing. Scott and Trevor came walking out to the field next. Mark got to his feet when he saw them approaching. So did I—just in case.

The four of us stood there. And then things broke open and the play took off.

"Sorry, bro," Trevor said.

"Me too," Mark mumbled.

"I deserved that punch. And I'm really sorry I missed that block, but I didn't do it on purpose."

"I know," Mark said. "Just don't do it again."

"And don't do it when the time comes for my secret-weapon play," Scott added.

We laughed.

"Don't worry, I've got your backs," Trevor promised.

"So do I," Mark said.

"We cool?" Trevor asked.

"We're cool," Mark said.

They locked hands in a dude handshake and pulled each other into a guy hug.

Scott did a fist pump. "Finally!" he cried. "Now sit down. It's time I tell you guys about Stonebreaker."

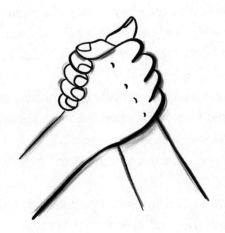

Randi

Gav and the rest of the guys were already on the field when we got out there. I wasn't sure what they were doing, but it looked like Scott was holding a powwow. I giggled at the sight.

When Scott heard us approaching, he stopped and turned around. "Oh, I forgot!" he squealed. "Tonight's activity is stargazing. Yay!"

"That's right," Mr. Beard said. "Let's gather in the middle of the field."

Scott ran to the middle. His talk with the guys was over now, but Gav and Trevor and Mark still stayed on the bench.

"No way," Natalie whispered. "Do you think Scott just laid down the law and whipped those two back into shape?"

She was referring to Trevor and Mark. They were laughing and joking—like old times. "I don't know," I said. "Scott can be unpredictable, and that's putting it mildly."

Natalie chuckled. "All I can say is thank goodness for whatever happened. Best friends work much better together than apart."

I'd been thinking the same thing, but not about those two. Maybe that was why her saying it rattled me.

SCOTT

"Find a spot and spread your blankets out," Mr. Beard said. "Then lie down on your backs, look up, and soak in the show."

I didn't have my blanket, and neither did the guys, because we'd all come out to the field early, but lucky for us, Randi and Natalie had great big ones and they let us share. We squeezed together like sardines and did what Mr. Beard had said. We started soaking in that sky.

It was still turning dark, so not all of the stars were out yet, but that was okay because not all the stargazers were there yet, either. Natalie took that opportunity to grab my phone and download my videos from the day. She got done right before Mr. and Mrs. Magenta showed up, surprising us.

"Mr. and Mrs. Magenta, what're you doing here?" I squealed.

"Thought I'd check on my players," Mrs. Magenta said, "and I also happen to love stargazing."

"If it's okay with you, we thought we'd join you for this activity," Mr. Magenta said.

"The more the merrier when it comes to stargazing," I said.

Mrs. Magenta smiled, but the way she was holding her belly made me wonder if she had an upset stomach again. But why would she be nervous? I held my breath and didn't say anything because I saw Mr. Magenta rubbing his hand on her tummy after they lay down, so I knew he was being a good husband and taking care of her.

It was close to dark now, so more stars had shown up. And a few minutes later there were more. And then more. And still more. Out there in the country, in that wide-open field where no other lights were bothering us, the sky went on and on and on—like it did at the beach.

"There's the Big Dipper," I said. "And the Little Dipper, too." I pointed.

"It's beautiful," Randi whispered.

"It sure is," Gavin said.

"What do you think about when you look up there?" Natalie asked the group.

I had my answer right away. "That I want to go up there," I said.

"You mean be an astronaut?" Natalie asked.

"Yup. I've been thinking about it ever since I read the book Mrs. Woods gave me."

"What book?"

"*Chasing Space*. It's the autobiography of Leland Melvin, a football player who became an astronaut for NASA. Leland says being an astronaut is a lot about teamwork and problem-solving, and I'm really good at those things and I'm a football player. So I could probably be an astronaut. It sounds fun—and they even have astronaut ice cream!"

"Scott, I wouldn't say this to just anyone, but you should go for it," Gavin said. "Space is about the only place I can think of that might be big enough for all of your energy and spirit."

"Amen to that," Trevor said.

"Indeed," Natalie agreed.

"It's either that or open a bake shop," I said.

They laughed.

"It's funny, but I could see you doing that, too," Gavin said.

"Just bring the cookies and cupcakes with you into space," Mark suggested. "You can even make it à la mode with your astronaut ice cream."

There was more laughing, but I thought that was a good idea.

"Who else?" Natalie asked. "What do you think about when you look up there?"

"I wonder if the stars foretell my destiny," Randi said.

"Maybe," Mrs. Magenta replied, "but remember, you can connect the dots and draw the picture any way you want. You're the artist. It's up to you."

Randi nodded. I liked that, too. Maybe I could find a picture of me catching that pass.

"How about it, Coach Magenta?" Gavin said. "What do you think about?"

"I search for the perfect star," she said. "The one that speaks to me. And when I find it, I think of my brother, Eric, and the baby that Mr. Magenta and I lost. But it's not sad, because when I find that star shining ever so brightly, twinkling, and looking down on me, I know it's them—and they're smiling."

We grew quiet after that because what Mrs. Magenta had said was something that made you think and feel. I liked her idea. That wouldn't be the last time I thought about it.

Randi

Stargazing turned out to be some pretty deep stuff. You didn't just shrug and move on after hearing what Mrs. Magenta had to say. I liked what she'd said about finding the perfect star. It was a happy-sad thought.

After talking for a while, we grew quiet and just lay there. The sky was incredible that night. There must have been a billion stars above us. It was nice to slow down and forget your worries and appreciate the natural beauty of our world. Told you it was deep. It was a unique experience, so I was surprised when Natalie brought it to an early end for the two of us.

"Randi, will you accompany me to the bathroom?" she asked.

"Now?" I questioned.

"Yes, now. This can't wait."

"Where're you going?" Scott wanted to know when we got up.

"If you'll excuse us, Randi and I have some business to attend to," Natalie announced.

180

Gav looked at me, and I shrugged. I sure didn't know what she was referring to.

"What kind of business?" Scott asked.

"Girl stuff," Natalie answered.

That seemed to do the trick, because Scott zipped it and no one else said anything. That was good because Natalie wasn't waiting either way. When I glanced back at her, I saw that she was already halfway across the field—and she wasn't slowing down. I was practically running, trying to catch her, and I wasn't supposed to be running. Something told me this was more than a trip to the bathrooms.

"Where are we going?" I called out to her.

No answer. She had her nose to the ground. Whatever it was, she meant business.

"Natalie, will you please wait?" I pleaded. "I can't go that fast."

Finally she stopped.

"Where are we going?" I asked again after catching up to her.

"Randi, sometimes a woman's got to do what a woman's got to do."

I started to say something, but stopped when I heard voices approaching. It was a group of boys from that other school.

"Hey, look," the first guy said to his buddies. "These fine young ladies must be lost. Should we *show them the way*?"

His group laughed at his macho-man routine. *What a jerk,* I thought. And his beard was dumb, too.

"We're not lost," Natalie said, unfazed. "In fact, we were looking for you."

"Sister, there's a long line of girls looking to get with me."

Uh oh, I thought. *This guy doesn't know who he's dealing with. He's toast.*

"Let me make this as simple as possible so your pea brain can understand it," Natalie said. "Number one: I'm not your sister; and number two: I'm most certainly not among the girls looking to get with you, nor is my friend—not in your wildest dreams. Rather, we're here on a matter of business."

"Business? What kind of business?"

"Do you happen to know what blackmail is?"

"Blackmail? Yeah, I know what that is."

"Okay. Explain it, then," Natalie challenged.

Macho Man opened his mouth and closed it.

"As I suspected, you haven't a clue. Nothing but rocks in your head."

Macho Man didn't like that and took a step toward us. I was ready to retreat, but Natalie wasn't backing down. She held her ground.

"Just in case you and your sidekicks here don't know, let me explain. Blackmail starts with me having a video of you bullying my friend—Peachy. You remember him?" Natalie held up Scott's phone as evidence. "Blackmail comes into play when I tell you what I want, or else said video will be turned over not only to your teachers but to the district attorney, whom I happen to know quite well. You'll be looking at one to two years behind bars for what you did."

Was that true? Or was Natalie making stuff up to sound more intimidating? Either way, it was working.

Macho Man glanced left, then right, looking to see what his buddies thought. They didn't say anything, but he still wasn't ready to give up. He made his next move.

"I'd say you're the one with rocks in your head. Gimme that phone." He stepped forward and reached for Natalie's arm. He was calling her bluff. Too bad Natalie was always way ahead of her opponents.

She sidestepped his attempt. "Do you honestly think I would've shown up here without making a copy of the video first? You're dumber than I thought. You can try to get this phone, but you still won't have all the evidence. And if you take the phone from me, then I guarantee you that the video will be turned over to school and law officials."

I watched Macho Man turn into Mousy Man right before my eyes. The color in his face drained, and his puffed-up chest deflated. He was beaten, and he knew it. I loved Natalie so much in these moments.

"You see, I'm way ahead of you, Stonebreaker. Welcome to blackmailing."

Stonebreaker? How did Natalie know this guy? What was on that video?

"Are you ready to listen now?" she asked him.

Mousy Man's chin dropped. He stood there staring at the ground, and gave the slightest nod.

"Great," Natalie said. "Here's how it's going to work. . . ."

N‍ATALIE K‍URTSMAN
A S P I R I N G   L A W Y E R
Kurtsman Law Offices

Brief #11
OCTOBER: A SIMULATION

Everyone is familiar with the adage "Don't judge a book by its cover." I have a similar personal mantra: "Don't judge a person until you've had her on the stand"—figuratively, of course. It's understood that when you put a person on the witness stand, you get to ask her anything you want. The result is that you get to know the person, which is exactly my point—get to know someone before judging. That was my philosophy, but sometimes I fell short. Camp was an important reminder.

I'm ashamed to admit it, but I'd prematurely labeled each and every one of our camp counselors as a hairy tree hugger. And while there was some truth to that, as the week progressed, I came to see that they were good people with a genuine passion for our planet who had much to teach us— and we had much to learn.

Lesson number one came at the conclusion of our first meal, when it was announced by the kitchen staff how many pounds of food waste they'd collected from our trays. I'm embarrassed to say it was close to a camp record. Improving on this became one of our class goals. We did simple things like eliminate trays; we opted for carrying only a single plate when getting our food, which resulted in us taking less food, thereby having less to waste. By being mindful, we made steady progress in this area over the course of the week—and that felt good.

Not only did we talk about food, but we tackled water conservation as well. This introduced a different adage; not my favorite due to its grossness, but effective nonetheless. "If it's yellow, let it mellow. If it's brown, flush it down."

"What if it's green?" Scott asked. "Sometimes mine is green. Or blue-green, especially after eating blueberries. I love blueberries."

"Well," Mr. Beard responded, "the short answer is, flush it, but I'd say we need to come up with a phrase to add to our saying. If you or anyone else thinks of one, let us know."

Scott nodded and gave an enthusiastic thumbs-up; he was on it. I was relieved when our talk moved on. I was not at all interested in discussing his variously colored scat. (Like how I chose that word? I learned that term during an animal tracking activity led by Mr. Beard.)

In addition to the meaningful conversations, this outdoorsy bunch led us in numerous activities. For example, the aforementioned animal tracking expedition, bottle rockets, yoga, knot tying, outdoor fire building, bird-watching, identifying edible plants, and stargazing, to name a few. All the activities were a mix of fun and interesting, but the simulation we did at the end of the week was by far the best. Why? Because it challenged my thinking and gave me a new perspective.

It started with each of us being given an index card that contained our pretend name and story. In short, each of us was homeless, for any number of reasons. Our goal was to seek assistance and get off the streets. That was to be accomplished by going to the different stations that were set up around the camp. Among the stations were a health clinic, a women's shelter, a regular shelter, the unemployment office, and more. It sounded simple to me, but that all changed once we began—and that was exactly the point.

At virtually every stop I encountered long lines and not enough help. And when I did get to talk to a person (one of the counselors engaged in role-playing), I often discovered that I lacked the required documentation and couldn't be helped, so I was told to go someplace else, where, inevitably, long lines waited. I failed to get back to the shelter in time on one occasion and found myself spending the night on the streets. (This was all role-playing, of course, but you get the drift.) The experience was incredibly annoying, frustrating, and depressing. After three rounds (which represented days), I was no better off. I was ready to quit—again, exactly the point.

After running the simulation, we gathered together and debriefed. We shared the stories from our cards. This part was eye-opening. Why? Because prior to the simulation, we'd all assumed that people on the streets had wound up there as a result of drug or alcohol abuse. Yes, that might be true for some, but not for all. Listening to one another, we learned that some of us were homeless because of mounting medical bills, because of running away from an abusive situation, because of a gambling addiction, because of a house fire or other natural disaster, because we'd lost money in the stock market, or lost our job, and more.

Here was the big takeaway. In some ways it seemed easy for a person to wind up homeless—and it wasn't always that person's fault—but it could be incredibly difficult to improve your situation once you got there.

Just think about that for a second—I sure did. And that wouldn't be the last time I thought about those lessons, either.

8

AFTER CAMP

Randi

I was looking forward to sleeping in my own bed. I was looking forward to my blankets and pillows, my slippers and shower, Mom's cooking, and my personal toilet. I'd had a good time at camp, but I'd roughed it long enough. It's funny how you end up missing the simple things in life when you're without them for a while.

Most of all, I'd missed Mom. We had plans for a nice dinner and a movie, but things changed after I got into the house. I dropped my stuff by the door and plopped onto the couch.

"Good to be home?" Mom asked.

"Yes," I said.

"So how was it?" she asked, sitting next to me.

I sat up, and that was when I spotted the flowers perched in our bay window. You couldn't miss them. It was a huge bouquet in a brand-new vase.

"Where'd you get those?" I asked.

"Oh, from Jacob," Mom said. "Aren't they beautiful?"

"He sent you flowers?"

She hesitated. "Actually, no. He brought them to me."

"Brought them to you? You mean, like, in person?"

"Yes. He came to visit while you were at camp."

"Came to visit? Did he stay here?"

Mom nodded.

"Where did he sleep?"

"Randi, I don't think that is any of your business."

That was all the answer I needed. I wasn't a little kid any-more. I knew how these things worked.

"Do you love him?"

She didn't answer, again telling me all I needed to know. This was beyond serious. We were talking potentially life changing. I stared at the floor. I wanted to be happy for Mom, but I was scared. The next step would be selling our house and moving so that Mom could be with Jacob. I couldn't let that happen.

"It scares me, too," Mom said.

Not the same, I thought.

"I don't want to do something stupid and get hurt . . . or see you get hurt," she said.

"Then take it slow," I warned. "I don't trust him."

That wasn't true, but fear can make you do terrible things. Mom looked hurt by my words, and that sent a shot of pain through my body worse than when I'd torn my ACL. I got up and went to my room. I didn't like what I'd done, but what choice did I have?

Trevor

Mark missed the broadcast on Monday morning, our first one since camp, but that wasn't because he was mad at me. It was because he had an appointment with his doc to see if he could play yet. He didn't make it to school until after third period, but I spotted him in the halls in between classes. I'd been looking for him all morning because I was dying to find out what the doctor had said. I ran up to him.

"Hey, bro. What did he say? Can you play?"

He frowned and shook his head.

My shoulders dropped. "No?" I mumbled. "Sorry."

He shoved me. "Dude, I'm joking. I'm back."

"You jerk!" I yelled.

"Ribs are completely healed." He patted them to show me.

I still felt terrible and responsible for him getting hurt, but man, I was pumped. It was going to feel like we were playing football on the same team again—for the first time all season.

"Strong side," I said, popping him in the chest.

"Left side," he responded, popping me back.

"Strong side!"

"Left side!"

The students walking by looked at us like we were nuts, but we didn't care.

"Strong side!"

"Left side!"

"Gentlemen!" Mrs. Carson yelled, charging out of her classroom. "This is not the practice field. Get to class."

"It's from the movie *Remember the Titans*," I tried explaining.

"I don't care. Get to class!" she ordered.

"Sorry. On our way."

I turned back to Mark. "See you at practice, bro."

"Later, dude."

I jogged to ELA. I hoped we had to do some of that mushy writing about our feelings, because I had the perfect poem in mind. It was titled "Bring on Stonebreaker."

NATALIE KURTSMAN
ASPIRING LAWYER
Kurtsman Law Offices

BRIEF #12
November: Firing on All Cylinders

In our first week back from camp, we featured Scott's videos on *The Razzle-Dazzle Show* every morning. I must admit, he captured a plethora of great moments—none more important than the bathroom episode, which I couldn't share, but that was okay because I'd found a good use for it anyway. His documentary was a huge hit. The seventh grade was already buzzing with excitement, and their turn was still a whole year off.

Of course, in addition to sharing camp videos during the broadcast, we also continued with our typical announcements, weather reports, and previews of upcoming athletic contests. I could tolerate a sports segment on the show as long as it wasn't the sole focus. Besides, to be fair, it would've been negligent, if not completely unacceptable, and maybe even a case of borderline censorship, if I hadn't made time to talk about the football team when they were still undefeated. Such an act could've been grounds for my termination. But to be realistic, the guys never would've let me get away with that. I would've had a mutiny on my hands if I'd tried.

All in all, it was a splendid week for the show. I definitely got the sense that people had missed us while we'd been at camp. Numerous teachers and students went out of their way to tell me so, which made me feel both appreciated and proud, but nothing meant more than when Mrs. Woods shared her praise.

"You've really got this *Razzle-Dazzle Show* firing on all cylinders now, Miss Kurtsman."

I smiled. "Thanks."

"Seems to me there was at least one important development at that camp not caught on Mr. Mason's phone." She was referring to Mark being around again. Mrs. Woods knew full well that something had been amiss and now it was fixed. She was still as sharp as a tack.

"Yes," I acknowledged.

"That's good. Now that you've got everyone on board, I'd say this show is ready for great things."

"What great things?"

"Oh, I don't know, but you'll figure it out. I've got no doubt about that."

Doing something of significance with *The Razzle-Dazzle Show* had been my goal from the onset, but suddenly there was pressure to deliver. It wasn't until the end of the week— Friday, to be exact—when I'd finally finished editing all of Scott's videos that I got around to thinking about what could be next. It needed to be special, whatever it was. It needed to open eyes and push thinking, like the homelessness simulation had done for me at camp. I had no way of knowing if Mr. Holmes had responded to my letter, but I'd promised Robbie that I'd be back to see him, so paying him a visit was next on my list.

SCOTT

I didn't stop smiling all week because so many people kept telling me how terrific my documentary was. Mr. Allen stopped me on my way to class—I thought because I was running in the halls—but he just wanted to talk to me. "Scott, the seventh graders are going to owe you. Your documentary is all the proof I'll need to convince the board to approve sending them to camp next year."

Boy, did that make me smile. "Thanks, Mr. Allen. That's super."

"No, thank you, Scott."

I sped off to class, and Mr. Allen yelled for me to slow down, but I was way too excited for that. My documentary was a hit—and the best parts of camp weren't even in it, like Trevor and Mark becoming best friends again. Their fight had been a doozy, with a real punch and some blood and a black eye, but that wasn't the good part. Their getting back together after the fight was the good part. It was good for *The Razzle-Dazzle Show,* for the Recruits, and especially for our football team.

One week with Trevor and Mark playing together again, and we looked like a whole new team. I dressed and participated in warm-ups for our next game, but after that I put my helmet on the bench and picked up my deluxe clipboard and play sheet. We didn't need a secret-weapon play against Morristown. We blanked them 45–0.

The only thing we were missing was Coach and Mrs. Woods.

Trevor

It's always a good feeling when all kinds of people—cheerleaders, parents, teachers, friends, classmates, you name it—offer congratulations and pat you on the back after a big win. You feel special in those few minutes, even more when your girlfriend happens to be standing next to you during it all. Man, I wanted to take Natalie's hand or throw my arm around her and pull her close, but she had a strict no-PDA policy—no public displays of affection. There would be absolutely none of that—and definitely no kissing. So we walked side by side from the field back to the school. Sounds boring, but that was when things got exciting.

"One more W and then Stonebreaker," I said, making conversation.

"Wait, Stonebreaker? The guy from the bathroom—"

I stopped dead in my tracks. Natalie's hand flew up to cover her mouth, but she'd already let too much slip.

"How'd you know about that?" I asked.

She sighed. "I wasn't going to say anything. I saw Scott's video from the bathroom when I was downloading his files to my computer. It was spotty and only audio in parts, but I saw enough."

"You mean, you saw those jerks pants him?"

"Pants him?" she repeated, not understanding.

"Yanking his sweats down," I explained.

"Yes."

"Whoa."

"Oh, I didn't see his you know, if that's what you're thinking. I saw his white butt, but not his—"

I laughed. "No, that's not what I was thinking, but thanks for clearing that up."

She punched me in the arm.

I waved my finger. "Naughty, naughty. No PDA," I teased her.

She punched me again, and I laughed.

"I didn't know he got all that on video," I said. "I forgot he had his phone recording."

"The boy documented everything at camp."

"I guess so." I worried that his video might've started with me on the pot, but Natalie didn't mention that, and I wasn't asking. I had a different question for her. "So what did you do after you saw it?" There was no way the answer was nothing. This was Natalie we were talking about.

"Blackmail."

"What?"

"Blackmail," she repeated.

"You know how to do that?"

"Of course I know how to do that! This is me we're talking about. How did you think I got Murdoch to be your assistant coach? I bring him breakfast and his mail from the office every morning before homeroom. Technically speaking, that's not blackmail, but you get the point."

"Really? You do that?"

"Yes. That's why I'm not always first to arrive for our broadcast, but you guys needed a male coach on the staff, and I got you one."

"But isn't blackmail illegal?"

"Depends. I wasn't asking for money, just cooperation, so there was nothing illegal about the deal I struck with Stonebreaker and those jerk boys from camp."

"What was the deal you made with them?"

"I threatened to turn the video over to school officials and law enforcement if they didn't leave Scott alone or if the picture that they'd snapped wasn't deleted."

I shook my head. Natalie was way badder than me. "I've said it before and I'll say it again, I'm sure glad I'm on your team."

"Trev, I'm your girlfriend. Of course you're on my team."

Sure wish I could kiss you, then, I thought.

"Hey, lover boy," Mark called from the school doors. "Let's go. Coach Magenta's waiting for you."

I turned to Natalie. "You sure you're glad we're back to being best friends?"

She smiled. "See you later," she said.

"See ya." I jogged to the building but looked back before ducking inside. And that was when she blew me another kiss.

"I saved it for after the game this time," she said.

"Good thinking, but maybe one of these times you can plant it instead."

She blushed, and I ran into the locker room before I died on the spot. I didn't know where I'd found the guts to say that, but I was kind of glad I had.

GAVIN

Come Sunday, it was time to get my butt to the Senior Center for another visit. Magenta and Woods were both in the habit of telling me that Coach was getting better, but he didn't make it to our game again, and sometimes seeing is believing.

I woulda told everyone else I was going, but I wasn't sure what kinda shape I was gonna find Coach in, and I didn't want to jump the gun by inviting more people if he wasn't up for it. If he was doing good, they could join me next time. The only Recruit to go with me was Scott. We always went together, but I made it clear we weren't beating around the bush. The plan was to find his grandpa and get to Coach's room—but when did things ever go as planned? We got to the center, and there was no Grandpa or Coach anywhere.

We raced down the halls, searching for them. Had something happened? Was that why everyone had disappeared? I jumped all the way to thinking terrible things, but I couldn't help it. I had firsthand experience with terrible things. Terrible things happened whenever they wanted to happen. There was no warning when it came to terrible things.

I charged ahead, looking for anyone, looking for answers. The Community Hall was empty, but suddenly we heard a burst of laughter nearby. We took off again and finally found everyone in the TV room. Mrs. Woods had brought the tape of our *Razzle-Dazzle Show,* and she had it playing on the big screen.

"You're watching our show!" Scott cried.

"Just finishing it," Grandpa said. "And we've already watched your game from yesterday. Mr. Magenta taped it for us."

"You boys looked terrific," Woods commented.

"Thanks," I said, glancing at Coach. Smoky was curled up on his lap, but Coach's gaze was zeroed in on us. I elbowed Scott to make sure he noticed. Coach was still tired and not talking much, but his eyes said it all. He knew it was us.

"I don't know squat about football," Eddie admitted, "but I've always said, if you need the world to know something, put it on *Good Morning America* with that Connie Stewart. Guess now I can say, 'Put it on *The Razzle-Dazzle Show.*' That Miss Natalie sure is something."

"She's the quarterback of our broadcast," Scott said.

"Gavin, you tell her and Miss Randi that Agnes and I were asking about them," Eddie said, "and we hope they're having fun stirring up trouble and chasing boys."

Agnes huffed. "You don't need to repeat that last bit."

"That's the important part," Eddie exclaimed.

Me and Scott chuckled. "I'll tell them," I said.

We found seats and watched the rest of our show and an episode of *Judge Judy* with them, and then Woods unlocked the brakes on Coach's wheelchair. "I can see Coach is getting tired, so we're going to head back now. We've had enough excitement for one afternoon." She started steering him toward the door, but Coach stuck his hand up for her to stop.

He nodded in my direction. That was his way of asking for me to do the driving. I was happy, surprised, and scared all at the same time. I walked over and grabbed the handles on his chair and pushed him out the door and down the hall. Mrs. Woods followed us, but she was the only one.

When we got to his place, Woods had me wheel Coach close to his recliner and put the brakes on. "I'll need you to help me get him into his chair," she said.

I didn't know how to do that or what I was supposed to do, but I wasn't gonna say no to her. I walked around to the front of his wheelchair. Smoky hopped down, and Coach leaned on me hard. He was heavy. But that was okay. I was ready to carry him.

"I thought you'd be watching football today," I grunted, trying to make conversation while I struggled to move him. "It's Sunday, you know."

Coach groaned as I helped him into his recliner. He leaned back, winded from the exertion. Smoky hopped into his lap again.

"Valentine," he rasped.

I leaned closer.

"Don't worry. I need to see how all this finishes up before I go anywhere."

I swallowed. "No time soon," I croaked.

"Not yet," he said.

I nodded. What else can a boy do in that moment, except try to be strong?

Randi

Gav called me when he got home from the Senior Center. I never even knew he was going, but he explained why he didn't tell any of us. I understood.

"So how is he?" I asked, referring to Coach.

"Better," Gav said. "He's better, but he's not the same. . . ." His voice trailed off.

My eyebrows scrunched. "How so?"

"I don't know. It's hard to explain. It's not like he's getting confused more often, but he's sleeping more. And he's weaker, too. He's just not the same."

"Do you think the rest of us should visit?" I asked.

"You should. I can't promise you'll get to see Coach, but Agnes and Eddie were asking about you and Kurtsman."

"Really?"

"Yeah."

"I'll tell Natalie we need to get over there."

Gav grew quiet. I waited for him to say something, but he

didn't. "Gav, what's wrong?" I said, sensing there was more. "Why'd you call?"

"Just got a bad feeling about Coach, that's all."

"Oh." I understood bad feelings. Mine wouldn't leave me alone. If anything, they were happening more and getting stronger. I was having nightmares about us moving now. And it didn't help that Mom and I weren't talking. It was the silent treatment all over again, except Mom wasn't being mean about it. I was the mean one. Mom was only trying to give me time and space, but she could give me all the time and space she wanted. That wasn't going to change how I felt.

"I guess there's not much I can do except visit him when I get the chance," Gav said.

"He's getting better, Gav. You said so yourself." That was me trying to say something comforting, but it didn't fool him.

"Yeah, I guess. I'll see you in the morning."

"Okay."

We hung up, and I sat there in the quiet, thinking about Gav and Coach, and then I heard Mom's voice coming from her bedroom. She was on the phone, giggling and carrying on. There was only one person who could make her laugh like that.

I had a bad feeling. A bad feeling.

9

PEP RALLIES
AND BUSINESS
MEETINGS

Natalie Kurtsman
ASPIRING LAWYER
Kurtsman Law Offices

BRIEF #13
November: Kids Klub #2

Monday's *Razzle-Dazzle Show* was nothing more than a week-end recap, definitely not the great things Mrs. Woods seemed to have no doubt we'd achieve, but it would have to suffice, because that was all the energy I could give to the show presently.

Here was the problem: Secretively I was immersed in two important cases. The first involved Scott. I wanted to find time to meet with Mr. Allen to inform him of the bathroom bullying Scott had endured at camp. I had told Stonebreaker I wouldn't hand over the video, but I'd never said I wouldn't tell. Getting Stonebreaker in trouble was not my motive, though I wouldn't have objected to that; rather, I simply wanted to make Mr. Allen aware so that he could keep an eye on Scott and also so that Mr. Allen had knowledge of that backstory before we went into our game against North Lake—in case this Stonebreaker bozo did anything egregious that violated our agreement.

My second case required a return trip to Kids Klub. I needed to know if Robbie's father had responded to my letter. As you can see, I was engaged in serious work, but unfortunately, none of it was appropriate for *The Razzle-Dazzle Show*. As previously stated, this was one video of Scott's that I couldn't put on our broadcast, and there wasn't anything for me to report about Holmes—yet.

"Natalie," Randi called, getting my attention after we'd finished with the show and were packing up. "Gav went and visited Coach yesterday, and he said Agnes and Eddie were asking about us. We need to go and see them."

Add that to my list of things to do, I thought. "I can't go today or tomorrow," I said, "but I'm free on Wednesday."

"I have PT on Wednesday. How about Thursday?"

"That will work. I'll make the arrangements."

"Great. See you later," she said.

"Bye."

Everything I'd told her was true. I'd made arrangements with Father to get dropped off at Kids Klub that afternoon, and I hoped to meet with Mr. Allen the next day after school. I'd purposely chosen Father to be my driver because he never asked too many questions, other than about my school day. Mother would've been interrogating me, wanting to know where everyone else was.

FYI: The answer to that question was "in the dark." No one could know I was potentially stirring up more trouble with Holmes.

All went according to plan. Father was easy. It was the first grader I was on my way to see that had my hands all sweaty. I could go toe-to-toe with the best of them; I could stare down a giant. Yet I was a bigger jumble of nerves than I would've been if I'd been going to see the president.

True, I'd had a heart-to-heart with Robbie the last time I'd visited, and he'd been eager to help me, but now I worried that he might be upset with me for taking so long to return. Nevertheless, the only way to find out was to face the music. I walked into the cafeteria where Kids Klub took place and found Robbie in his usual spot. He was busy reading his joke book again.

I reached inside my bag and pulled out a different joke book I had picked up at the local bookstore. I was prepared. I held it in my hand and walked across the floor.

"Hi, Robbie," I said. When he looked up, I showed him the book. "I thought you might like to read some new jokes."

"Are they any good?"

"Why couldn't the toilet paper cross the road?" I asked.

He shrugged.

"Because it got stuck in a crack."

He laughed. "That's a good one," he said, taking the book from me. "Thanks."

"You're welcome."

I sat down next to him, trying to be as nonchalant as possible. Robbie found another joke he liked and told it to me. We laughed. Then he went back to searching for more. I leaned over. I found a funny one on the bottom of the page and pointed. He read it, and we laughed again.

I confess that I had gone to see if Robbie's father had received my letter and given Robbie a written a response, but sitting side by side with Robbie and laughing over silly jokes was worth my trip. To see him smiling and happy was what was important.

I decided not to mention his father. If the best I could do when it came to Mr. Holmes was help his first-grade son, then that was fine by me. I slid closer, and we continued with the jokes until it was time for me to leave.

"Robbie, I've got to go now."

Hi shoulders slumped. "You do?"

"I'm afraid so. My father just texted to tell me he's here. Thanks for letting me hang out with you this afternoon."

No response.

"Don't worry. I'll come and visit again."

"Really? You promise?"

"Yes, I promise." I mussed up his hair, and then I got to my feet and started toward the exit. I only made it halfway before—

"Natalie, wait!"

I stopped and turned around in time to see him scurrying to his backpack. When he pulled out a folded envelope, I gasped.

He came running over to me with it. "I almost forgot, but don't worry, nobody else saw it."

"Thank you, Robbie." I slipped the envelope into my bag. "I'll be back soon," I assured him.

"Bye."

I smiled, and then I turned and hurried out the door, passing Brian on my way to the parking lot. He was headed inside to volunteer. I waved hello but didn't stop for small talk. No time. I needed to get to the office ASAP so that I could read Mr. Holmes's response.

SCOTT

Mr. Allen wanted to meet with me on Wednesday. I guessed the pressure of the football team going undefeated was finally getting to him and he probably wanted to talk about it. I understood. It wasn't easy. That's why Gavin and me were putting in extra time now. The Warriors were down to this weekend's game, and then it was Stonebreaker. Other than Gavin, Trevor, Mark, and me, no one else on the team knew about the beast. Coach Magenta was a firm believer in one game at a time, so she didn't want us telling the guys anything about the Titan's ferocious linebacker until North Lake was next up on our schedule. All I knew was I had to learn to catch if my secret-weapon play was ever going to be called. I was hauling in about 50 percent of Gavin's passes now, but that was with no one else around and no defense breathing down my neck—and no Stonebreaker looking to maim me. Add that stuff to the mix, and I was going to have trouble breathing, forget catching a pass.

"Scott, how're you doing?" Mr. Allen asked.

"Good," I said. "How're you doing, Mr. Allen?"

He chuckled. "You know, Scott. I don't see you in here that much anymore. I miss our chats."

"Is that why you invited me down here?"

He chuckled again. "Always to the point. Scott, I heard about what happened at camp with that Stonebreaker kid."

I gulped. "You did? Trevor told you?"

"No. Actually, Natalie told me. Apparently your phone recorded the incident and she saw it when transferring files to her computer."

"It did?"

"Yes. I didn't see the video, and Natalie assures me that no one else has, but she felt the need to tell me about it because she wanted me to check on you and make sure you were okay. She was concerned."

"Oh."

"Scott, I did contact the principal at North Lake to tell him what had happened. Brutus Stonebreaker has been suspended from their next game. I intend to push for more, but politics has gotten in the way, since he's their star player."

I gulped again. "Mr. Allen, don't push for more. Stonebreaker needs to be on the field when we play them. If he isn't, then people will always say we only won because he was missing. The team won't get the credit we deserve and neither will Coach Magenta. Please."

"Are you sure?"

"Yes," I said, even though I was already shaking on the inside. Stonebreaker was going to be out for blood after getting suspended.

"Okay," Mr. Allen agreed. "If that's what you want."

"Thank you."

"Now tell me about football," he said.

This was the part I'd been waiting for. I skooched forward in my chair. "Well, we've got to win this weekend, and so do the Titans—without Stonebreaker, but they should—and then we're going to have a huge Thanksgiving showdown. The Titans are undefeated, too. They've got a very tough team this year. It's going to be epic."

"Yes, everyone's certainly getting pumped up," Mr. Allen said. "Here's what I've been thinking. If you guys pull off another win this weekend, then we're going to hold a historic pep rally before the epic Thanksgiving showdown."

"Really? A pep rally?" I exclaimed. "With cotton candy and stuff?"

"You guys win, and I'll make sure we have cotton candy," Mr. Allen promised.

"Oh boy," I squealed. I was so excited, I spilled the beans and told Mr. Allen all about my secret-weapon play even though it was a secret, but he crossed his heart not to tell anyone. I told him how my play was progressing and what I was scared about. And then Mr. Allen gave me some great advice.

"Scott, every person who's brave enough to attempt something great, whether it's writing a book or giving a presentation, running for public office or serving as principal, singing a solo or catching a pass, will battle self-doubt along the way. There will always be that little voice whispering negative thoughts. That's normal, but you can't listen to it. You must quiet it. Do you know how to do that?"

"Plug my ears?"

Mr. Allen laughed. "You need to remind yourself that even

if you do fail, it will be okay, because the trying is the important part. You'll become better and will ultimately succeed as a result of what you've learned from failing, so don't be afraid of it. And after you've tried once, you'll know you can do it again."

"But if I drop the pass, I'm not sure I'll get another chance."

"Maybe not on the football field, but by going for it, you're going to be ready for even bigger and more important things later on."

"Like what?"

"That, I can't predict, but I know this: Whatever it is that life has in store for Scott Mason, it's going to be great."

"Like going into space?"

"Like going into space," he said.

I smiled.

"You should get back to class now."

"Okay. Thanks, Mr. Allen. It's been nice visiting with you."

"You too, Scott. Good luck to you and the team. And keep your eye on the ball."

"I will. Thanks." I sped away. I wasn't in a hurry to get to Mrs. Carson's boring class, but I was too worked up about a pep rally to even think about slowing down. We had to win this weekend—for cotton candy!

Trevor

I blew it. I finally had things back the way they were supposed to be with Mark, and then I went and screwed it up with Natalie. Why did I have to say that about not blowing her kiss? Now she was acting all weird, pretending to be busy after school so that she could avoid me.

It wasn't until Scott came flying into the locker room and started rattling off about his meeting with Mr. Allen that I stopped to consider that maybe Natalie was telling me the truth. Stats Man was all jazzed about some pep rally and cotton candy that Mr. Allen had promised we'd have before our Thanksgiving rivalry if we won our final regular-season game, but I was still stuck on the fact that he and Mr. Allen had had a meeting.

"Wait, you met with Mr. Allen?" I asked. "Why?"

"He wanted to check in with me to see how things were going, and then he told me about the pep rally—and he promised cotton candy! Can you believe it?"

Scott couldn't stop talking about the pep rally, and I couldn't stop thinking about Natalie. She must've said something to Mr. Allen, because why else would he want to check on Scott? That was cool of her, but that still only gave her an alibi for one day—not every afternoon.

I'd blown it. Me and my big mouth. I'd had to say something about a kiss. Idiot. How was I supposed to fix this mess? Getting in a fistfight with Mark was the thing that'd helped get us talking again, but I didn't think slugging my girlfriend was the way to go.

So what, then?

GAVIN

Scott couldn't have been more excited if our locker room had turned into a doughnut shop. The kid was going a mile a minute about Mr. Allen's pep rally idea and cotton candy and snow cones and music and games and, and, and—

"Whoa. Slow down, wild man," I said. "We've got to win this weekend first. Otherwise, none of that stuff happens, right?"

"Yeah," he said, "but it's going to be awesome."

"This weekend first," I reminded him. "Get ready and get out to the field. We need to work on your secret-weapon play."

Coach Magenta was right. All the greats talked about taking it one game at a time. It was hard, but it was what you had to do, or else you were bound to slip up. If I got to thinking about Stonebreaker and our big matchup, I started getting just

219

as excited as Scott—but it wasn't our next opponent or Stonebreaker that was my main concern right now. It was Coach and his health.

Everybody had their reasons for wanting to win. It coulda been for Coach Magenta, it coulda been just 'cause you hate losing, it coulda been for Scott or yourself or your teammates. All good reasons, but the person I was playing for was Coach. Us winning was keeping him going. Us winning was helping him get better. That might sound crazy, but it was the truth. And don't ask me how I knew it. I just did. If you'da helped him into his chair, felt his grip on your arm, and had him look hard and deep into your eyes, you'd understand too. Trust me.

NATALIE KURTSMAN
ASPIRING LAWYER
Kurtsman Law Offices

BRIEF #14
November: Business Meeting #1

I was no stranger to surprising letters, having received several important ones containing pertinent information from Lake View Middle School over the previous two years, but this handwritten note from Mr. Holmes was in a category all its own—and it was only four words. *I'll talk to you.*

I couldn't stop thinking about it, and yet it was only a single sentence. I didn't know what to do. Mr. Holmes's note spurred all sorts of questions. What if the man I had grown to despise the previous year wasn't all bad? Or was I being gullible? What if Mr. Holmes was trying to lure me in with deception? Clearly he knew a thing or two about deceiving people. But what if he was being honest this time? I felt guilty, angry, and confused—but most of all, I was conflicted. As previously stated, I didn't know what to do.

This ongoing dilemma with my conscience was all-consuming. I had to address it—and soon! I'd become so distracted and preoccupied by it that I'd barely talked to Trev, and I even canceled on Randi. I was in no shape to go to the Senior Center on Thursday; Eddie and Agnes would see right through me. When I told Randi I had to cancel, I blamed it on my parents, which was a lie, but it kept her from asking too many questions, and I promised her we'd go on Sunday.

After several days of getting nowhere, somewhat reluctantly I came to the conclusion that I needed Mother's help. I prided myself on my independence, but the fact was that I needed Mother if I was going to accomplish anything. Simply put, there were too many rules and regulations when it came to prisons for a kid to do much. Besides, Mother would be sworn to secrecy because of the attorney-client oath. I scheduled a business meeting with her for after school in the conference room at the office.

"Okay, Natalie, what is this all about?" Mother asked.

I started explaining, beginning with my wonderings about Mr. Holmes. "Truthfully, my questions first commenced shortly after meeting his youngest son, Robbie," I said. "The boy is adorable. He and Meggie Davids are two peas in a pod."

Mother never interrupted. She sat and listened and let me talk. I told her about the visit that Randi and I had had at the Senior Center and how that had gotten me thinking harder about Mr. Holmes, which had led to me organizing our first trip back to Kids Klub so that I could see Robbie and secretly discuss my plan with him. I confessed to mailing a letter to Mr. Holmes in one of Mother's business envelopes so that the sheriffs would regard it as lawyer-related material and be more apt to leave it alone. And then I told Mother about my second trip to see Robbie—and the note he'd given me.

"Here it is," I said. I slid the paper across the table.

Mother held my gaze, then put on her glasses and glanced down at it. "You're always up to something, aren't you?"

"I try to be. Something important, anyway."

Mother chuckled. "I'd say this qualifies." She removed her glasses and sighed. "Natalie, you're special. You're determined to uphold the law and seek justice, but you're also full of compassion. That is a rare combination. You strive to understand the whole person—the human being. You want to read all the pages, not just the summary. I'll warn you, this will likely leave you feeling conflicted many times over, as you see and deal with more and more cases, but don't give up. Don't change—not one iota."

I swallowed. "Conflicted is exactly how I feel."

Mother nodded. "I know."

"Does this mean you'll help me?"

She reached across the table and grasped my hands. "I'll try."

"I need to go and see Mr. Holmes, but prison policies won't allow it."

Mother sat back. "Clearly, meeting with Mr. Holmes is the next step," she mused. "I've got it. You'll need to accompany me as my assistant. They can't deny you then."

I smiled. "How about as your partner?"

"Don't push it."

Randi

There hadn't been a whole lot for me to look forward to this year, but going to see Eddie and Agnes was always fun, so I was disappointed when Thursday came and Natalie canceled on me. Natalie was the best when it came to delivering the truth, but she was terrible at lying. I didn't believe for one second that it was her parents' fault like she'd claimed. There was only one explanation for her canceling last-minute—she was up to something. She tried making it better by rescheduling for Sunday, but I was still skeptical. I wasn't sure what was going on with her, but I trusted that destiny would reveal her secret soon enough.

The nice thing about going to the Senior Center on Sunday afternoon was that it wasn't just Natalie and me going, but Gav and Scott, too. That didn't necessarily mean we'd see each other, because Coach was usually in his room and not hanging with Eddie and Agnes, but today was different. Everybody was in the TV room when we got there—Coach and Mrs. Woods, Scott's grandpa, Eddie and Agnes, and Mr.

and Mrs. Magenta. Natalie and I were the first to arrive, but Gav and Scott showed up not long after us, during a commercial break.

"Hey, look what the cat dragged in," Eddie said. "You boys are just in time to watch our show with us."

"Is it football?" Scott asked. "Today's Sunday."

"Football!" Eddie hollered. "Good heavens, no! We're watching *America's Funniest Home Videos.*"

"I love that show!" Scott exclaimed.

"How'd it go yesterday?" his grandpa asked. "You boys still undefeated?"

"We won," Scott answered, "but it wasn't easy. It was so cold in Oak Falls that I was peeing icicles after the game."

My stomach hurt, we laughed so hard after that comment.

"You're lucky you didn't get frost bite on it," Eddie teased. "They might've had to cut it off."

"Ahh!" Scott shrieked, grabbing himself.

I laughed even harder then. When I finally got myself to stop, I felt like I'd gone through a core workout.

"Shhh!" Agnes hissed. "Our show's on."

We settled in and got ready to watch—everyone except Gav. His eyes were on Coach, not the TV. Coach seemed okay, but how much was he really present was always the question. He hadn't said anything so far.

"Ha! Ha! Ha!" The room burst into laughter. I turned back to the TV and saw a replay of the video that had everyone in stitches. There was a little girl dressed in her mother's high heels and jewelry with makeup all over her face.

"And who're you supposed to be?" the camera person asked.

"I'm Mommy!" she squealed.

"You want to be Mommy when you grow up?"

"I'm going to be a big girl and have a big butt just like Mommy."

Oh. My. Goodness. We laughed harder the second time around.

"Kids say the darnedest things," Eddie said.

"But they're so cute," Agnes replied. "Melt my heart, they do."

"I've got one of those at home," Gav said. "Melting hearts is her superpower."

"I've got one on the way," Coach rasped, taking all of us by surprise. Suddenly he was with us.

"You've got what on the way?" Gav asked.

"A baby," Coach croaked.

"Coach, you're not pregnant!" Scott squawked. "That's impossible!"

"I think he means *the family* has one on the way," his grandpa explained.

"Mrs. Woods, you're pregnant?" Scott screeched. "I didn't know people that old could have babies."

"Ugh! Unbelievable," Natalie groaned, running out of patience. "Scott, not Mrs. Woods." She pointed.

His gaze landed on Mrs. Magenta. She was all smiles, her hand on her belly. "Coach Magenta," he said.

She nodded.

The rest of our afternoon was a mix of laughs and celebration. Mrs. Magenta was going to have a baby! She was barely showing, and I only ever saw her with coaching stuff on, so that explained why Natalie and I hadn't noticed. Apparently

Scott had seen her dealing with morning sickness many times but had never put two and two together. He'd thought it was her nerves getting the best of her on game day. Sometimes he was so silly—and clueless.

I was glad Natalie and I got to spend time with Eddie and Agnes and that we got to see Coach and everyone else. We had fun, but boy, it sure seemed like Natalie's brain was somewhere else. I just had a feeling—and I could usually trust my feelings, which was something that scared me even more.

Natalie's dad gave me a ride home from the center when we were done visiting. I thought it was weird when Natalie got out of the car with me.

"You don't need to walk me to the door," I said.

"I know, but I need to tell you something."

I knew it, I thought. I waited.

"I won't be coming to school in the morning, so I need you to be ready to run the broadcast." She handed me a copy of the script.

"Why aren't you coming?"

"I can't tell you. I'm bound by law, but I hope to be able to explain soon."

We reached the front step, and I stopped and faced her. "Natalie, are you okay? Does this have anything to do with Mr. Holmes?" I'd been concerned that she was going to try contacting Mr. Holmes back before camp, but now she was missing school and claiming to be bound by law and I was suddenly leery again.

"Yes, I'm okay, but I can't say anything more, so please stop asking."

I sighed. "I'll take care of the show. Be careful."

"Thanks."

Before I got into the house and before she reached her dad's car, Natalie remembered one more thing. "Hey, Randi. You do realize we need to go shopping for baby stuff now?"

I smiled. It was never boring with Natalie. I loved that about her.

She waved, and then she climbed into the car and they drove away. *Please be careful,* I thought.

10

THE THANKSGIVING SHOWDOWN OF THE CENTURY

Randi

The *Razzle-Dazzle Show* team gathered in the broadcast room Monday morning, but as she'd promised, Natalie was a no-show.

"Where's Natalie?" Scott was the first to ask. "We're supposed to go live in ten minutes."

"She must be running late," Mark said.

"But she's never late," Gav countered.

"Where is she?" Scott repeated. "Trevor?"

"I don't know," he snapped.

"We can't run the show without her," Scott whined. "Something must've happened."

Panic was beginning to set in. And confusion. Natalie had known this would happen. That was why she'd warned me. I half smiled. The girl was always two steps ahead of us.

"Mr. Mason, calm down," Mrs. Woods said. "Miss Cunningham was about to tell us what's going on."

She must've seen that I was the only one not freaking out.

Mrs. Woods was another one who always seemed to be ahead of us.

"Natalie is fine," I told the group. "She has an appointment this morning."

"An appointment!" Scott screeched. "What kind of appointment?"

"I don't know, but we can't worry about that. We've got a show to put on the air. Here's today's script." I passed out copies. "I'll cover Natalie's position. The rest of you do what you always do. We've got this."

There was a moment's hesitation, like the Recruits weren't sure we could pull this off, but Mrs. Woods jumped in again. "Okay, you heard Miss Cunningham. We've got our backup QB calling the plays today. Are you going to fall to pieces or rise to the challenge?"

"Let's go!" Scott cheered. "We've got a show to save!"

A little football talk was all he needed. The ball was snapped, and we got cracking. Scott did his weather segment and ran through the morning announcements, and then I took over and gave a weekend recap, with special emphasis on the guys' big win.

"They're calling it the Snowbowl," I said. "I'm talking about our football team's game that took place in the tundra at Oak Falls on Saturday." (I was making that up, but Scott really liked it.) "With the win, our Warriors have finished the regular season without a blemish on their record, setting the stage for a huge contest on Thanksgiving against an undefeated Titans team from North Lake. The game is already being billed as the Thanksgiving Showdown of the Century and is expected to be the biggest clash in the history of this storied rivalry. To maximize our school spirit and to get us completely psyched, Mr. Allen has decided it's time for our first-ever Thanksgiving pep rally. Stay tuned for details on that in the days to come. In the meantime, Lake View Middle, pat our players on the back, congratulate them, and wish them good luck. I'm Randi Cunningham. Have a razzle-dazzle day, Warriors."

The broadcast ended, and the guys slapped high fives. We'd done it.

"Randi, you were great!" Scott exclaimed.

"Thanks. You too."

I felt like I'd just finished competing. I was a mix of thrilled and relieved, but there wasn't any awards ceremony to run off to. Instead we had to get to class. I started gathering my things.

"Randi, you really don't know what kind of appointment Natalie had to go to?" Trevor asked before leaving. Mark was with him, and Gav was standing nearby. Scott had already Tasmanian-deviled out the door.

I sighed. "I really don't know, but she's up to something."

I wasn't sure if Trevor liked that answer or not, but he nodded. There wasn't much else I could say or he could do. "Great show today," he said. Then he and Mark turned and left.

Gav had to meet with a teacher, so he was leaving right behind them. "You were the perfect star today, Cunningham," he said. "I'll see ya later."

"See ya."

That left just Mrs. Woods and me in the room. "Great save today, Miss Cunningham."

"Thanks," I said.

"Miss Kurtsman knew she could count on you. That's why she entrusted her anchor role to you."

I nodded.

"We should all be so lucky to have such friends. Miss Kurtsman made that comment about Mr. Mason, and I'm saying it about you. I know you're focused on winning more gymnastics championships, and I have no doubt you will, but you're much more than a gymnast, Miss Cunningham. You're one of the best friends I know of. I saw it in the way you befriended Miss Kurtsman and Mr. Mason in sixth grade, I saw it with Mr. Davids last year, and I saw it again this morning."

I looked up at her, but I didn't say anything. I couldn't. "Have a good day, Miss Cunningham."

I nodded, and then Mrs. Woods quietly walked out the door. You would think hearing such nice things would've made me feel extra special, and it did, but boy, it also stirred up all kinds of emotions.

What kind of friend would I be if I moved away and left the Recruits behind? If I left Gav behind?

And what kind of daughter was I for the way I was treating Mom?

Natalie Kurtsman
ASPIRING LAWYER
Kurtsman Law Offices

BRIEF #15
November: Business Meeting #2

I would never advocate for skipping school. I'd received five perfect attendance certificates thus far and had been on my way to number six, but this was a necessary sacrifice. Mother believed it would be easier to convince the sheriffs that I was her assistant if we visited Mr. Holmes on a weekday, because wouldn't I have been in school otherwise?

My heart kicked into high speed the moment we pulled into the prison parking lot, and it started beating even faster after I climbed out of the car and began looking around. I'd seen a cell tower before, but somehow the one next to this place seemed gigantic—and eerie. The single row of tiny flowers growing in front of the concrete fortress did nothing to make the building feel inviting. Intimidating was more like it. But the single most unnerving site was the chain-link fences erected beside the main building, encompassing what was commonly referred to as the prison yard. The fence had to be twenty or thirty feet tall, and scariest of all, lining the top of the chain link for the yard's entire perimeter were coils of razor-sharp barbed wire. It was terrifying.

Mother stopped outside the entrance. "Ready?" she asked.

I pulled in a deep breath. "Ready," I said. But I was nowhere near ready.

We walked through the door, and I was shocked to see a metal detector only a few feet away. Next to it was an X-ray machine for bags and purses. It was similar to airport security, except there were no lines and this felt way more serious. The sheriff on duty came out. I noted the name on his badge—Sheriff Martin.

"May I help you?" he asked.

"Yes, I'm Gloria Kurtsman, attorney, and this is my assistant, Natalie." Mother handed him her ID. "We're scheduled to meet with Mr. Holmes."

The sheriff glanced at Mother's ID and gave it back to her. Then he looked at me. "This is your paralegal?" he asked, incredulous.

"Assistant," I corrected him, preferring that term. "Yes, I'm young, but I also happen to be an expert at law. Thank you for your role in helping us to uphold it."

He cracked a grin. "Well, according to policy—"

"According to policy, attorneys and assistants are permitted to meet with prisoners, so you'll let us meet with Mr. Holmes now," I said, and smiled. "Please. I don't believe you want an ageism lawsuit on your hands."

Sheriff Martin needed a second to recover, but he managed to find his voice again. "You—you are correct. That is our policy," he stammered. "Go ahead and place your bags on the belt and step through the metal detector. One at a time, please."

We did what he'd asked, and then we were inside. It was that simple.

Sheriff Martin showed us to the meeting area and told us to have a seat while he went to inform Mr. Holmes that there was an attorney here for him. "Sheriff Martin," I said, stopping him before he was gone. "Will you please tell Mr. Holmes that Natalie is here to see him as well?"

Sheriff Martin cocked his head, giving me a peculiar look. "Sure thing," he replied.

Mr. Holmes had the right to refuse to see anyone, and I worried he might do that if he thought only Mother was here, but based on his note, if he heard my name, he would agree. I held my breath and waited—for three very long minutes—and then the door opened and Mr. Holmes entered the room and took a seat across from us. Sheriff Martin stayed so that he could supervise our visit, but he sat far enough away that we had privacy.

"Who else have you told?" Mr. Holmes growled, eyeing Mother.

"No one," I said, trying to sound brave.

"Mr. Holmes, I'm Gloria, Natalie's mother. Natalie is crafty, but she's also smart. Given prison policies, there was not much she could do for you on her own, so she came to me for help. I'm bound by attorney-client privilege to keep everything we talk about today confidential. Natalie and I made the same agreement before she told me anything about your case."

"Why are you doing this?" he asked.

I swallowed. "I met Robbie."

"How's my boy?" Mr. Holmes asked, his tone softening.

"He's good, but sad," I said.

Mr. Holmes sighed. "I need your help."

"We're here to listen," I assured him.

He took a deep breath and started at the beginning. "When I lost my factory job, I lost our health insurance with it. Being a hairdresser, my wife, Stephanie, didn't get insurance at her job. So buy new insurance, you say. Not so easy when you're out of work and can't afford it. I got the coaching position, but that paid next to nothing.

"We went along like that for a while, until Robbie fell out of a tree and broke his arm. That scared me like I'd never been scared before. Me and Steph scraped together enough money to pay for his ER visit and all, but that was a close call. If he'd needed surgery or if any other terrible thing were to happen, we were doomed. I couldn't let that happen to my family. So I found a way.

"I took enough money from the booster club that I was able to get our boys on a plan, but I never did that for me or Steph. That was next. It was easy until you came along. You and your friends and all your questions."

"This is not Natalie's fault," Mother interjected, defending me.

"No, it's not," Mr. Holmes admitted, hanging his head. "I'm the one responsible for my bad decisions, and I've made many. I don't want to blame anyone; I only want to make sure my family is okay."

"Keep going," I said.

"A few weeks ago I had a scare. I started sweating and having crushing chest pains. I couldn't breathe. I was feeling numb and tingly. I thought I was having a heart attack. I thought I was going to die.

"The guard found me and got me help. The doc here checked me out and told me I'd had a panic attack. Most likely brought on by all my stress and worrying. I got a full exam, and found out my blood pressure was through the roof and my cholesterol was bad. I'm lucky I'm in here, because they got me the meds I need and I'm going to be okay. What scares me is Stephanie. She hasn't been to a doctor in forever. She could be like me—or worse. She's got some family history stuff that should be monitored.

"I need her to be okay. My boys need her. Can you help her? Please?"

Mr. Holmes had gone from being a scary and coldhearted man to a desperate and helpless one. His story could've been on any one of our index cards at camp. He was one accident away from losing everything.

"We'll try," Mother told him. "We'll try to get her help."

"Thank you," he said.

Mr. Holmes didn't stick around after that. He pushed back from the table and left the room.

Mother and I also left—with a lot to think about. I didn't know how I felt. Mr. Holmes certainly had made mistakes, and had done many wrong things, but he'd done them to protect his family. Yes, his anger toward Gavin was not acceptable or easily forgiven, but when a person feels helpless, one can see how he might end up on Holmes's path.

"Natalie," Mother said when we got into the car. "Mr. Holmes just shared a lesson with you that you'll likely never learn in school: life is not always fair."

If school wasn't going to teach students that, then maybe *The Razzle-Dazzle Show* could? My plan for helping Mr. Holmes was already beginning to take shape.

Trevor

Randi had told me Natalie was up to something, so I started thinking that maybe the fact that she'd been kind of ignoring me had nothing to do with me. That should've been good news, but it just got me worrying more. Not about the big US, but about Natalie. I couldn't imagine what she was up to this time—and when Randi told me that she'd asked and Natalie wouldn't tell her because she was sworn to secrecy under lawyer law (whether really true or not, Randi couldn't say), I believed it. It was Natalie we were talking about. So I didn't bring it up when I saw her, but I hoped to find out the story "soon," which was what I guessed she'd told Randi. Well, "soon" showed up faster than I'd expected, and not at all *when* I expected.

Brian and Madison were over for dinner. Brian had the night off from class. Mom was doing a lot of talking, because having them there always got her excited. She liked Madison a lot. So did I. She was way cooler than Brian's old goons, Chris and Garrett—and way hotter, too. Mom was going on and on about Thanksgiving plans, telling everyone when dinner was going to be served and what we were having and making sure Brian was coming—and Madison was invited, too, of course. Like I said, on and on.

"I've got it, Mom. Don't worry. We'll be here," Brian promised.

"Right after Trevor's big game," Madison added.

I smiled. Told you I liked her.

"You guys ready for that Stonebreaker kid?" Brian asked.

"How'd you know about him?"

"Oh, I've got my ways, don't you worry," he said, giving me a hard time.

"No, really. How'd you know?"

Brian smirked. "I was maybe talking about you at work and one of the guys mentioned that his son plays for the Titans. Said they're undefeated and that their Stonebreaker kid is a real bruiser. He showed me a picture of the kid that was in one of the papers. He did look tough."

"You were talking about me?"

"I said maybe, and don't let that go to your head. You know who else I saw?"

"Who?"

"Your girlfriend. She was at Kids Klub not long ago. That little boy you guys visit told me she'd come to see him."

Robbie. Robbie Holmes. What are you doing now, Natalie? I wondered.

"You kissed her yet?" Brian asked, trying to embarrass me.

Madison jabbed him in the side with her elbow. Normally my brother's heckling would've irked me, but I didn't even respond. My brain was too busy trying to figure out what Natalie could be doing with little Robbie Holmes.

"Brian, stop," Mom said, trying to stick up for me, but she just made it worse. "He's too young for that."

"Oh, really?" Dad said. "Too young? I can't seem to recall, when was your first kiss, Dorothy?"

"You hush up. That's not important," Mom snipped.

"Mom!" Brian squawked.

Madison jabbed him again.

"You be quiet too," Mom warned my brother. She pushed back in her chair. "Time to clear the table. Madison, would you mind giving me a hand?"

"Sure thing, Mrs. Joseph."

"Kiss-up," Brain teased.

Madison jabbed him hard for that one. Then she got up and carried a pile of dishes into the kitchen. Dad got Brian talking about classes and work, and I took that chance to slip away from the table.

I wasn't staying quiet much longer. Maybe I didn't have the guts to kiss Natalie, but once I was done with football, the gloves were coming off and I was demanding answers.

Her clock was ticking.

SCOTT

I got to interview Mr. Allen about our first-ever school pep rally on *The Razzle-Dazzle Show*. Everybody was asking questions—teachers and students—so the interview was a way to get answers. It was my idea.

I started with a very important question. "Mr. Allen, there's going to be cotton candy, right?"

"There will be cotton candy," he confirmed.

"Good. You promised."

"Yes, I did," he agreed.

"What else can you tell us?" I looked at my notes. "When is it going to be?"

"I've scheduled the event for next Wednesday, our last day of school before Thanksgiving break."

"That's only twenty-four hours before the showdown," I said.

"Yes, I know. I've decided that holding the pep rally during school hours makes the most sense. Chances are that nothing productive will be happening the day before break anyway, especially since we only have a half day, and the daytime means we can get the whole school involved."

"That's awesome!" I exclaimed. "No boring social studies!"

"I'm glad you agree," Mr. Allen said, and chuckled. He went on to explain some of the details. Our pep rally was going to include several different contests between grade levels. One was a float contest that kids could sign up to work on. I would've done that, but it was during practice. Another competition was a cheering contest, to see which grade had the most spirit, and another was a team relay race through an obstacle course. At the finish line you had to run through a poster of the Titan mascot. And after that it was cotton candy.

My interview with Mr. Allen was a big hit. Natalie decided the best way to continue building excitement for the pep rally and our big game was by doing different showdown-related stories on our broadcast every morning—and that meant a feature on the beast. Once Natalie caught wind that Stonebreaker was a transfer and repeating eighth grade, she went wild. This hot-topic issue was the sort of thing she ate up. You should've seen her on our show.

Natalie started slowly. She did a very thorough job of presenting all the different arguments for and against transfers, painting a clear picture of the debate, but then she finished with a bang. She left no doubt about where she stood on the issue. "It's unfortunate, but our league is behind the eight ball on this because there is no policy on transfers, so you can say what you want, but if you ask me, this Stonebreaker addition is borderline cheating. The Titans couldn't beat us fair and square last year, so they went and found a fifteen-year-old transfer to help them get the job done this season. I can't wait until Coach Magenta and the guys show them it still wasn't enough."

I'd never expected Natalie to dish out trash talk, but boy, was she good at it. You could hear cheers and hoots from all over the school after she said that. It wasn't even the pep rally yet, but she had Lake View Middle psyched and ready to go.

Problem was, *I* wasn't ready. Stonebreaker had been chasing me in my nightmares, and now he was starting to come after me in all of my daydreams—and I did a lot of daydreaming in school, especially in Mrs. Boringest's class.

To make matters worse, the same day our Stonebreaker segment ran on *The Razzle-Dazzle Show*, there was a story about him on the local evening news. Those same TV people who'd come to our field when Coach Magenta had first gotten the job were talking to Stonebreaker now. He'd already broken the state record for most tackles in a single season—and he hadn't even gotten to play in their last game!

"Brutus, congratulations on your outstanding year," the reporter said. "But what do you say to the people complaining about you being a transfer?"

"They're a bunch of poor losers," he growled. "If they'd won, they wouldn't be saying anything. Nothing but crybabies. And the people over at Lake View are only whining because they're scared—and they should be, because the pain train is coming." He flexed his muscles for the camera, and I almost peed my pants.

The reporter's eyes got big. "What are your thoughts on going up against an undefeated Warriors team and their star quarterback?" she asked next.

Stonebreaker snarled. "The Warriors are gonna pay the

price for me sitting out last game—and it's gonna hurt. That Davids kid better run fast, because I'm gonna be breathing down his neck all game long."

That scared me half to death, and he wasn't even talking about me. Natalie had been trying to watch out for me by telling Mr. Allen, but she'd only gotten the beast angrier.

"He's ugly," Mickey said.

"Yup," Dad agreed.

"My goodness, he's got a beard," Mom cried. "Look at him. Is he really only fifteen?"

"That's what they say," Dad said.

"He wants to beat your team up," Mickey observed.

"Thanks, Captain Obvious," I said, and gulped.

"Scott, you'd better not get on the field with that—"

"Ugly mean guy!" Mickey yelled, finishing Mom's thought.

Dad laughed, but not me. That night I dreamed that the poster at the end of the pep rally relay race was Stonebreaker, and it tackled me and ate all my cotton candy while I was pinned to the ground. I woke up kicking and fighting against my blankets.

I didn't fall back asleep for the rest of the night. I didn't want to. I didn't eat breakfast in the morning, either—and Mom had doughnuts. My stomach didn't feel good. It was full of nerves. I didn't throw up, but I was feeling yuckier than Coach Magenta with her morning sickness.

I wanted the pep rally, but I wanted the Thanksgiving showdown to be over more. Forget the secret-weapon play. That was a lost cause. I was a lost cause.

GAVIN

Coach Magenta had told the team about Stonebreaker, and we were working on a plan to deal with him, but after his story hit the news and the guys saw him on TV, they were nervous. You could probably say some of them were even scared. Scott was the worst. He fell to pieces. He went from catching close to 80 percent of my passes to dropping almost all of them again. We needed his head in the game, and I had a feeling we might need his secret-weapon play before we got done.

I found Magenta after practice and told her I was worried about the guys—Scott, especially. "This Stonebreaker kid is in their heads. They're starting to crumble under the pressure."

"Don't panic, Gavin. This is normal. As long as you remain confident and keep leading us, we'll be okay."

"All right," I said. I trusted her, but I kept thinking about the team. Maybe that's why I was the one to come up with the brilliant idea this time. I had to 'cause everybody had Stonebreaker on the brain. Well, if they wanted Stonebreaker, they were getting him.

I remembered seeing a picture of our rival in Dad's newspaper. I found it when I got home from practice and cut it out. I gave the picture to Woods the next morning at school and asked her to make me a bunch of photocopies. I took the copies and made every player on our team tape one onto the front of his helmet. I taped the extras all over the locker room. Stonebreaker was staring at us from everywhere when I got done. The guys got used to seeing him on the field. They got used to blocking him, tackling him, and running from him.

"He's no match for your wits or my arm, and he's definitely no match for your speed," I promised Scott.

I don't know if he believed me, but we kept working on his play. And as he got more and more comfortable with Stonebreaker glaring at him, he started catching my passes again.

"You're ready, Stats Man," Coach Magenta told him after our final practice. "Our secret-weapon play is in the plan."

I fist-bumped him, but inside I was hoping we didn't need his play. I didn't want something bad to happen—and if Stonebreaker ever got his hands on Scott, it would be real bad.

SCOTT

Mr. Allen deserved an awesomest-principal trophy. His pep rally was the best.

He called all students and faculty down to the gymnasium shortly after homeroom. I ran so that I could get a good seat in the bleachers, but I didn't get to stay in my spot for long. Mr. Allen had our team gather in the hallway outside the gym while everyone else went inside. We were still standing in the corridor when he got things started. We could hear him on the other side of the doors because he was using a microphone.

"Do I have sixth grade here?" he called.

"Yeah," they chirped.

We laughed.

"Oh, come on," Mr. Allen bellowed. "This is a pep rally. I need to hear you. Do I have sixth grade here?"

"YEAH!" they screamed.

"That's more like it," Mr. Allen responded. "How about seventh grade?"

"Ahh!" they shouted.

"And eighth grade?"

"Woot, woot!"

"All right," Mr. Allen said. "Are you ready to get our un-defeated Warriors psyched for tomorrow's showdown? Are you ready to let them know we're behind them?"

The gym exploded in screams and shouts and cheers. I got goose pimples.

"Okay, then," Mr. Allen said. "Please welcome your Lake View cheerleaders."

The doors to the gym flung open and our cheerleaders paraded inside. Somebody dressed in a Warrior mascot costume was with them. I'd never seen that before. It must've been a brand-new purchase. Our cheerleaders put on a performance that got the student body all fired up.

"Let's hear it for our cheerleaders," Mr. Allen said when he took the microphone again.

More craziness and yelling.

"And now let's meet our team," Mr. Allen shouted. "First up, number twenty-two, Justin Lopez."

Justin walked through the doors, and the gym erupted.

Mr. Allen announced each player one by one, saving the eighth graders for last. Mark and Trevor got huge responses. And when Gavin got called, it felt like the roof was ready to come off the place. I thought Mr. Allen had forgotten me, because I was the only one left in the hall—but I was wrong.

"And last but not least. Let's hear it for Stats Man, Scott Mason."

I walked through the doors, and the noise almost knocked me down. I saw the team gathered in the middle of the floor.

I ran to join the huddle, and then we started jumping up and down and cheering with everybody else.

When the noise died down, Mr. Allen grabbed his microphone again. "Now it brings me the utmost pleasure to introduce our spectacular coach, the first female football coach in state history, the extraordinary Coach Magenta!"

The gym went bananas, but it wasn't just more noise. I saw all the teachers on their feet, giving Coach Magenta a standing ovation, and all the students quickly followed along. It was a screaming, cheering standing ovation.

Lake View Middle was in a frenzy, but I thought I heard the faint sound of a banging drum. *Boom. Boom. Boom.* The sound grew louder, and I could tell that other people heard it, too. *Boom! Boom! Boom!*

Mr. Allen directed the cheerleaders and our team into the bleachers, and then he hurried over and opened the gym doors. The high school marching band marched in next. Our pep rally went from awesome to super-awesome.

The band put on an incredible performance, and afterward we had our cheering contest to see which grade had the most spirit. I screamed my head off, and we won. Mr. Allen presented our grade with a new trophy—the bronze warrior. That's when I realized that our pep rally marked the beginning of a new tradition. It felt really awesome to know we were the first ones to start it.

The final event of the pep rally was the team relay race. I was running anchor for our squad. Gavin put me in that position because the last person had to sprint across the floor to the finish line, and I was the fastest. But the last person also had to run through a poster of a Titan, and as I got closer, I saw that someone had taped the picture of Stonebreaker over it—the same face that had flattened me in my nightmares.

Coach Magenta had told me I was ready and that my secret-weapon play was in the plan, but it wasn't until I tore through Stonebreaker that I believed her. We won the relay race and I got my cotton candy, and it tasted so good.

GAVIN

The guys who land in the Pro Football Hall of Fame all have something in common. They've all played in big games. And the ones who've been lucky enough to line up against other greats in those contests have had parts of their legacies written in those moments.

Maybe I was only in eighth grade, but I knew that this Thanksgiving showdown was where my legacy would start. If things didn't go well, my story could die on the field, and if Stonebreaker got ahold of me, I could die, too, but if things went our way, then the writing next to my name in the Hall of Fame would begin with this game. If things went like I'd dreamed, this game would be worthy of mention in the Hall of Fame, not just 'cause of me and Stonebreaker, but also 'cause Magenta would cap off an undefeated season in her first year—and as the first-ever female coach in our state history. Any way you sliced it, this was a big game. Huge. It was a game that would be talked about for a long, long time—maybe even forever. But the best part wouldn't be in any of those conversations. The best part happened before the opening kickoff.

When I led the team to the sideline after warm-ups, I spotted Mrs. Woods standing near the bleachers. Scott's grandpa was next to her. And in front of them, perched in his wheelchair, wearing a winter hat and with a blanket covering his lap and legs, was Coach.

I jogged over. "You made it."

"Coach insisted we come," Mrs. Woods said.

I swallowed.

"Ready, Valentine?" Coach croaked.

I nodded.

"Fight hard," he said.

"Till the last play," I promised.

"Hi, Grandpa," Scott said, joining us. "Hi, Coach. Hi, Mrs. Woods."

"We came to see your secret-weapon play," Grandpa said.

Scott gulped.

"He's ready," I said, patting him on the shoulder pads.

Scott's grandpa winked at me. "Go get 'em, boys."

I locked eyes with Coach one more time, and then me and Scott turned and jogged back to the sideline.

"What do you say we win this one for the old-timer?" Coach Magenta said.

"And for you," I added.

The officials called captains, and I walked to the middle of the field for the coin toss. That was when I came face to face with Stonebreaker for the first time.

"You Davids?" he said.

The brute was even bigger in person. "You Stonebreaker?" I responded.

"You'll know after I hit you the first time."

I wasn't about to let his trash talk psych me out, but you better believe I was nervous. Once I stepped into the huddle for our first possession, all that went away, though. It got replaced by the eye of the tiger. Welcome to legacy time.

We put together a solid opening drive. We had a string of good plays, including a couple of tough runs from Mark and a big completion on my first pass, but then we were forced to punt after Stonebreaker stuffed us on third down.

Our defense answered the call. Trevor and Mark showed they could hit and tackle just as much as Stonebreaker. When I saw that, I got pumped.

The first half was everything it was supposed to be, a battle between our top-ranked offense and the Titans top-notch defense. We had a few strong drives, but still no points to show for it. The score was notched at 0–0. Stonebreaker was definitely the best we'd seen, and he hit harder than anyone else we'd played against—I could vouch for that. He knocked the snot out of me on one sideline tackle, but I did what the greats do. I hopped right back up and showed him I wasn't backing down. That play mighta been the most important one of the first half, 'cause after my teammates saw that, they were ready to go and fight with me—and for me.

The second half was more of the same, a back-and-forth battle. We still hadn't found the end zone, but by the fourth quarter we were putting together longer drives, which meant Stonebreaker stayed on the field, getting more and more tired.

We got the ball back with less than five minutes to go, and Coach Magenta dialed up our no-huddle offense. It was her genius idea to put this into our offensive game plan over the last week of practice 'cause she knew we might need it. Stonebreaker's tongue was dragging like Otis's. We got inside the red zone, which meant we were less than twenty yards from the end zone. We were so close, I could taste it—and I got too excited. I put too much pep on my next pass, and it bounced off Trevor's hands. Stonebreaker made a huge interception off the tip and ran it out to the forty-yard line before I knocked him out of bounds. He didn't pop up right away 'cause he was exhausted.

I glanced at the game clock on my way back to the sideline. I went from tasting the end zone to choking on a probable tie. We didn't have overtime in our league, so our only chance was to get a quick stop and get the ball back right away.

Randi would claim what happened next was thanks to destiny, and maybe that was part of it, but it was Coach Magenta who had made sure we were always the better-conditioned team, and boy, did that make a difference. Trevor refused to quit. He was so mad about that interception that he ripped through the line and sacked the Titan's QB on third down. The ball was knocked loose, and Mark was there to recover the fumble. We had seventeen seconds and no time-outs. This was it.

"Okay, Scott. It's time," Coach Magenta said.

He looked at me, and I nodded.

"I can't. I'm not ready," he squeaked.

"Scott, if you try and fail, it's okay," Coach Magenta said. "But if you don't try at all, that's going to be hard to live with.

That will always bother you. Not trying is not okay. You've got to try—for us, but more for you. You can do this."

He gulped. "Mr. Allen told me the same thing."

"Well, he's a smart guy," Coach Magenta said. "After all, he hired me for this job."

Scott chuckled.

I looked at Coach Magenta with the eye of the tiger, and then I pulled Scott along and we jogged out to the field and stepped into the huddle. I didn't even need to call the play.

"Catch the ball, and we'll do the rest," Trevor promised. "We've got your back; you know that. We've always got your back."

We broke from the huddle and lined up in trips right, with Scott just off the line of scrimmage. The ball was snapped. I took a one-step drop and turned and threw him a beauty. The ball hit Scott in the chest and popped straight up into the air.

Stonebreaker was charging like a madman. If Scott had seen him, he probably woulda peed his pants right there on the field, but the kid never took his eyes off the ball. It flipped end over end and fell back down into his hands. He tucked it under his arm like I'd taught him and turned up field. He'd lost valuable time by not making a clean catch. The defense was closing fast. This play was designed as a quick hitter, not a slow-motion play. But Scott had never been worried about the running part; it had always been the catching part. He'd made the catch. Now the race was on. He sidestepped the first defender and put the burners on. Stonebreaker's outstretched arms grazed Scott's back, but that was as close as he got. Scott was a magician doing his disappearing act—there one second, and gone the next. The Titans never had a chance.

I raised my arms in the air. There would be a sentence in the Hall of Fame about the Warriors stats man and his secret-weapon play, hailing Scott Mason, the perfect star on that fateful afternoon.

Randi

My favorite part of the game was after Scott scored the game-winning touchdown. He didn't do a big spike with the football or any kind of end zone dance or celebration. He found the nearest official and ran over and handed him the ball and shook his hand. Meanwhile, his team was going nuts, jumping and hugging, and the crowd in the bleachers was jumping and hugging, too.

Natalie and I got down and ran onto the field. I found Gav and threw my arms around him. "You were great," I said.

"Thanks."

I didn't want to let go. I didn't want to lose him, but he eased up, so I stepped back. "I had to find you before everyone else gets to you," I said. "You're going to be busy for a while."

Sure enough, Meggie was right behind me, running up to hug her big brother. We laughed.

I looked around and spotted Natalie hugging Trevor. Maybe it was the energy and craziness of the moment, or maybe Trevor really couldn't wait any longer, but he asked her right there on the spot, "Natalie, what's going on with Robbie Holmes? Are you okay?"

Her answer was not one that anyone could've expected. Natalie raised onto her tippy-toes and planted her lips on his. She kissed him! Beautiful-looking Natalie had her arms wrapped around a sweaty, grass- and dirt-stained football player—and she was kissing him. My mouth hung open, but no one was more surprised than Trevor. He was all smiles when it was over.

"Everything's great," Natalie said. "Stop worrying."

I was pretty sure the only thing Trevor was thinking about after that was Natalie's lips, but that performance definitely left me wondering what she was up to.

Trevor

Natalie kissed me! She kissed me. Right on the fifty-yard line. Forget "no PDA."

"Everything's great," she said. "Stop worrying."

What can I say? I did. I wasn't thinking about anything but our kiss.

Scott was the star—but I was the man!

11

THE ACCIDENT

NATALIE KURTSMAN
ASPIRING LAWYER
Kurtsman Law Offices

BRIEF #16
December: Starring Robbie Holmes

By the end of my meeting with Mr. Holmes, one thing was made clear: his family was his main concern; they'd always been his top priority. So the question became how to help.

By Thanksgiving I'd spent considerable time with Robbie Holmes and had captured a host of valuable moments with him on video. I used our school break to get those videos in order and edited so that they were ready to roll when we returned to school. Robbie was the perfect approach. He was going to soften everybody up with his cuteness, and then I'd hit them with the rest of the story. I had lots of energy behind me, not only as a result of our big win but because after the game Mr. Allen had informed me that the league's superintendents had committed to establishing a policy with stricter guidelines about transfers before the next school year. Our show had helped make a difference, and we were going to do it again.

"Ladies and gentlemen," I said, calling my broadcast team-mates to attention. "Welcome back. I hope everyone enjoyed the break, but now it's time to get to work; we've got a big week ahead of us. I know some of you have been wondering what I've been up to. You're about to find out." I began handing out the day's script. "You'll note that I've carved out additional time for my segment this morning so that I can introduce my new story."

"What is it?" Scott asked. "Is it a feature about our big game?"

"No, my piece is not about your game," I said, "but if you look at the script, you'll see that there is also an extended block for Randi to do a sports recap, and we can definitely do more about the game throughout the week. I know there is loads we can talk about related to that incredible victory, so don't worry."

I peeked at Trev and saw him staring at the floor and smirk-ing. It was obvious what play he was recalling, but our smooch was definitely not something we'd be covering on the show.

"Okay. Places, everyone," I said, kicking us into gear. "Let's make sure we're ready to go."

I glanced at Mrs. Woods, and she winked. She knew about one of my surprises, but not both.

We ran through the normal segments of our broadcast—lunch menu, school announcements, Scott's weather report, and Randi's sports recap—and then it was time for the first surprise.

"Good morning, Lake View Middle," I said, greeting my viewers. "We're taking extra time on today's show to intro-duce a new story, but before we get to that, I'd first like to invite our favorite retired teacher and broadcast supervisor, Mrs. Woods, to the set for a special announcement."

Mrs. Woods walked out and stood before the camera. "Since Coach Magenta can't be here this morning, she asked me to share a letter she received from the football coaches association." Mrs. Woods looked down and read from the piece of paper she was holding. "'Dear Coach Magenta, we are pleased to inform you that Gavin Davids has been selected to play in the state's inaugural eighth-grade all-star game. The game will be held inside the Lake Region Dome on artificial turf. More details coming soon. Congratulations.'"

Mrs. Woods smiled and offered Gavin her compliments, while Scott started cheering wildly. Trevor, Mark, and Randi followed suit, but I took that as my cue to quickly resume with the show before the wheels fell off the bus.

I slid back in front of the camera. "Thank you, Mrs. Woods, for that exciting announcement, and congratulations to Gavin. Now it's time for me to share a new story with you—one that begins with my friend Robbie."

Mark clicked on the designated link, and our screen cut to the first video I had uploaded. It was a shot of Robbie at Kids Klub. "Can you tell us your name?" I could be heard asking.

"You know my name, you silly."

The Recruits giggled.

"Yes, I know your name, but my many classmates watching this might not know you," I said.

"I'm Robbie. Can I tell your friends a joke?"

I remember not expecting him to say this, but once he had, I'd known that it was perfect. Robbie's joke of the day would become our new segment. "Sure, okay," I said.

"Why did the chicken cross the road?"

"Why?"

"To get to the stupid person's house."

I waited for more, but that was it. "I don't get it," I said.

"Knock, knock," he said.

"Who's there?"

"The chicken!" Robbie screeched.

We were supposed to stay quiet on the set, but the Recruits couldn't keep from laughing out loud at that. My plan was working.

"Got any more?" I asked Robbie.

"I've got one for you. What kind of underwear do reporters wear?"

"Gee, I don't know," I said.

"News briefs!" Robbie squealed.

I heard laughter coming from across the hall after that one. The screen cut away from Robbie and came back to me in the broadcast room. "You can expect to hear more from Robbie throughout the rest of the week. He's only part of an important story that needs to be told. I'm Natalie Kurtsman, saying, 'Have a razzle-dazzle day, Warriors.'"

Our show ended, and I glanced around the room. Robbie had put a smile on everyone's face—but those smiles quickly faded when we saw Gavin's scowl. You could feel the tension in the room. This was serious, but I'd known that going in.

One by one my teammates left. No one said a word—not even Scott. *What have I done?* I wondered.

The only one who said anything was Mrs. Woods. She was my coach, and she knew just what I needed.

"Miss Kurtsman, I realize you're determined to become a

lawyer, and I have no doubt that you could make an exceptional one, but it seems to me you might be more interested in helping people than perhaps you are in laws and bureaucracies. Don't sell yourself short. Being a lawyer is a respectable job and a major accomplishment, and in no way do I intend to minimize that, but you can be more. You can use your lawyer background to make a difference for humanity. That's what you're doing now. And as you can see, such pursuits won't be met without controversy, but you need to keep going.

"Keep going, Miss Kurtsman."

She patted my arm, and I looked up through wet eyes to see her leaving.

"Thank you," I whispered.

Trevor

Those segments with Robbie Holmes that Natalie was playing on our morning show were fun, but after a few days, the fun was wearing off. It was time for her to move forward. Gavin still hadn't said anything, but he didn't need to. His cold silence said it all. I didn't want some fight going down that had me needing to choose sides, so I tried talking to Natalie about it when we were walking to class.

"Natalie, you weren't there during football last year. Mr. Holmes was really bad to Gavin. I mean, really bad. Racist bad. Full of hate. You bringing him up again . . . I just . . . I don't want anyone to get hurt or upset. That's all."

"Trev, that's sweet," she said, taking my hand in hers. "I plan to reveal the rest of the story tomorrow, so don't worry."

Natalie was smart and sneaky. She made me forget about everything just by holding my hand. And to make sure I stayed distracted, she gave me a peck on the cheek before ducking into her classroom. It was quick, and no one else was around to see it, but, man, it did the trick. Gavin and Mr. Holmes were out of my mind until our next broadcast, when Natalie got in front of the camera and finally came clean.

"Friends, rather than share more of Robbie's jokes again today, I'd like to share the rest of his story. It's time."

She paused to let that sink in. It was weird. I could almost feel the school growing quiet and getting serious.

"My friend Robbie's full name is Robbie Holmes," Natalie continued. "If his last name sounds familiar, that's because his father is our former football coach. Mr. Holmes currently resides in prison because of an embezzling scheme that was uncovered here last year.

"It was never my intention to dig deeper into Mr. Holmes's past, but after meeting Robbie, I felt torn because I really liked the boy. The more time I spent with him, the more I began to wonder about Mr. Holmes. How could the father of this wonderful little boy commit such a crime? Something felt amiss. I suspect some of you may be thinking and feeling the same things, and you've only just met Robbie, so imagine how strong those emotions were for me.

"Those of you who know me will attest to the fact that I have a hard time letting questions go when I don't have the answers. Getting answers is what I do. In this case, that required meeting with Mr. Holmes. I won't go into the details of how I managed to pull that off, but I did, and here's what I learned."

Natalie went on to explain Mr. Holmes's complicated story. It sounded like something straight off one of our cards at Nature's Learning Lab—Natalie even said so herself. This stuff was real.

"Let me be clear," Natalie said. "I'm not asking you to help

Mr. Holmes, but I am asking you to consider helping his family. To help Robbie, whom you've all grown to adore.

"Mr. Holmes's story is a lesson for all of us, a reminder that life is not always fair. Perhaps our story can show something different. Sometimes in life people can get lucky. Sometimes in life, good people can make all the difference.

"I have already established a GoFundMe page for the Holmes family. Details are on your screen now. The money raised will be used to get Mrs. Holmes a medical checkup and to help address any health-related concerns. If possible, the Holmes family might be able to restart health insurance, which would be the ultimate goal.

"How about it, Lake View Middle? Let's see what we can do. I'm Natalie Kurtsman, asking, How big are your hearts? Have a razzle-dazzle day, Warriors."

I can't say I liked Mr. Holmes any better after listening to Natalie's piece that morning, but I did ask Mom and Dad to donate to the GoFundMe page.

GAVIN

After getting the exciting news about the all-star game, I was outside throwing with my tire target every chance I got. Before and after school and first thing Saturday morning.

"I'd have you help me give the van an oil change," Dad said, "but I guess you can do that next time. I know you've got this big game to get ready for." He patted me on the back and walked around the side of the house to crawl under his plumbing van.

I kept throwing. My hands were ice cold and I couldn't grip the ball good, but that was no excuse. Brett Favre became a legend because of his great play and the toughness he showed in braving the brutal cold at Lambeau Field. If I was going to be like him, I needed to start training now.

But it didn't matter how many pep talks I gave myself. It wasn't working. I got madder and madder with each throw I missed. I couldn't manage a tight spiral, and I couldn't hit the freakin' target. And getting mad just got me thinking about Kurtsman and her Holmes stuff all over again, and that turned mad into angry. And then stupid Otis had to show up. Meggie had gone with Randi to some gymnastics clinic that Randi's gym was hosting, so the dog was bored and had to bother me. He grabbed my football and tore around the yard.

"Gimme my ball," I growled.

Otis shook his head, and slobber flung from his mouth. He got down low, shaking his rump high in the air. That stupid dog thought I was playing. He was dead wrong.

"Give it," I ordered, raising my fist. That did it. Otis dropped the ball and shrank away from me. I'd never raised a fist to him before. It scared him—and me. I'd just threatened to hit him, but I would never hit him, no matter how mad I got. Realizing what I'd done made me feel even worse.

"I'm sorry, Otis. I'm just not in the mood for playing." I grabbed my slobbery football and punted it over the house. "Get out of here," I said. I wanted to be left alone.

Otis tore around the house after the ball. Nothing coulda stopped him. This was his favorite game.

A football bounces in unpredictable ways. It might go end over end, or it might take erratic sideways hops. It can go every which way. And Otis was a big dog. As big as a small horse. He was too big to stop on a dime, especially when charging after a football that was bouncing all over the place—even a football that bounced toward the van your dad was underneath.

Dad had the jack positioned where it was stable and safe, and the block of wood was behind the back tire to keep the van from rolling. Safety first. Always safety first. But that jack wasn't built to withstand a crushing blow from the side.

The collision between dog and van sounded like a high-light reel hit from the NFL. Otis crunched the door when he ran into it. He hit with such force that he pushed the van sideways. He rammed it so hard, the jack that Dad had had holding the front end off the ground—the jack that had been positioned where it was safest so that nothing could go wrong—tipped and fell over. My entire world toppled in that moment.

Dad's yell was a sound I'd never heard before. It echoed off the hills and pierced my heart. I tore around the house faster than Otis had run. "Dad!" I cried.

I slid on my knees and peered under the van. Dad was as white as a ghost. There were beads of sweat dotting his fore-head, and blood was trickling down his cheek. The left front wheel was on top of his hip, pinning him to the ground and crushing him under all its weight. Dad was done yelling, but the low moans coming from him were even scarier.

I knew the "scared" you felt when you were afraid of get-ting in trouble. Or the kind that made you yell, like when you were on a roller coaster or spooked during a scary movie—the kind of scared you got to laugh about later. And I knew the scared that happened before a big game. But this kind of scared I'd only ever felt once before. This was the kind you felt when you were afraid you might lose one of the most impor-tant things in your life—forever.

I'd heard of people becoming superhuman in times like this, becoming stronger than any NFL lineman. I jumped to my feet and grabbed the front bumper. I lifted up on it with all

271

the strength in my body. I tried. I willed myself to do it—but it was hopeless. I couldn't get it to budge.

"*Niño*, the jack. Use the jack!" Mom screamed from the porch. She dropped the phone and came running. "We have to get it off him!"

I got down and found the jack. I slid it into position, where it was safe and stable like Dad had taught me. His breaths were shallow. My eyes blurred. I pumped on the handle, and the van rose into the air.

Mom slid underneath on her belly, and Otis army-crawled in next to her. He knew Dad was hurt. He nosed Dad's shoulder and licked his arm. If dogs could talk, Otis was definitely saying "sorry."

"It's okay, Otis," Mom said, petting him behind the ears. "He's going to be all right." Otis rested his big head on Dad's chest, and I swear, me and Mom smiled for a second.

The sound of sirens rang in the distance. I listened to them growing louder and closer.

"The ambulance is on its way," Mom said.

"Hang in there, Dad. Fight," I urged.

Randi

We got back from the gymnastics clinic just in time to see Mr. Davids getting loaded into the back of an ambulance. There was an oxygen mask covering his face, and he looked as white as the sheets covering him.

Meggie jumped out of the car before Mom had even stopped. She ran into Gav's arms, and he held her tight. "Daddy got hurt, Megs, but he's going to be okay."

My heart ached—for the intense love I was witnessing between big brother and little sister, for Mr. Davids and Mrs. Davids, and for Mom. I didn't want to be upset with her anymore.

All at once Mrs. Davids broke away from her husband's side and hurried into their house. Seconds later she came running back out with her purse.

"Mom, I'm coming, too," Gav said.

Mrs. Davids stopped and gripped his shoulders. "*Niño,* you need to stay here with Meggie and Otis. I promise I'll get you to the hospital as soon as I can." Her voice cracked.

Gav bit his lip. I could feel how badly he wanted to go, but there was no time to fight.

Mrs. Davids bent and kissed Meggie on the forehead. "Everything's going to be okay, *mija*."

Meggie wrapped her arms tighter around Gav.

Mrs. Davids glanced at me next. "I'll stay," I said.

"Thank you, Randi." She squeezed my arm, and then she ran and hopped into the back of the ambulance. They closed the doors behind her and sped away. Otis stood at the end of the driveway watching them until they disappeared.

"Randi," Mom called from the car. "I'm going so that I can be there for Carla and give her a ride home when she's ready."

I wanted to run and hug her and tell her how sorry and scared and everything else I was. I wanted to tell her how much I loved her—but I only nodded.

Mom drove off, and the three of us plus Otis were left standing in the driveway. When you feel this kind of shock and confusion, you don't do much talking. You kind of turn into a zombie. Gav and Meggie weren't saying anything, and neither was I. We shuffled into the house and sat in the living room. The TV was on for noise, but that was it. Gav was in the chair, gripping his football, staring into space. Meggie cuddled with Otis on the floor. That was the first time I ever saw that dog not wagging his tail. I'd held it in as long as I could. I cried silently.

We stayed that way for hours, not talking and not moving. I didn't know what to do. I thought back to what Mrs. Woods had told me. I tried to be the best friend I could. I made a pot of mac-n-cheese around dinnertime even though none of us felt like eating. Even Otis skipped out on it. That tells you how sad he was. I cleaned up, and then I helped Meggie get into bed. Otis stayed with her, so I returned to the living room.

At some point later in the night, Gav and I finally drifted off to sleep. I woke with a crick in my neck when I heard Mom and Mrs. Davids talking in the kitchen. Gav sat forward in his chair. He was awake now, too. We made eye contact, but we didn't start talking. Listening to what was happening in the kitchen was more important.

"What am I going to do?" Mrs. Davids asked. The desperation in her voice was loud and clear. "Michael's already had one surgery, and the doctor said he's likely going to need more. We can't afford the ambulance ride, let alone surgeries."

"Carla, insurance will cover all that. You don't need to worry," Mom said, trying to comfort her.

"Jane, Michael and I don't have health insurance. We have the kids on it, but it cost too much for the two of us. I missed a lot of work with everything that happened last year, and we had to make some hard choices. We wanted to find something again. In case. But it's not easy to read through all those forms. I was trying . . ."

She broke into sobs.

I looked over at Gav.

"My card at Nature's Learning Lab said I became homeless after I was in an accident and couldn't afford my medical bills. I didn't have health insurance," he said.

"That doesn't mean anything," I scoffed.

"Stop pretending, Randi. If that's not destiny giving me a warning, I don't know what is."

"Fine. But that doesn't mean it's your destiny," I said, trying to keep him positive.

"It will be if we don't find the money."

"Hey, maybe Natalie can do one of those GoFundMe pages for your family, like she did for the Holmeses."

"That's barely raised anything," Gav said. "We're gonna need way more than that."

He was right. I sagged on the couch. "What're you going to do?" I asked, my voice barely above a whisper.

"I don't know, but whatever it is, it's gotta be big."

SCOTT

It was Sunday, but I was out of bed extra early because I had a big day ahead. There was lots on my to do list. First up was practice at Gavin's house. I was training him for his upcoming all-star game. I wasn't going to be on the sideline, but I'd told him I would still be his eyes from the bleachers. I had come up with a series of hand signals so that we could communicate through sign language. Silent communication had worked for the Recruits once before, so I knew we could do it. After our workout we were going to the Senior Center for dinner with Grandpa and Coach. It was going to be an exciting day.

Mom dropped me off at the Davidses' but didn't come to the door. Ever since I'd gotten my phone, she'd stopped doing stuff like that because I could call or text her if I had a problem.

I knocked and heard someone come running from inside the house. *Gavin's excited, too,* I thought. *This is going to be great.*

The door flew open. "Scott! What're you doing here?" Gavin groaned. He looked surprised to see me.

My shoulders slumped. "We're training today, remember?"

"No," he moaned. "Scott, I can't practice today." He stomped away and left me standing there.

"Why not?" I said.

I stepped inside and saw Meggie sitting next to her big dog. She was wearing her jacket and a hat and gloves, and she had her backpack on, too. Randi was also there. She was helping Gavin fill his bag with sandwiches and water bottles and other stuff.

"What's going on?"

Gavin sighed. "Scott, there's been a change in plans."

"What do you mean? We're supposed to practice."

"Scott, my dad got hurt yesterday. Hurt bad. We've got to go and get him help."

"In the hospital, hurt bad?" I asked.

Gavin nodded.

"But won't they help him?"

"It's more complicated than that."

"We need money to pay for my daddy's hospital bills," Meggie said. "He doesn't have inchurents. So we're going to get money."

Now I understood. "So you're going to the bank?"

"We don't have enough money in the bank," Meggie said. "We're going to *Good Morning America* so I can get on TV and save my daddy."

"Oh." I thought about that for another second, and then it hit me. "You're the new secret-weapon play!" I exclaimed. "That's perfect. Nobody will expect it.

"But wait. Today's Sunday," I suddenly remembered out loud. "That show isn't on until tomorrow morning. Why are you going now?"

"'Cause that show is in New York City," Gavin said, "and that's not exactly right around the corner."

"Oh yeah. New York City!" I exclaimed. "We're off to the Big Apple!"

"No," Gavin snapped. "Scott, you can't come. This . . . I don't want you to get in trouble."

"I'm the guy calling plays for this outing, not you. Consider this an audible. I'm coming, and that's it."

Gavin groaned. "We don't have time to fight about it. If you want to come, fine. But you made the call, not me."

"I made the call," I said, and smiled.

Gavin threw on his coat and backpack, and Randi got her stuff, too. Meggie squeezed her dog. "We'll be back soon, Otis. Be a good boy."

Otis lay down and whimpered. He was bigger than Stonebreaker, but he was acting smaller than me. I didn't know why yet.

We walked outside and climbed into Mrs. Davids's car. I got into the back with Meggie, Randi rode shotgun, and Gavin hopped behind the wheel. I got my phone out and started recording.

"Scott, gimme that stupid thing," Gavin hissed. He snatched my phone and ran inside the house and got rid of it. Then he came running back out and jumped into the car, and away we went.

"My phone," I whined. "What'd you do that for?"

"We can't risk your mother tracking you and coming to find us. We've got one chance to make this Hail Mary work."

"But I was going to make a documentary like I did at camp. We could put it on *The Razzle-Dazzle Show* and—"

Randi handed me her phone. "Use mine," she said.

Gavin glanced over at her.

"It's a good idea. It could help," she said.

I grinned.

"Whatever," he grumbled. "Just make this part quick, 'cause I'm not supposed to be driving. I don't have a license, in case you forgot."

I hadn't thought about that. This was the most dangerous thing I'd ever done—except maybe getting on the football field with Stonebreaker. We were breaking the law. Good thing Natalie wasn't with us. I hoped she wouldn't want to arrest us when we got home.

GAVIN

Eddie had said if you wanted the world to know something, then put it on *Good Morning America*. So I was getting Meggie on that show if it was the last thing I did. After that, everything hinged on her superpower ability to melt hearts. Scott was right. She was our secret-weapon play—and we needed a touchdown.

Turns out that wasn't the only miracle we needed. Our first close call showed up way before I was expecting, when the gas light suddenly came on. I'd never even given that a thought, but there wasn't anything I coulda done anyway. The bottom line was, we needed fuel—or else we weren't making it very far.

I pulled off the next exit and found the near-est gas station.

"Oh, thank goodness," Scott said. "I've gotta go potty like you can't believe."

Meggie giggled.

"Are you kidding me?" I hissed. "This has to

be fast, and I mean fast, 'cause the last thing I need is someone to notice me driving."

"I'll be fast," Scott promised. "It's diarrhea that I feel coming on, so it's going to fall right out of me."

"Gross!" Randi yelled.

Meggie started laughing. Nothing about this was funny, but if you thought about all we'd been through in the last twenty-four hours, her smiling instead of crying was probably the biggest miracle.

"Make it quick," I warned him.

He took off, and I hustled inside and paid the cashier. I only gave her five bucks 'cause I needed to save as much money as possible for the rest of the trip. I hurried back outside and grabbed the hose.

Scott got there as I was finishing up, but that was already too late. The old man at the pump across from us was staring at me. "C'mon. We gotta get out of here," I hissed.

Meggie musta noticed the old man, 'cause she rolled down her window. "My brother's a late bloomer. We're not sure if he'll ever need to shave."

The old man chuckled. Meggie had used her magic.

"Oh, be quiet," I said to Megs, trying to play along. I looked over at the man and shook my head.

"Don't worry, kid. I was a late bloomer, too. Don't rush shaving. Once you start, you'll wish you never had to do it."

I closed the gas cap and put the hose back. I gave the old man a wave, hopped into the car, and drove away.

That was enough close calls for me—but we were just getting started.

Randi

The train was my idea. It's what Mom and I took when I had to go to New York City for my knee surgery. We parked in the garage next to the station because then we didn't need to worry about paying until we came back.

"Okay. Grab your stuff and let's go," Gav commanded.

"I've never been on a train before," Scott said, sounding excited. This was the next big event on his field trip.

"Me neither," Meggie chimed.

Gav looked at me and shook his head.

I smirked. As much as he didn't want Scott tagging along, I was happy we had him—and I know Meggie was, too. Her superpower might've been her ability to melt hearts, but Scott's was his ability to keep us laughing and calm. Without him, this would've been too intense. Without him, there would've been no documentary—and that turned out to be ingenious.

Once we made it into the station, I took the money from Gav and went to make our purchase. Piece of cake—except for one problem. He only had enough cash for three tickets, not four. Oh well. I wasn't about to give up that easily. Friends don't quit on each other. I bought three tickets and led the way out to platform five. I didn't say a word to the others because the less they knew the better.

I remembered from my trip with Mom that you didn't actually need a ticket to get onto the train. The conductor came by and collected them after you were already on your way. So that made it simple. We were going to ride the rails like they did in the old days. Add that to the list of laws we were breaking.

Our train pulled up, and we boarded with everyone else. We found a set of open seats and sat down. The doors closed moments later, and the train lurched forward. This was it. There was no turning back. Now it was time for outsmarting the conductor—but I hadn't figured that part out yet.

"It reeks in here!" Scott exclaimed. "I feel like I'm choking on a ninety-year-old fart."

"Yucky," Meggie said, and giggled.

I couldn't have agreed more. The train was far from luxurious. The floor reminded me of the school cafeteria, and the blue-and-red seats were made of cracked plastic that just pinched, poked, and scratched you, but the stink was by far the worst. It stunk of dirty old air. Air that had been trapped inside those doors since its beginning and had never escaped, making it incredibly stuffy. The odor was suffocating, but the real challenge came when Meggie said she had to use the bathroom.

"Now?" Gav said.

"Yes. I've been holding it all morning. Randi, can you take me? Please."

Walking on a moving train was no easy task, especially when you've got a less-than-perfect knee, but who could say no to Meggie? Hopefully, no one. Our entire plan was counting on that, and I wasn't about to jinx it.

"Okay," I agreed.

"Thank you," Meggie said.

And then it hit me—or destiny did. The bathroom was the perfect place to hide. I glanced ahead, searching for a sign. Instead I spotted the conductor. I saw him through the windows in the connecting doors, slowly making his way toward us. I turned around and looked in the other direction, and that was when things got more serious. There was a woman wearing a stiff blue hat collecting tickets in the car behind us. This was a big train, which meant it required two conductors. One started in the front while the other started in the rear. They worked their way to the middle until they bumped into each other.

"C'mon." I grabbed Meggie's hand and led her down the aisle. We headed in the direction of the male conductor since he was farther away.

When you're traveling straight on a moving train, it's not bad, but as soon as the track makes a sudden turn, you get thrown to the side. Meggie and I held on to the corners of the seat backs as we moved forward, doing our best to keep our balance, but one of those sharp turns was a little too much for my knee and peanut Meggie. We got tossed into the lap of a newspaper-reading businessman.

"You girls all right?" he asked, helping us back to our feet.

"Yes, thank you," I said.

"Sorry about your paper," Meggie added.

"That's okay," the man said. "It's nothing but the same old depressing news about our economy and health insurance."

"We could tell you all about that," Meggie replied.

"We're looking for the bathroom," I cut in. Meggie had already said too much and had him curious. We were supposed to stay unnoticed.

"It's in the next car," the man said, his eyebrow raised. "Just keep going."

Meggie and I smiled and hurried on, but I was terrified. Since the bathroom was in the next car, that meant we had to go through the connecting doors, bringing us closer to the conductor, but that wasn't the worst of it. Nothing scared me more than those connecting doors—not even back tucks on the beam.

The first door had to be pulled open and the second one pushed. Much easier said than done. I gripped the handle and leaned back, pulling with all my weight and strength. I got it open just enough for Meggie and me to slip through, and then it slammed shut, trapping us in the area between connecting doors—on a moving train! Just so you understand, we were standing on a rubber floor made of two separate panels, each extending from the car it was attached to. The panels shifted up and down in different rhythms as the two cars jockeyed side to side. The thunder of the train and the beating noise of air whipping by filled the space all around us. And just below, the ground raced by in a blur. Walking from one car to the next felt like playing with death, and yet Meggie was giggling. She found it fun. Not me!

I held my breath and lowered my shoulder. I leaned into the second door, again using all my weight and strength. It barely budged, but we slipped through the opening. The million-pound door sucked shut behind us, and I breathed a sigh of relief—because we were alive, but also because destiny had finally given me a break.

The bathroom was right there. I lifted the small silver lever and slid the door open. We ducked inside before the conductor ever laid eyes on us. I closed the door and locked it. We were safe, tucked away inside the most disgusting bathroom I'd ever seen. It was a porta-potty on wheels, but I told Meggie to make herself comfy because we weren't leaving.

It had to be the worst way to travel, stuck in a moving porta-potty, but Meggie was a trouper. Fighting to keep my balance every time the train jerked one way or the other was harder than staying on the beam, and my knee was aching by the end, but we made it.

"GRAND CENTRAL TERMINAL," the mysterious train voice announced.

I sighed. "Finally." I looked at Meggie. "Ready?"

"Yup," she replied, as excited as ever, eager for the adventure ahead.

I slid the bathroom door open, and we melted in with the rest of the passengers getting off. We found Gav and Scott, and I relaxed. I hoped the hard part was over—but we had a long way to go yet. Mr. Davids was still stuck in intensive care, and destiny had much scarier things waiting for me.

GAVIN

We got off the train and hurried up the platform and into Grand Central Terminal.

"Wow," Meggie said. "This place is huge."

"Everything in New York City is big," Randi said, looking around.

"Gavvy, look at the ceiling. Look at all the constellations. How do you think the artists got them up there?"

"I don't know. C'mon." I pulled her along. I wanted to get us over to the side, where we would remain undetected. The place was massive, made of what looked like beautiful white marble or stone, but Meggie was definitely going to catch people's attention if she kept standing there gaping at the ceiling like that. Everyone would find that cute.

"Gavvy, how do you think they got up there?" She was still talking about the stars and the artists.

"Angels," Scott answered. "New York City has lots of them."

Meggie didn't say anything. She musta liked that answer. I did. We were gonna need the help of angels to save my father.

"All right, listen," I said. "Here's the plan. We're making the trip to Times Square now so that we know how to get there in the morning."

"So this is like our walk-through practice on the day before our game?" Scott said.

"Yes, exactly, but we need to hustle, 'cause it's getting late in the day, and I want to be back here before dark."

"Why back here?" Scott asked.

I sucked in a deep breath. It was time. I had to tell them eventually. "'Cause this is where we're sleeping."

That was the first I'd told any of them about that part of the plan. I'd known from the beginning that we'd have to find some random place to crash 'cause we didn't have enough money for a hotel, and Grand Central Terminal looked and sounded better than the streets.

"We're going to be like Claudia and Jamie in *From the Mixed-Up Files of Mrs. Basil E. Frankweiler,*" Meggie said.

"I love that story!" Scott squealed.

I shook my head. *Saved by a book,* I thought. *Mrs. Woods would be so proud.* I glanced at Randi, and she shrugged. What choice did we have?

Scott used Randi's phone to pull up a map with directions to Times Square. "Okay," he said, pointing. "That way."

We walked through the doors, leaving our home-for-the-night behind, and stepped out onto Forty-Second Street. We were hit smack in the face with New York City. Let me tell you, this was a lot for a small-town boy to take in.

"Wow," Meggie said. It was a lot for my little sister to take in, too.

Standing across from us like a wall of defensive linemen

were buildings so tall, you had to strain your neck back to glimpse the tops. Taxicabs darted in every direction, bullying their way through traffic and blasting their horns. And everywhere you turned there were people. People, people, and more people.

"C'mon. We'd better keep moving before we get run over," I said. Stonebreaker had never sacked me, but standing in the middle of New York City people traffic was definitely a way to get knocked to the ground.

I took over holding the phone so that it didn't get dropped or stolen, and led the way. I counted the intersections but didn't see any signs for Times Square. I was beginning to get nervous that I'd somehow missed it, when all of a sudden there it was, off to my right. We'd made it. We entered the world of bright lights and colors. Signs shone everywhere, advertising

different companies and stores. Massive billboard-like television screens hung in several locations, broadcasting previews of upcoming movies and events.

"Is this it?" Meggie said, her eyes wide with wonder.

"This is it," I said.

"It's pretty."

"Look!" Scott exclaimed, pointing.

He'd spotted the *Good Morning America* studio. Even now, with little activity going on, the place looked very official. It made me anxious.

"Gavvy, there it is!" Meggie squealed, hugging me.

"There it is," I said. "Tomorrow morning we've got to get here and get you on TV. It's our only chance at saving Dad."

She squeezed me, and I squeezed her back.

"Okay," Randi said. "Let's go spend the night under the stars with all those angels, so that we're ready for our big day."

"C'mon, Scott," Meggie said, skipping off. "We're going to sleep under the stars with the angels."

"Thanks," I whispered to Randi.

She grasped my hand, and we didn't let go, not until we'd made it back to Grand Central Terminal.

Mrs. Mason called, wondering if I'd heard from Scott or had any idea where he might be. The answer was no; I certainly didn't know Scott's whereabouts. I found her call odd but didn't think much of it—that is, until I heard her voice shaking.

"Thank you, Natalie. Please let me know if you hear from him," Mrs. Mason choked.

"I will," I said. I was about to ask if everything was okay, but she hung up.

I texted Randi to see if she knew anything but received no reply. Somewhat annoyed by that, I resumed my preparations for the next day's broadcast, but I found it increasingly difficult to focus, the longer I went with no response from her. Mrs. Mason had been genuinely concerned. What was going on?

Eventually my phone buzzed. Finally a text—but not from Randi.

> Trevor: mrs. mason wuz just here w/ randi's mom looking for scott randi gavin and meggie, know where they r?

> Trevor: they were pretty worried

I promptly replied: No.

And then I sent him a second text: Let me know if you hear from them.

> Trevor: 👍

I wouldn't say I was worried just yet. I qualified more as curious—very curious, to be exact. I didn't believe anything bad had happened; on the contrary, I had the feeling my friends had disappeared together and were entangled in some devious plot. Hence my curiousity.

It was only a few minutes after I'd received Trevor's text that Mrs. Mason and Ms. Cunningham arrived at my house. I heard Mother greeting them.

I walked out of my bedroom, knowing they were looking for me. "I don't know where they are," I said. Mother looked at me, clearly puzzled. "Randi, Gavin, Meggie, and Scott have disappeared," I explained, bringing her up to speed. "Trevor texted me."

Mother turned to Mrs. Mason and Ms. Cunningham for verification. They nodded.

"Gloria, why don't you sit down with Natalie. Let me fill the two of you in on what's happened," Ms. Cunningham said.

I flinched. It was the tone of her voice. For the first time, I began to worry. Maybe something bad had happened.

Ms. Cunningham started at the beginning and gave us the full story. *How much can one family be asked to endure?* I wondered, thinking of the Davidses. I'd been wrong not to worry.

Very wrong. Mr. Davids was in intensive care. He'd already undergone one surgery to repair a tear in his liver, and he was going to need at least one additional surgery to fix his broken leg. He was in rough shape, but the dire financial situation that this put his family in was far worse. It had the potential to be tragic.

I felt my phone buzz. I excused myself and hurried to the bathroom. I'd just learned from Mrs. Mason and Ms. Cunningham that Scott's phone had been left behind and that Randi's phone had had the location settings turned off so that she couldn't be tracked, so who was texting me? Curiosity replaced worry again. My friends didn't want to be found. What were they doing?

I locked the door and pulled my phone from my pocket. Finally, some answers.

> Randi: Don't tell ANYONE! PLEASE!

> Randi: In NYC. Very important. Sending you videos to explain.

Whoa! This was insane! What were they doing in New York City?

I waited for the videos to come across, but staring at my phone didn't speed things up. There were tiny bubbles on my screen, which meant Randi was replying—or sending—but it was taking forever. How big was the video? Didn't she know not to make it too big or else it wouldn't send? And how many was she sending? I hoped she knew enough not to send several at once. If I waited in the bathroom much longer, it would raise suspicion.

I began texting her a response, but before I finished, the first video suddenly came across. I quickly deleted all that I had typed and opened it.

Already I was confused. The text was from Randi, but the video had been taken by Scott. They were in a car—and Gavin was driving! Were they out of their minds? Gavin was breaking the law! He could get arrested!

"Meggie, can you say hi to the camera?" Scott asked.

She waved.

"Got any jokes for us?"

Was he taking a page out of my book, getting viewers to love her before spilling the whole story? I'll admit, I was flattered—but still over-the-top concerned.

Meggie shook her head. Just seeing her made me smile—but she looked sad.

"Can you tell everyone your name and what we're doing?" Scott asked.

"My name is Meggie Davids," she told the camera. "My brother is Gavvy. Gavvy's best friend is Randi, and she's with us. So is Scott. He's behind the camera.

"My daddy got hurt bad in an accident yesterday. He's in intensity care in the hospital. We're on our way to save him now. I'm the secret-weapon play. Don't worry, Daddy. We're going to get help."

The video ended.

I wanted to scream. That was like a chapter ending on a cliffhanger. Only, with a book you could keep reading. Not so with videos. I had no choice but to wait for the next one—and I had no inkling when it might show up. Torture!

Of course, my immediate dilemma was what to do now? Should I tell Mrs. Mason and Ms. Cunningham or keep it secret? The first thing Randi had texted was not to tell. I certainly wasn't going to give away their location, but Randi also didn't know how worried her mother and Mrs. Mason were.

I considered telling them that I'd heard from Randi and that everyone was safe, but if I did that, they were sure to bombard me with questions. I was trained to withstand the toughest interrogation, but keeping quiet, at least for now, meant escaping the questions altogether. I made my decision and left the bathroom and returned to the living room.

I promised Mrs. Mason and Ms. Cunningham that I'd let them know if I heard anything, which I planned to do later, after Randi had sent additional videos. I didn't enjoy withholding the truth, but I was confident in my plan. Besides, I'd be in a better position to share news and ease their worries after I had collected more information.

As soon as Mrs. Mason and Ms. Cunningham left, Mother grabbed her purse and car keys and told me she was going to the hospital to check on Carla and Mr. Davids. With so many questions circling about my friends, I'd almost forgotten about Mrs. Davids. She had a husband in the intensive care unit and two children missing. That was too much. I had to ease some of her burden.

"Mother, tell Mrs. Davids that Gavin and Meggie are okay," I said.

She froze. "Natalie, do you know something?"

I looked away. I had to. "Mother, please. Just tell her."

Obviously I knew something. Mother stood there, one eyebrow raised, scrutinizing me, deciding what to say next. "You come to me if you need help—or if your friends do. Is that clear?"

I nodded. "Thank you."

Mother held me in her gaze for another second, and then she turned and left for the hospital.

My phone buzzed.

Randi

The first thing we did when we got back to Grand Central Terminal was plop down at a table. We hadn't stopped to eat all day, and we were starving, but before eating, I took a minute to send Natalie our first texts and video. We knew our parents would be worrying, but we also had to be careful not to give ourselves up. After my message went through, I pulled the peanut butter sandwiches and granola bars from my bag. Our food was warm and a bit smooshed, but it still tasted good.

During dinner, Meggie and Scott told me all about Claudia and Jamie, the brother-sister combo in the book *From the Mixed-Up Files of Mrs. Basil E. Frankweiler*. Apparently, in the story they hide in a bathroom inside a museum.

"Is that what we're going to do, Gavvy?" Meggie asked.

"You know it," he said. "I've already checked it out. The men's bathroom is a lot cleaner than anything else I've seen, and the handicapped stall is big enough for all of us to hide in there. Plus we can lock the door."

"And we have a toilet, so we won't have to worry about that for later," Scott pointed out.

I wasn't about to sit on any toilet in front of him, nor was I going to let him do his thing while Meggie and I were in there, but I didn't make a fuss.

"Why not the girls' bathroom?" Meggie asked.

"Because it's always busier than the boys'," Scott said.

I chuckled. Wasn't that the truth.

Gav was smart and had brought a deck of cards, so after dinner we hung out at the table playing Go Fish until things got quiet, and then we made our way into the bathroom and hunkered down. We talked in hushed whispers, waiting for the night-shift custodian to show up. We figured he'd be our challenge, but Gav and I had a plan.

Finally, after about an hour, the custodian banged through the bathroom door with his cleaning supplies. The handicapped stall was the last in line, so we had locked one of the earlier stall doors to see how he handled the situation. That way we'd know what to expect when he came to our locked door. We had planned to crawl under the stalls, scurrying from one to the next in order to stay hidden, but that wasn't necessary because this guy was lazy. One tug on the first locked door, and he gave up.

When he came to our door, it was the same. "Darn kids playing jokes again," he muttered. "Guess you'll wait to get cleaned later with your friend down there," he told our stall. He moseyed away, whistling as he left.

After he was gone, we let our giggles out and relaxed. It didn't take long for Scott and Meggie to fall asleep, but Gav and I stayed awake for a while. We sat with our backs pressed against the wall, talking.

"What're you thinking?" I asked him.

He didn't answer right away, but I waited. I could see him forming his thoughts. "I didn't like Kurtsman doing that story about Mr. Holmes. I was pretty mad about it."

"I know. Why didn't you say anything?"

He shrugged. "I like conflict on the football field, but I don't like it with my friends."

"Are you still mad about it, her doing the story?"

"No. It's crazy, but it seems like Mr. Holmes and my dad are more alike than they are different. They were both just trying to take care of their families during hard times.

"Kinda makes me wonder, how many wars have been fought between people that when you get right down to it are really the same? I mean, wouldn't most fathers say their children and families are what's most important to them?

"My dad has always taken care of us. I've gotta make this work tomorrow, Randi. I've got to do this for him."

I rested my head on Gav's shoulder. We were done talking after that. I counted his breaths until I fell asleep.

12

MEGGIE'S SECRET-WEAPON PLAY

Trevor

Natalie's hot, and I'm not just saying that because she's my girlfriend. Her looks alone make her intimidating, but add her kick-butt-and-take-questions-later attitude and she can be downright scary, which is why you don't hear a lot of people talking about her being hot. But trust me; she is.

That's why I got nervous when she showed up for our broadcast on Monday morning not looking like herself. Gavin, Randi, and Scott hadn't made it yet, and Natalie looked exhausted. Her eyes were bloodshot.

"Natalie, what's going on?" I whispered.

"Miss Kurtsman, cutting it close this morning, aren't you?" Mrs. Woods said. "Any idea where the rest of our Recruits might be? We're getting close to showtime."

Natalie sighed. "There's too much to explain right now, but the others won't be joining us. I've been up all night preparing for today's show, which should answer all of your questions."

"You mean they're still missing?" I said.

"No, they're not missing. I know exactly where they are.

But not now, Trev. We need to do the broadcast. This will be the most important show we've ever done. I've got a series of videos saved to our folder. When I cue you, play the first one. Just go in order after that."

I glanced at Mark and Mrs. Woods. "Okay," I said.

"Got it," Mark replied.

"Last thing," Natalie said. "Toward the end of the broadcast, I'll need you to cut to live TV. Channel ABC. Can you do that?"

"No sweat," Mark said. "We've got this."

"Good, because we're out of time," Mrs. Woods said. "Let's razzle-dazzle 'em, Miss Kurtsman."

Natalie got positioned behind her desk, and Mark and I adjusted the cameras and sound.

"We're live in three, two, one," I said.

"Good morning, Lake View Middle School. I'm Natalie Kurtsman. I come to you today with urgent news about our quarterback and dear friend, Gavin Davids. There was a serious accident over the weekend involving Gavin's father. His family is in desperate need of our help. I know I've leaned on you to help Robbie Holmes and his family, but—"

Natalie's voice cracked, and she had to stop talking. I don't know if she'd planned that, but it worked. She didn't need to say anything more because we could feel that it was real bad. She tried.

"Gavin's—"

That was it. That was all she could get out. Her jaw started quivering, and you could see that she was fighting tears. Natalie nodded in my direction, and I hit play on the first of her videos.

Meggie Davids appeared on our screen. She greeted us from the back of a car—a car that her brother was driving! Meggie gave us the lowdown on what was happening. She made us chuckle, but she also made a knot form in my throat. When the video ended, Natalie spoke again from behind her desk. She'd regained composure and pressed on.

"Mr. Davids was on the ground underneath his plumbing van on Saturday morning, performing some routine maintenance, when by freak accident Meggie's very large dog, Otis, collided with the side of the vehicle, causing the jack to collapse and the van to fall on top of Mr. Davids. Mr. Davids was rushed to the hospital by ambulance and went into immediate surgery to repair a tear in his liver and to stop internal bleeding. He had a second surgery to fix his broken leg last night."

Natalie nodded, and I cut to the second video. This clip showed footage from the train, Grand Central Terminal, and Times Square. It was clear that this was Scott's work. After making his documentary at camp, he knew exactly what to do. I felt like I was on the journey with my friends. With every minute that passed I became more worried, surprised, excited, and hopeful for them. I wasn't with Gavin and Meggie, but I sure was rooting for them.

The video ended, and we cut back to Natalie. "I just came from Saint Mary's Hospital this morning," she said. "Mr. Davids is doing well but remains in the intensive care unit." She nodded, and I clicked on the next link, and an image of Mr. Davids appeared on the screen. I'll tell you one thing, a picture of somebody in intensive care is not a happy sight.

"Let me reiterate. Mr. Davids is doing well, but he clearly has a long road ahead," Natalie continued. "His family, on the other hand, is in even greater peril. For whatever reason—and we should not judge—Mr. Davids does not have health insurance. Gavin's family will be stuck paying all of his father's medical bills—which are certain to be significant. That is a financial burden that even the wealthiest of families would struggle to meet. There is simply no way the Davidses can pay that debt. They need help—and Gavin and Meggie have gone to find it."

Natalie paused. Her phone was buzzing. She quickly pulled it out and read the screen. Then she took a deep breath and looked back into our camera.

"I've just received word from Randi Cunningham that our friends are outside the *Good Morning America* studio. We're going to break from our broadcast and go live to see what happens. Cross your fingers, say a prayer—do whatever it is you do—but let's hope little Meggie Davids is able to capture America's heart with her secret-weapon play. Her family's life depends on it."

GAVIN

I grabbed Meggie by the hand. It was time to save our dad—and our family. We pushed through the door, leaving Grand Central behind, and stepped out onto Forty-Second Street. But instead of finding the sun's glare reflecting off the skyscrapers, we were met by pouring rain. The sky was dropping sheets of water. Within minutes, we were soaked all the way through.

"Nothing a football player can't handle. Right, Gavvy?" Megs said, wiping the rain from her eyes.

"That's right!" Scott cheered. "This is nothing compared to our Snowbowl. Let's go."

I glanced at Randi 'cause she was the one with the map on her phone, except there was no map 'cause the bad weather and these crazy tall buildings were teaming up to block satellite reception. It didn't matter, 'cause Megs and Scott weren't waiting. They were already hurrying down the sidewalk.

Me and Randi followed them. Randi kept trying to get her phone to work, but still no luck. I didn't say anything, but after walking several blocks, I started getting nervous. It was like the city had transformed overnight. Nothing looked familiar under these gray skies. This was the trickiest defense I'd ever played against. I couldn't tell if we were going the right way or not. I couldn't even remember the name of the street where we were supposed to turn.

"We're almost there," Scott cheered. "C'mon!"

Why was I worried? Scott was even better at reading defenses than me. He didn't need a phone or a map. One trip, and he had this route programmed into his brain.

He turned at the next corner, and I immediately recognized the place. Even in these miserable conditions, Times Square was lit up and looked alive. I wasn't surprised to see a mob of people already crowding the studio, but missing was the swarm of signs waving back and forth, looking for airtime. They'd been replaced by umbrellas. As soon as Megs pulled her poster from my backpack, I understood why. Her marker SAVE MY DADDY letters had leaked all down the paper.

Megs shrugged. "I can still use it," she said.

I shielded my eyes from the rain and watched my little sister snake her way through the people. Even wearing the same clothes that she'd had on all day yesterday and slept in on a bathroom floor, even as a drowned rat, she was still the cutest thing I'd ever seen.

Meggie made it to the front just as the crowd erupted, yelling and cheering. The weather-man and camera guy had come outside. She joined the frenzy, and the show went live.

All I could do now was watch and hope.

BRIEF #18
December: Saving Mr. Davids

Mark switched the feed, and suddenly all of Lake View Middle was watching *Good Morning America*. I gasped. The camera was following the weatherman as he made his rounds with the crowd outside the studio. I frantically searched the people, desperately trying to find Randi or Gavin. They weren't there.

"What's that sign?" Trevor asked.

"Where?" I screamed.

"There." Mark pointed.

I saw her streaky letters. "It's Meggie!" I squealed. "She's there!"

"She made it," Mrs. Woods said, relieved.

"Hi. What's your name?" the weatherman asked a random person.

There was small talk, and then he moved down the line.

He stopped at another random person. "Hi. Where are you from?"

More small talk before he moved on again. "Hi. What's your name?"

More small talk, but instead of moving down the line, the weatherman stepped back. "Okay, how about a check on the weather? In case you couldn't tell, here in New York we're looking at rain—and lots of it. It will be cats and dogs all day. The sunshine is out west, where you'll be enjoying a gorgeous week. And down south you'll be warming up in temperatures reaching the high seventies.

"Now here's a look at your local news and forecast."

The show cut to our local meteorologist and reporter. "Quick," Mrs. Woods urged. "Switch the feed back to Natalie. You've got to tell everyone to keep watching."

We scrambled into position, and Mark gave me the go-ahead. "Don't turn off your TVs," I implored. "We spotted Meggie Davids in the crowd. She's there—and she's got one last chance to get the weatherman's attention. This is it."

The screen went black, and Mark reconnected us to *Good Morning America* just in time.

"We're back in the pouring rain," the weatherman could be heard saying, but the camera wasn't on him yet. "Before we go back inside to get out of this nasty weather, I've got to ask about this sign. The rain has all but ruined it, so I'm having a hard time reading it. Can you tell us what your name is, how old you are, and what your sign says?" he asked someone.

Who was it? We still couldn't see!

"My name is Meggie Davids," a strong little voice said. "I'm six years old, and my sign says 'Save My Daddy.'"

Suddenly the camera connected, and we could see Meggie on TV. Lake View Middle erupted in cheers. Cries of joy and celebration could be heard from every corner of the building. Tears sprang to my eyes.

"My daddy got hurt in a bad accident, and he's in the hospital in intensity care, and he needs surgeries. I'm here with my brother and Randi and Scott. We broke lots of rules to get here because Gavvy is only thirteen and he's not supposed to drive, but we had to make it because my daddy doesn't have health inchurents, and without America's help our family is going to lose everything. Eddie—she's an old lady at the senior center where my brother and his friends visit—she said if you ever want the world to know something, then just get it on your show—so that's what I'm doing. My daddy needs help. Please."

Meggie got all of that out, and then her voice cracked on the last word and she fell to pieces. I lost it. I was sobbing. Meggie hadn't just tugged at the heart; she'd broken it—all the way.

The weatherman lifted Meggie over the iron railing and held her in his arms. He hugged her and then he turned and faced the camera. "America, we're going to help."

The camera panned the crowd. People were cheering and crying and applauding. And then a chant rang out: "Meg-gie! Meg-gie! Meg-gie!"

We watched the weatherman carry Meggie toward the studio, and they disappeared inside.

"Okay, Natalie. We've got to bring it back to you now," Trev whispered.

"Bring us home, dude," Mark said.

I giggled and wiped my eyes.

"In three, two, one," Trev said.

I looked directly into the camera. "You can help by going to Meggie's GoFundMe page. I set it up yesterday. Details are on the bottom of the screen.

"I'm Natalie Kurtsman, saying, 'Have a razzle-dazzle day, Lake View Middle.'"

What else was there to say? Either Meggie's play had worked—or it hadn't. Only time would tell.

SCOTT

After Meggie got whisked away by the weatherman, Gavin and I high-fived, and Randi gave us a hug. Our secret-weapon play had put us in the red zone. Now we needed America to do the rest. We did a little end-zone dancing to celebrate, and then we waited. Randi had texted our moms earlier, and my mom was on her way, but for now we were stuck standing in the rain.

"Gavvy," Meggie suddenly called from the studio door. "Gavvy, you've been invited inside. Randi and Scott, too."

Saved. Meggie was a team player. I didn't know where we were going, but I was happy to go anywhere as long as it got me out of the cold. The rain was turning to sleet, bringing back memories of the Snowbowl. To my delight, there was a tray of cookies in the room where they took us, and some nice woman served us hot chocolate.

I was on my fourth cup when I heard Mom's voice. "Scott."

"Mom!" I yelled, spilling my cocoa. I jumped up and ran to her, and she grabbed me in a giant hug.

"You had me worried sick." She held my face in her hands. "Are you okay?"

"Yes. I'm sorry you were worried, Mom, but we had to get Meggie here to ask for help. It was our secret-weapon play. And I had to come to make a documentary of it so Natalie could use it on our show."

"It's my fault, Mrs. Mason," Gavin said. "Don't blame Scott."

"Get over here," Mom snapped at him. "And you too," she told Randi. She pulled all three of us close and squeezed us tight together. It was hard to breathe. "You scared us to death, but no moms could be prouder of their children," she whispered to us.

I looked up at her. "We did it, Mom," I said.

"You did it," she replied.

Wait till I tell Grandpa this story, I thought.

GAVIN

The *Good Morning America* people brought me in with Megs so they could get the full story. I filled them in. I asked to do it without Meggie present, 'cause like Scott had said after his fire, what you don't know can't hurt you.

After I got done talking, they wanted to meet Randi and Scott, and we told them about Kurtsman and Trevor and Mark and *The Razzle-Dazzle Show*. Randi showed us that Kurtsman had a GoFundMe page set up for Meggie, and when we looked, we saw something none of us expected—money was already being donated to it. My legs got wobbly, and I had to sit down.

Before the *Good Morning America* broadcast ended that morning, they replayed Meggie's clip on TV and shared information on how to help by going to her GoFundMe page. The team at the show wished us good luck and promised to check in on us real soon, and then we left with Mrs. Mason.

I'd broken a bunch of different laws dragging my little sister and Randi and Scott all the way into New York City, and I'd made us spend the night hiding in a bathroom stall at Grand

Central Terminal, but I still hadn't faced the scariest part of it all. That was waiting for me.

Mrs. Mason led our return trip, but she didn't take us home. We went straight to the hospital, 'cause that's where Mom was. She was sitting with Randi's mom in the family-lounge area on the intensive care floor. When we walked in, Mom jumped from her chair and rushed over to us. I felt small in her arms. I didn't want her to let go.

"It's okay, Mommy. We went and got help," Meggie whispered.

"I know, *mija.*" She held Meggie's head against her belly and looked at me.

"Sorry, Mom—"

"*Niño,*" she said, cutting me off. "A parent does whatever he can, whatever it takes, to protect his family—and so does a special son."

I swallowed against the knot in my throat.

"Your father wants to see you," she said.

I swallowed again. Was he mad? Did he blame me for the accident?

"I'll show you where he is."

Randi gave my hand a quick squeeze. This was it. This was the scariest moment. I woulda rather played against Stonebreaker with no pads and no helmet.

I took a deep breath and followed Mom out of the lounge and around the corner. It was a short walk. We stopped outside Dad's room. Mom kissed me on the cheek and gripped me by the shoulders so that she could look at me square. "Your father is doing okay, but he doesn't look great, *niño*, so be strong."

I took a deep breath and stepped inside.

Randi

Mrs. Mason and Scott left, but Mom and I stayed at the hospital until Gav returned from seeing his dad. He wasn't gone that long because Mr. Davids was very tired. I was usually good at knowing how Gav was feeling and what he was thinking, but it was hard to tell when he came shuffling into the lounge.

"What did Daddy say?" Meggie asked.

"He said he'll see you soon and to take care of Otis."

Hearing him mention Otis made my eyes get wet.

"Okay," Meggie said.

"Let's go home now," Mrs. Davids said. "We'll give Daddy a chance to sleep, and you two can take a shower and get some rest, too. We'll come back later."

I held Gav's hand and walked with him on the way out. "He told me he was proud of me and to stay strong," Gav whispered.

Mrs. Mason had told us the same, but I don't think Gav believed it until he heard it from his father. He looked at me, and I smiled. "It's going to be okay," I said, giving his hand a squeeze.

I felt him squeeze back.

I got into the car with Mom, and exhaustion hit me full force—and so did a batch of funny feelings.

Trevor

Under normal circumstances school would've been slow and ultra-boring in the couple of weeks before Christmas, but not with Natalie. That girl never stopped.

The Razzle-Dazzle Show was business as usual. Natalie wasn't done helping the Davidses. She did a feature interview with Gavin, then with Randi, and then with Scott. I thought she'd saved Scott till last because his part had been the least important, but I was wrong. Randi made you feel sad and kind of mushy, and I felt really bad for Gavin when he mentioned missing the all-star game because of everything that had happened, and that was all good because feeling sad and mushy and bad was important for getting people to care and want to help, but it was Scott who stole the show.

Natalie didn't even need to ask him any questions. He did it all by himself. "You know what?" he said. "I think Santa Claus came early this year. I checked Meggie's GoFundMe page this morning, and people are still donating. Her secret-weapon play was the best of all time."

"Scott, wait until you see this," Natalie said.

"What is it?"

"A surprise."

"I love surprises!" he shrieked.

"I know," Natalie said. She pointed to Mark, and he clicked something on his computer screen. Whatever she had planned was a surprise for me too. Suddenly an image of Stonebreaker and some of his teammates popped up on our screen. It was a video message. Mark clicked play.

"Hey, Davids. We're sorry to hear about your dad," Stonebreaker said. "We saw the video of your sister on *Good Morning America* and wanted to help. Our team did a fund-raiser, and we'll be donating to your GoFundMe page.

"It's cool that Mason had my back and made sure I got to play in our game, especially after what I did. We can be rivals on the field, but much respect off it," Stonebreaker said. "And, Davids, sorry you missed the all-star game. You belonged there."

The video ended, and Mark cut back to Natalie.

"Wow," Scott said, clearly stunned. "Stonebreaker did that?"

"Actually," Natalie said, "the Titans aren't the only team to donate. Every team you played has contributed."

"Holy smokes! That's awesome! I told you Santa came early this year!"

He had all of us laughing—including Gavin. And, boy, did that feel good.

Bottom line was that Meggie had killed it with her secret-weapon play, and Scott had stolen the *Razzle-Dazzle Show* broadcast, but Natalie was the hands-down MVP behind the scenes—and she wasn't done surprising me yet. After we'd packed up and were heading to our first-period classes, she sprang it on me.

"Trev?"

"Yeah?"

"Would you be interested in going to the soup kitchen on Friday? The one your brother and Madison told us about."

"You mean . . . like . . . just the two of us?" I sputtered.

"Actually, there's this girl in my math class. Her name is Abby. She thinks Mark is cute, so I was thinking maybe they could go with us?"

"You mean . . . like . . . a double date? With my best friend?"

She nodded. "Sure. We're going to help the homeless, but we'll call it a date. Maybe we can get some ice cream afterward or something."

"Scott was right. Santa did come early."

Natalie giggled. "I'll tell Abby. You tell Mark." She waved and ducked into her classroom.

I stood there, and then it hit me. Natalie had proven me wrong yet again. It was possible for the problem to also be the solution. Was there anything my girlfriend couldn't do? I didn't think so.

I turned and headed for my classroom. I wondered if Santa might also be able to deliver a second kiss.

Randi

Mr. Davids made it home just in time for Christmas. I was there when Gav wheeled him up the temporary ramp he'd built and into the house for the first time. I thought my heart had already been smashed to pieces, but it shattered all over again when I saw Otis's reaction. The dog started whimpering the moment he saw Mr. Davids, and he lumbered over and pushed his big head into Mr. Davids's lap. Mr. Davids rubbed Otis's ears and told him it was okay and that he was okay. I'm not exaggerating when I tell you that Otis's tail immediately began wagging. Otis licked Mr. Davids on the arm, and his tail got going faster and faster until he got so happy, he couldn't hold it in any longer and he let out one of his thunder barks.

Mr. Davids was stuck using a wheelchair to get around, and he would be for a while, but no one was complaining. We didn't need any reminding that it could've been worse. If that van had fallen on his neck or head, we would've been raising money to pay for his funeral service, not his surgeries and recovery. Speaking of money, America had delivered. Meggie's video from *Good Morning America* had gone viral. People were still donating.

Truthfully, that was all the happy news and present I needed for Christmas. If you had asked me beforehand, I would've told you that all I wanted was for Gav's dad and family to be okay. That was it. But Jacob was in the giving spirit.

He arrived on Christmas Eve, and at dinner that night—with me sitting right there—he got down on one knee, pulled a glittering diamond ring from his pocket, and popped the question.

"Yes!" Mom cried. "Yes!"

Jacob slid the ring onto her finger and they kissed.

I darted from the table and ran to my room. I flung myself down onto my bed and buried my face in my pillows. And I let it out. I finally let it out. I cried and cried, until I felt Mom touching me.

"Randi, what's wrong?" She rubbed my back. "Randi? I know you don't hate Jacob or distrust him, so what's got you so upset?"

I wiped my face and sat up. My tears didn't stop, but neither did I. "I can't move, Mom. I know you love Jacob, but I can't move. I can't leave my friends. I can't leave Gav." I fell apart, sobbing all over again.

"Oh, Randi." Mom pulled me close. "We're not moving, honey. I wouldn't ask you to do that. Is that what you've been worrying about?"

"Yes," I croaked against her shoulder.

"Randi, I'm not going to uproot you now. Jacob doesn't want that, either. He wants to come and stay with us."

"Really?"

"Yes. You're getting ready to start high school, and you're right, you've got a very special group of friends—especially Gav."

I sat back and wiped my face again. And then I told her about the funny feelings that I'd been having. "Mom, is it okay if Gav feels like more than a friend sometimes? I don't know how to describe it, but it's just different with him."

"Yes, it's okay. Feelings can be confusing, but one thing is for certain—you and Gav have a special relationship. What comes of those feelings, only time will tell, but something tells me you will always be in each other's lives."

"Should I say anything to him—about my feelings?"

"That's a tough question. You can . . . but I wouldn't. The two of you have been able to read each other for as long as I can remember, so maybe let destiny handle this one and save the talking."

"Mom, I really like Jacob."

"Me too."

"I'm sorry. I was scared."

"I know. It's okay. You've been through a lot this year. Hopefully we're over the hump now and it will be smooth sailing from here."

We hugged once more, and Mom stood up to go back downstairs with Jacob.

"Mom, don't tell Jacob I was upset, okay?"

"Don't worry, honey. I'll take care of Jacob."

I went to wash my face before rejoining them downstairs. I still had a lot of questions, but they could wait. The biggest one had been answered. I wasn't moving.

13

SUDDEN NEWS

NATALIE KURTSMAN
ASPIRING LAWYER
Kurtsman Law Offices

BRIEF #19
January: An Epiphany

It was a successful double date, but you'll get no kissing and telling from me.

Moving on. Once we got past the holidays and things slowed down a bit, Mother and I agreed it was time we went to see Mr. Holmes again.

Sheriff Martin remembered us from our previous visit, so he didn't have any concerns. We still had to pass through the metal detector and send our bags down the X-ray belt and adhere to all the other rules, but I wasn't questioned again. Instead I was welcomed.

Mother and I took our positions in the visitors' area and waited. Suddenly I became nervous. What if Mr. Holmes declined to see us because he was angry? We'd told him we'd be back sooner, but life had gotten hectic after Mr. Davids's accident. Had we broken his trust? I was prepared to hear that he was refusing the meeting, but the door opened and he appeared.

Mr. Holmes took his seat in the chair across from us. "Wasn't sure I'd be seeing you again," he said. "Your family have a nice holiday?"

"Mr. Holmes, I apologize for not returning sooner—" Mother said.

"We had every intention," I cut in, "but Mr. Davids got hurt in a terrible accident, and we've been busy helping his family."

"I saw that story," Mr. Holmes said. "How's he doing?"

"Better," Mother replied. "He's home now, but he still has a long road ahead."

"And his kids?" Mr. Holmes asked.

"His children and wife are well. Everyone's just relieved that Mr. Davids is on the mend."

"That's good," Mr. Holmes said. "I had Stephanie donate some money to their page. It wasn't much, but we did what we could."

I was lucky that Mr. Holmes was staring at the table, because I did not do a good job of hiding my surprise when he said that.

"When you get locked up, you tend to have more time for thinking. Self-reflection, I guess you'd call it." He paused. "Stealing that booster club money was bad, but the way I treated his kid was worse. And when you get right down to it, me and that Davids guy aren't all that different, are we? Shows how ignorant I was."

epiphany (noun): a sudden insight into the essential reality or meaning of something

One could disagree with me, but I do believe that Mr. Holmes had had an epiphany. Clearly he had done some serious self-reflecting! It was a moment met by silence because it was that significant.

"Mr. Holmes, I also created a GoFundMe page for your family," I said when it felt okay to speak again. "I did it shortly after my first visit here. I shared video clips of Robbie and told your story on my morning news show at school. Everyone fell in love with Robbie, but I wasn't able to raise as much as I'd hoped. The page is still active, though, so there's always a chance for more."

Mother showed him a printout of Robbie's page with the most recent balance listed. Mr. Holmes couldn't take the paper because of visitor rules, but he saw it. Must have been that all the reflecting a man got to do in prison had made him softer, too, because his eyes got wet almost immediately.

"You did this?" he said, looking up at me.

I nodded. "Yes."

"Thank you."

"I'll be contacting your wife," Mother said. "There's enough there to help her get a physical. Then we'll see what we can do about an insurance plan. We're going to make sure she's healthy."

"Thank you," Mr. Holmes said again, and then, abruptly, he stood and turned away. He made haste toward the door.

Mother and I made no attempt to stop him. We began

gathering our things. Clearly this meeting was adjourned. But then—

"Natalie," Mr. Holmes called. He'd paused at the doorway and was looking back at me. "You'll be in the high school next year, right?"

"Yes," I answered.

"If you see my older boy, maybe you can tell him his dad says hi and that I'm sorry."

My eyebrows pinched. I was confused.

"Nicky won't come and see me. He's angry. Can't blame him."

The man was in prison because of his own poor choices, but I couldn't help feeling bad for him. "I'll tell him," I said.

Mr. Holmes nodded, and then he turned and left.

Not surprisingly, I'd say that the word that best summed up how I was feeling when leaving the prison that afternoon would be "conflicted"—or maybe "torn." This was hard.

Randi

"We're calling it a wrap, people," Scott hollered, trying to sound all professional after another airing of *The Razzle-Dazzle Show*. We'd been back to school for a couple of weeks and had found some semblance of normalcy after a crazy December—but for Natalie, "normal" meant "boring," so she'd decided it was time to drop her next big idea on us.

"Before you all run off, I have an announcement," she said. "With the exception of Scott, who sees his grandpa on a regular basis, the rest of us are long overdue for a trip to the Senior Center. I propose a visit this weekend."

"I'll second that motion," Mrs. Woods said.

"All in favor, say 'aye,'" Scott yelled.

"Aye!" we shouted.

Done. It was that easy because we all agreed it was a great idea—but I knew better. "Hey," I whispered, getting Natalie's attention when we were packing up. "What's the hidden agenda this time?"

"What do you mean?" she said, playing dumb.

"I'm sure you're sincere about wanting to see Eddie and Agnes, but I know you better than that."

She giggled. "I think we should throw Mrs. Magenta a baby shower, but I've never attended nor planned one before, so who better to ask for advice than Eddie and Agnes?"

I smiled. "Told you," I said.

"Yeah, yeah. So, what do you think?"

"What do I think? I think we're going to throw her the best baby shower ever."

"I know. I can't wait."

The six of us carpooled, so we arrived together. We found Eddie and Agnes and everyone else hanging out in their new favorite spot—the Community Theater. Long gone were the days of the Community Hall.

"Well, if it isn't our favorite troublemakers," Eddie announced when we walked in.

"Troublemakers?" Natalie repeated. "Who're you calling troublemakers?"

"Well, you sure don't let the grass grow under your feet," Eddie remarked.

We smiled. She was right about that.

"Sit down," Agnes ordered. "These old rascals won't let us put anything on but some stinky football."

"Stinky? Agnes, this is the NFL playoffs," Mrs. Magenta said. "Dad never misses these games."

I glanced at Coach. He sat in his wheelchair, staring at the TV, but I wasn't convinced he was watching. Mrs. Woods and Mrs. Magenta were by his side. Gav took a seat near them, but I wasn't sure if Coach even knew he was there.

"Oh, enjoy your foolish game," Agnes said. "Eddie and I would rather hear all about Connie Stewart and *Good Morning America* anyway."

"We were watching when Meggie stole the show," Eddie whispered.

I started from the beginning, with the accident. I kept my voice low and that part short because Gav didn't need to hear it all over again. He'd been asked to tell the story too many times already. Eddie and Agnes were fine with the abbreviated version, but they wanted all the juicy details about our adventure trip, especially when it came to New York City and *Good Morning America*.

"Wow!" Scott suddenly yelled. "Grandpa, did you see that? They just ran my secret-weapon play!"

"I saw it," his grandpa responded. "Didn't look as good as you running it."

I thought that was sweet.

"Dude, that was sick," Mark said, giving Trevor five.

The guys were going on and on about that big play, but not Coach. I could sense Gav worrying.

Natalie elbowed me, getting my attention. "We wanted to ask you to help us with a new project," she mentioned to Eddie and Agnes.

"Are we getting paid?" Eddie asked.

"Very funny," Natalie replied. Then she lowered her voice to a hush and filled them in. "We would like to throw Mrs. Magenta a baby shower, but we're not sure what to do. We've never attended one."

"Well, you've come to the right women," Agnes said. "Eddie and I know just what you'll need."

"That's right. We're the party animals," Eddie said.

"Ugh!" Agnes groaned.

Natalie and I fell into a giggle fit. Those two never stopped. They were too funny. It took us a minute, but after we got ourselves calmed down, we refocused and turned serious again.

We spent the rest of the afternoon planning the shower, and we got Mrs. Woods in on the action. She told us where Mrs. Magenta had registered, which meant she had gone through a store and selected all the items she and Mr. Magenta needed and would like. Natalie pulled the registry up on her phone, and we couldn't believe how much there was on it. You need a lot of stuff when you're having your first child—a high chair, car seat, Pack 'n Play, crib, diapers, baby books, bath stuff, clothes and bibs, and on and on. We went through her list and came up with a solid game plan for who would get what, because presents were the whole point of a baby shower. We decided when to have the party and what the theme and food and activities would be. Mrs. Woods wanted to have the party in the Community Hall so that all residents at the Senior Center could attend and so she could keep an eye on Coach. It was a productive meeting, so Natalie was quite pleased.

There were two minutes left in the football game when we finished, so I convinced Natalie and Eddie and Agnes to watch the end with me. The Steelers had the ball and needed to get into field goal range to kick for the win. They made a couple of quick passes and got out of bounds to stop the clock. Then they tried Scott's secret-weapon play once more. The guy for the Steelers danced down the sideline and into range before stepping out of bounds.

"Go! Go! Go!" Trevor yelled.

"That's how you do it," Scott cheered. "That's how you run my play!"

"That's great clock management by Roethlisberger," Gav said, talking about the quarterback for the Steelers.

"And heart," Coach croaked.

Gav's face lit up. That was the first Coach had said all day, but it was enough for Gav.

The Steelers' kick was successful, and the boys went nutso hooting and cheering. They didn't even care who'd won. It was just an exciting finish.

"Okay, Coach," Mrs. Woods said. "What do you say we get you back to your room for some rest now?"

Coach reached for Gav before Mrs. Woods wheeled him away. "Valentine," he rasped. Gav leaned closer, and Coach grabbed his arm. Coach's voice was weak, so the rest of us couldn't hear what he was saying, but I could tell from Gav's face that whatever Coach was saying carried weight.

Coach released Gav's arm and closed his eyes. Then Mrs. Woods wheeled him off.

"What'd he say?" Scott wanted to know. "What'd he say? Was it something about football?"

Gav shook his head, but that was all the answer we got. He needed to hold that moment close and not talk quite yet. He'd share when he was ready. When the time was right.

GAVIN

Those *Good Morning America* people didn't lie. They said they'd check on us again, and they did. After we got Dad home and made it past the holidays, someone from the show called and talked to Mom. The short story is that one of their main reporters, Connie Stewart, came out to our house to do a follow-up story.

Getting interviewed for an important TV show like that was a pretty big deal, so there were a lot of players involved. Ms. Stewart's team included lighting and makeup and camera people. It was like she was the quarterback of an offensive unit, except they didn't ride together on a bus like we did. They had a string of cars. Me and Megs greeted Ms. Stewart when she got out of hers, and we showed her into our house. Mom and Dad took over from there.

The rest of her team got busy carrying in their equipment and setting up. There was a whole bunch to do to get ready, even more than in pregame warm-ups.

I wanted Woods and Magenta and the Recruits here for

this, but that didn't happen 'cause of bad timing. The girls were at the Senior Center for Magenta's baby shower. Kurtsman and Randi had helped plan the whole thing. Trevor and Mark made it over, though, and Scott was on his way, 'cause guys didn't normally go to that shower stuff. But if you want to know the truth, I woulda gone if I coulda 'cause I hadn't stopped thinking about Coach since our last visit. It wasn't just what he'd said but how he'd said it. "Keep making me proud," he'd rasped, making it feel like goodbye. I wanted to get back there, but I hadn't made it 'cause things were busy with Dad being banged up, and I needed to be home.

"Hi!" Scott cheered when he arrived. "Did you bring those yummy cookies and pastries like you had in the studio?" he asked the first person he saw.

The woman shrugged.

"Check in the kitchen," I told him. "Trevor and Mark are in there now."

He beelined. I woulda joined them, but it was my turn to get ready. The makeup crew sat me down and blasted me with their bright lights. Then they started messing with my hair and putting stuff on my face. Meggie loved it, but not me. The only makeup I ever used was eye black. I looked worse after all their fussing, but Connie Stewart was happy, so the filming began.

The taping of the show went well. Connie Stewart talked to everyone in our family. She had a conversation with Mom and Dad together. Then she talked to Meggie and Otis, and then me. She chose to have me go last, and I was fine with that 'cause I was nervous. Scott told me it was training for when I was gonna be in front of all those cameras on Monday Night

Football, so I'd better get used to it. That did the trick. I liked that thought.

When it was my turn, the first thing I did was thank everyone who'd helped save us, 'cause Mom and Dad had taught me about manners. Then Connie Stewart asked me her questions, and I knew the answers until she asked me the big one. "Gavin, have you learned anything from this experience that you'd like to tell the people watching?"

I stopped, taking a minute to think.

"Ms. Stewart, we make a big deal out of how different we look and sound, but when push comes to shove, I think we're a lot more alike than we are different. I know a father who I swore was nothing like my dad, but turns out he's a lot the same. Richard Holmes made mistakes and tough choices for his family after he lost his factory job. Maybe he did things my dad never would, but like my dad, he was trying to protect his family in hard times. It's crazy to think we have so much fighting in the world when so many of us want the same thing. I don't know if that makes any sense."

"It makes plenty of sense, Gavin."

"Mr. Holmes has a son my age and a son, Robbie, who's Meggie's age. Robbie and Meggie are friends. There's a GoFundMe page for the Holmes family, too. Natalie did a story on them for our *Razzle-Dazzle Show* and we've started raising money, but not as much as they need. Maybe some of the people watching your show would want to help them a little—'cause what I've learned, Ms. Stewart, is that love really is greater than hate."

I guess you could say that was me forgiving Holmes and trying to help him. I can't really describe it, but I felt different after I got done saying those things. There was some dark piece inside me that sorta let go and disappeared.

Ms. Stewart smiled when I stopped talking. Then she looked into the camera and finished things up. "We grown-ups aren't always smart enough to listen to our children. Or to even give them a chance, for that matter. I hope we know enough to listen this time.

"I'm Connie Stewart with the story behind the little girl who stole our hearts. Thank you for watching."

Trevor

It was cool getting to hang at Gavin's to watch the taping of Connie Stewart's special segment for *Good Morning America*. The camera dudes and computer nerds let Mark and me check out all their equipment, and they showed us how to use it. We learned a few tricks and got some ideas for our show. Like I said, it was cool, but things got more exciting after Natalie texted.

> Natalie: Big news: Baby shower ending early; Mrs. Magenta's water just broke!!

I elbowed Mark and showed him my phone. "What's this mean?"

He shrugged. "Must be a pipe burst in the Senior Center. Bummer. I hope Mrs. Magenta's presents didn't get ruined."

I shoved him. "You moron. Read it again." I stuck my phone in his face. "It says Mrs. Magenta's water broke, not the Senior Center's."

"What's that mean?"

"That's what I asked you. Man, you're hopeless sometimes."

"Why don't you text her back and ask her?" he suggested.

"I can't. She's busy." But for real I didn't want Natalie to think I was stupid.

Just then Scott came waltzing in from the kitchen, shoveling another cookie into his mouth. I was desperate. "Psst," I hissed, getting his attention and calling him over with my finger. "They had to end the baby shower early because Mrs. Magenta's water broke," I whispered.

"Really?" he squawked, spitting cookie bits everywhere.

"Yes," I said, "and be quiet. They're taping, remember?"

He nodded and gave me a thumbs-up.

"What's it mean that her water broke?"

"It means Mrs. Magenta's going to have her baby now."

"What? Now? How do you know that?"

"I saw it happen in the grocery store once. A pregnant lady's water broke, and it went everywhere."

"What went everywhere?" Mark asked.

"A baby is surrounded in a sac of water that protects it while it's in the mommy's belly," Scott explained. "When the sac breaks, the water spills out and then the baby comes next. They had the Mississippi River right there in aisle nine."

"The water comes from inside the woman?" Mark asked, making sure he had it straight.

"Yup."

"Dude, that's nasty."

"That's life," Scott said.

So that explained Natalie's text, but it also left me with a new question. A scary one. Fortunately, Natalie and Randi showed up right then, so I didn't have to rely on Mark and Scott for my answer.

"Did you get my text?" Natalie asked when she came in.

"Yes," I said. "Natalie, Mrs. Magenta wasn't supposed to have her baby yet. Will it be okay?"

"She's early, but close enough to her actual due date that everything should be okay. It's not like the old days, Trev. Hospitals are equipped and ready for these things."

I sighed. "That's good."

"It's sweet that you're worried," she said, grasping my hand.

Whew, I thought. *She thinks I'm sweet, not stupid.* I smiled. I could've stayed like that for the rest of the day, but Gavin finished up his interview and came to check on us—and Connie Stewart was with him.

"Hey, you made it," he said when he spotted Natalie and Randi.

"The shower ended early because Mrs. Magenta's water broke. She's on her way to the hospital to have the baby," Scott said, reporting the facts.

"Whoa," Gavin said.

"She's okay, Gav. Don't worry," Randi added.

He nodded.

"Are these your friends?" Connie asked, looking us over.

"Yes," Gavin replied.

"Well, since they're here, I think we should do a quick segment with them, too."

"Great idea!" Scott cheered.

"With us?" Natalie said, sitting up tall and straightening her skirt.

"You must be Natalie?" Connie said.

"Yes. It's a pleasure to meet you, Ms. Stewart."

"Likewise," Connie replied. She turned to Randi next. "So you must be Randi. And you must be Scott." He was easy to pick out. "Which means you guys must be Trevor and Mark, though I'm not sure who's who."

"I'm with stupid," Mark said, pointing at me. I swear, he was the goof-off king.

"So you're Mark." She had him pegged.

After our quick introductions Ms. Stewart brought us into the filming area, and we taped a short segment. She had us tell the camera our names and she asked a few questions, and then she closed things down with a Natalie-style monologue. And it was a good one.

"America, these are modern-day kids with old-school values. When a friend needs help, they are there for one another—time and time again. I hope their story inspires you like it has me. I'm Connie Stewart, and on behalf of the Recruits, I'm saying, 'Have a razzle-dazzle day, America.'"

NATALIE KURTSMAN
ASPIRING LAWYER
Kurtsman Law Offices

BRIEF #20
February: Baby Magenta

Mrs. Magenta had a baby boy. He surprised everyone by deciding to show up four weeks ahead of schedule, but we were excited to have him here. I'd told Trevor his coming early was no cause for alarm, but that wasn't entirely true.

Four weeks is early—no matter the advancements we've seen in medicine and technology—so there were risks and potential complications present. For instance, the baby's lungs wouldn't be mature yet; he might have jaundice, which meant he'd be yellow in color; he might not be feeding well, and he'd probably be tiny. On the bright side, all of these issues were manageable. But still, I saw no point in telling Trevor any of this and giving him reason to worry when worrying wouldn't do the baby any good, so I kept it to myself. (You might say I was following Scott's playbook from the fire fiasco; I'll give credit where credit is due.)

What I failed to realize about the baby coming early was that it also meant he had to be kept in the hospital. I expected him to be there for a few days and then go home with his proud parents. Not the case. Premature babies, such as Mrs. Magenta's son, sometimes needed to stay in the hospital until they were finally strong enough to go home. Mrs. Magenta was allowed to leave, but what new mother wants to leave her baby behind? She and Mr. Magenta traveled back and forth every day, spending as much time as they could with their newborn son.

I had wanted to go to the hospital on the night Mrs. Magenta's water broke, but that was clearly out of the question. First off, labor can take a long time, especially with the first baby. Apparently I made Mother and Father agonize for close to fifteen hours before I decided to come out. And second, to reduce the risk of infection for a premature baby, there were no visitors allowed. Thus, we were forced to wait.

Perhaps you've noticed that I haven't mentioned the baby's name yet. That's because he arrived before Mr. and Mrs. Magenta had settled on one. So while waiting for the green light to be able to visit the little guy, I used *The Razzle-Dazzle Show* to enlist everyone's help in finding the perfect name. After three weeks, I had collected enough suggestions that I could've published a baby-naming book—even after discarding the duplicates—but Mr. and Mrs. Magenta didn't need my book by then.

"This is Eric Wesley," Mrs. Magenta said, introducing her newborn son to us when we were finally able to visit her at home. He was absolutely precious, swaddled tight and nestled in her arms. Mr. Magenta stood nearby, gloating; he was a very proud father.

"I thought he didn't have a name yet," Scott said.

"He didn't, not until a few days ago, when Mom brought Dad here to meet him for the first time. When I put the baby into Dad's lap, Dad smiled and muttered Eric's name. That's when I knew."

"So he's named after your brother?" Scott said.

"Yes."

"Then who's Wesley?" he asked next.

"Dad," Mrs. Magenta answered.

"Coach's name is 'Wesley'?"

"Yes. And this little guy is Eric Wesley, named after two of the best men I've ever known."

"I think you've given him the perfect name," Gavin said.

"Me too," Mrs. Magenta agreed.

After getting all of his questions answered, Scott kept his distance, as did the other guys. They did the look-not-touch thing. It was funny to see them more petrified of a little baby than they had been of Stonebreaker. So it was just Randi and me who took turns holding him, and that was fine because it meant we got to hold him longer.

"I think I see a future gymnast," Randi said when she had him in her arms.

"I see a lawyer—or president," I commented.

"Quarterback," Gavin chimed.

"Maybe a pop star?" Trevor mused.

"Archaeologist," Scott said. "And scuba diver. And—"

"No," Mark said, cutting him off. "You're all wrong. Dude's going to be a garbage man by day and race car driver by night."

"Ugh," I groaned.

"Wrong," Mrs. Magenta said, which made us laugh.

"Eric will be anything he wants," Mr. Magenta said. "The sky's the limit—but we hope he's like all of you."

Until that moment, I wasn't sure I'd ever thought of myself as a role model—maybe because I didn't have any younger siblings—but I liked the idea. I left her house feeling quite happy. I wished I could've held on to that feeling for a little longer, but a heavy dose of sad was next in line.

SCOTT

The best part about going to Mrs. Magenta's house was all the food. When you have a baby, people make you all kinds of stuff. Mr. Magenta had two lasagnas, a chicken parm dish, and some crazy casserole thing to eat, but I helped him with his brownies and cookies.

It was nice to see Mr. and Mrs. Magenta and their new son, but it was boring, too. Babies don't do anything. And you can break them if you don't do the holding part right. It's not like tucking a football under your arm. So the only ones who held him were Randi and Natalie because they weren't chicken.

"Babies are good at eating, sleeping, and pooping," Mr. Magenta told me. He must've noticed I was bored.

"Those are impressive stats," I said.

"Next time I'll show you how to change a dirty diaper," Mrs. Magenta teased. "It'll be your new secret-weapon play."

"No, thank you," I replied. "No amount of practice will get me ready for that."

Everyone found that funny and laughed, but I wasn't fooling

around. Changing dirty diapers sounded scarier than Stone-breaker.

Even though baby Eric was boring, I had fun visiting. I liked when we surprised the baby with our present before leaving. We gave him a copy of *Charlotte's Web* signed by all of the Recruits.

"Thank you," Mrs. Magenta said. "This will be our first read-aloud. It's perfect."

"My favorite is the goose, goose, goose, and the way she talks, talks, talks," I said.

There was more laughing after that, but not from the baby because he was still boring. He was sleeping. We took that as our cue and said our goodbyes and left. Everyone headed home, but not me. I was going to the Senior Center because we were having dinner with Grandpa. I'd planned to tell him all about our visit because he still hadn't met the baby, but we never got around to talking about that stuff.

The Senior Center wasn't the same place when we got there that night. All the fun and smiles and happy faces had stayed at Mrs. Magenta's. I remembered Grandpa being sad and lonely before he moved there, but I was too little to re-member much of what he looked like after Grandma died. If I could remember, I'd bet he looked like what I saw when I got to his room.

Grandpa's eyes were red like he'd been crying and rubbing them, and he was sitting all alone in the dark and quiet.

"Gampa, turn the lights on," Mickey shouted.

"Dad, is everything all right?" Mom asked. "What's wrong?" She took the words right out of my mouth.

"We lost Coach this afternoon," he said.

GAVIN

When Mom said Scott was on the phone, I was kinda confused. I'd just seen him at Magenta's, so I didn't know why he'd
be calling. But you know Scott. When I picked up the phone
and said hello, he didn't waste any time beating around the
bush. He came right out and told me.

"Coach died."

14

GRIEVING AND HEALING

GAVIN

It was sudden. Real sudden. But that's how life can be some-times, and I'd been shown that more than once already. That's why you have to play every play like it's your last. That was Coach's advice.

I was beating myself up after he died. I knew something like this could happen, but I'd still never made it back to visit him. And now it was too late. Game over.

But it wasn't game over for me. Somehow I was supposed to find the strength to keep playing 'cause even after bad stuff happens, the world keeps spinning. The sun keeps rising and setting, and you need to keep on keeping on. Well, that's easier said than done. Mom and Dad saw that I was hurting pretty bad and came into my room to check on me after they said good night to Megs and Otis.

"Hi, *niño*." Mom spoke softly.

"Hi," I said.

"How're you holdin' up?" Dad asked, wheeling his chair closer.

I shrugged. I woulda started crying if I tried talking.

Mom sat next to me on my bed. "*Niño,* after coming to America, I never made it back home to see my mama and papa before they passed."

I looked at her. I never knew that.

"I know how you feel."

My eyes blurred.

"You need to give yourself time to grieve," Dad said, "but don't keep beatin' yourself up. Coach knew you were busy bein' a great son, doin' everything you could to help me and your mom and sister. He was proud of you, not mad at you."

"You made Coach's life better, and he made yours better," Mom said. "You shared a very special friendship. Remember that and feel good about the time you did have together. Hold tight to those memories."

She kissed my cheek, and Dad patted my leg. They said good night and turned out my lights.

One thing I learned is that getting through rough patches takes time, but it also takes family and friends by your side. I had the best family. They made me feel lucky even when I was down in the dumps.

NATALIE KURTSMAN
ASPIRING LAWYER
Kurtsman Law Offices

BRIEF #21
February: The Elephant in the Room

Not to be boastful, but one of my strengths is planning special events, such as the joint wedding vows renewal the previous year or, more recently, Mrs. Magenta's baby shower, but I was not interested in planning Coach's funeral. It most certainly qualified as special—extra special, even—but I didn't want to get involved; it didn't feel right. I shared my reservations with Mother and Father, and they assured me that was probably for the better.

"Sometimes you need to know when to take a backseat," Father said. "You don't want to step on anyone's toes, especially during personal times such as these. Your role is to be there to comfort and listen as needed."

You're likely familiar with the often-heard catchphrase "Mother knows best." Well, I'd like to add, sometimes a father knows best. I decided that the smartest way for me to fulfill my role was by continuing to do what I knew best. *The Razzle-Dazzle Show* had to go on.

Mr. Allen was a team player and filled in for Mrs. Woods while she was out, and we continued to bring Lake View Middle our broadcast. I thought it'd be wise if we kept it simple as we made our way through rough waters, so we stuck to the basics: the weather, announcements, and sports recaps. To be honest, it was all rather bland and melancholy. But we had the antidote for that—Scott.

Let me introduce another often-spoken metaphorical expression: the elephant in the room. Simply put, this expression is used when referring to the thing that is on everyone's mind but no one is acknowledging or talking about—except when you have Scott.

"Don't you think we should do something about Coach?" he asked after one of our shows. He just came right out and said it.

Our response was stunned silence. Coach was the elephant—the thing we weren't talking about because we didn't know how and we didn't want to upset Gavin.

"When somebody important and influential dies, TV news shows usually put together a tribute to honor that person. Don't you think we should do something like that for Coach?" Scott continued.

The cat still had our tongues, but then . . .

"Yes," Gavin croaked. "Yes."

That was all the okay we needed. We got to work.

SCOTT

Not everyone at school knew Coach like we did, but after watching our tribute, they were going to feel like they did. We came up with the best game plan.

My job was to video people at the Senior Center sharing memories of Coach. I got that job because I'd already proven I was good at it. I started with Eddie because she was the first person I saw when I got to the center, and I was too excited to wait. I also talked to Agnes and Grandpa. These were my favorite things they said.

Eddie: You know, I'm no slouch. I'm still pretty sharp. I've gotta be since I'm dealing with Agnes all the time. But I was no match for Coach. That man was a quiet thinker. He was always paying attention, always looking ahead, and always looking out for his family. Even when he got confused, family was on his mind.

Agnes: What a person says tells you a lot about him. A person's actions can tell you even more. But seeing how other people respond to a person reveals the most—and there wasn't anybody in Coach's company who didn't love him dearly and want to hang on to every word he said. He was special.

Grandpa: *How lucky I was to have met Coach. When Ellie, my wife, died, I lost my best friend. Coach showed me you can have more than one best friend in a lifetime. I'll miss him.*

Natalie worked with Trevor and Mark to edit my videos, and they added music to the background to make them even better. Grandpa was able to get us Coach's old scrapbook, so Gavin and Randi went through it and found different pictures and memorabilia to include in our film. Trevor and Mark added Gavin's narration in those parts.

My camp and Big Apple documentaries were really good, but when we got done, Coach's tribute was a step up. It was perfect—and I wasn't the only one who thought so.

Trevor

It was Scott who came up with the idea for the tribute, Gavin who gave the okay, and Natalie who immediately put us to work. The cool thing was that Mark and I got to use a few of the tricks we'd picked up from the *Good Morning America* crew. We added music and Gavin's voice in places and even adjusted backgrounds in parts. We did a bang-up job. The end product was really something. It made all of us feel good inside.

After seeing our film, Mr. Allen did a cool thing. He got in touch with Mrs. Woods and Mrs. Magenta and told them they needed to see it. We didn't know that until they showed up one morning before *The Razzle-Dazzle Show.*

"Mrs. Woods? Mrs. Magenta? What're you doing here?" Scott exclaimed.

"We came to tell you something," Mrs. Woods replied.

"Are we in trouble?" Scott asked.

"No," Mrs. Magenta said, and chuckled.

"We came to thank you for your touching tribute to Coach," Mrs. Woods continued. "It's . . ."

"Perfect," Mrs. Magenta finished.

"Yes, perfect," Mrs. Woods agreed. "We'd like to invite all of you to join us for a celebration."

"A celebration?" Scott repeated.

"That's right. Instead of some sad old funeral, we'd like to have a day where we celebrate Coach's life," Mrs. Woods explained, "inspired by your tribute."

"Like a party?" Scott asked.

"Sure," Mrs. Magenta said. "We'd like to have it on the high school football field, where Dad coached. Will you help us plan it? Maybe you can be our videographer?"

"Yippee!" Scott cheered.

I'm not usually the one to come up with the big ideas, but I did this time. It hit me as soon as Mrs. Magenta mentioned the football field. I made Mark hang back with me after we finished with the broadcast that morning, and I told Mr. Allen what I wanted to do.

Randi

Mom and I swung by Gav's house after dinner one night because that's what friends do, they check on each other. I said hi to Meggie and Otis and Mr. and Mrs. Davids, and then I went and found Gav. He was outside by his tire target, but he wasn't throwing passes. He was sitting with his back pressed against the tree. I sat next to him.

"This reminds me of the bathroom stall," I said.

Gav nodded.

"What're you thinking this time?" I asked.

He shrugged.

"I heard that if someone dies in your dream, it means a baby is going to be born."

"That's random."

"Not really," I responded.

"Did someone die in your dream?"

"I don't know."

"What?"

"Gav, when I first realized how close Mom and Jacob were

becoming, I got really worried and scared. I thought Mom was going to make us move so that she could be with him."

"You mean, move away for good? Like, forever?"

"Yes."

"Why didn't you say anything?"

It was my turn to shrug. "I don't know. It stirred up all kinds of feelings. I started having bad dreams. In one of them I was in a packed car with Mom, driving down the highway with tears streaming down my cheeks. I was reaching for you out the back window, but I couldn't touch you. You were saying something. I could see your mouth moving, but I couldn't hear you. And then we crashed and the car flipped and rolled and I flew through the air. Then I woke up."

"You think you died?"

"I don't know, but that was the last dream I had before Mrs. Magenta's baby was born."

"You're not moving, right?"

"No."

"Good. Losing you would be the worst, especially after just losing Coach."

I almost said something about my confused feelings then, but I didn't. And I felt like Gav was close to saying something, too, but he didn't. And that was okay. That was enough.

"Are you looking forward to Coach's celebration?" I asked.

"I am. I think it's gonna help me say goodbye."

I reached over and took his hand. We stayed there, quietly sitting together for a long while after that.

15

A CELEBRATION

Natalie Kurtsman
ASPIRING LAWYER
Kurtsman Law Offices

```
BRIEF #22
March: The Celebration
```

Given that Mrs. Woods and Mrs. Magenta decided that a celebration of Coach's life was the best way to say goodbye, I'd
say Father's advice about taking a backseat had been incredibly wise. I hadn't ever had reason to ponder death before,
and I definitely wanted to be respectful of people's beliefs,
but putting someone into the ground for the rest of eternity
did strike me as rather morbid. I much preferred the idea of
cremation, which was what Mrs. Woods and Mrs. Magenta
had decided. There were several reasons for that: (1) It was
Coach's game plan, (2) Mrs. Magenta wanted to keep her
father's ashes in a special urn alongside her brother's—Eric
had been cremated—so that she could take them with her
should she and Mr. Magenta ever move again, and (3) Some of
Coach's ashes would be spread on the football field where he'd

spent his days coaching and where, unbeknownst to us, some of Eric's remains had been scattered years before.

Thus, Warrior Field became the site of Coach's celebration. Not where I would want my ashes sprinkled, but very fitting for Coach—perfect, actually. Also perfect was the weather on the day of the ceremony. It was chilly, but sunny with a slight breeze. The slight breeze was key because a stronger wind had the potential to blow Coach's remains all over us—a truly mortifying thought. According to Scott, however, it wasn't the sun or breeze but the presence of seagulls covering the football field when we first arrived that was perfect. After he got done explaining, I had to agree.

He and I had this conversation before anyone else showed up. It should come as no surprise that it was the two of us who were the first to arrive. We were there early not only because that was in our nature, but also because we had important roles for the day. Scott was the videographer, and Mrs. Woods had asked me to be the emcee (master of ceremonies). Of course, I'd agreed.

As people arrived, my first task would be to hand out the programs I had created. It wasn't that we needed the program, but I wanted everyone to have something to take with them to remember the day. For me personally, the program wouldn't be necessary, though. There was a moment that occurred before the ceremony even took place that will be forever stamped in my brain.

Many people came to celebrate Coach. Some I knew; many I didn't. There were quite a few of his former players who made the trip, which I found very touching. There were even some old coaches he'd played against, and Director Ruggelli brought a busload from the Senior Center. But when I saw Mrs. Holmes and Nicky and Robbie, a swell of feelings and emotions flooded my body. I couldn't explain how they'd found out about the ceremony or even why they'd chosen to attend, but none of that mattered. I stood frozen and watched Nicky go up and shake Gavin's hand. I watched Mrs. Holmes hug Mrs. Davids. And through blurry eyes, I watched Robbie walk up and present me with a single flower.

Coach's celebration had brought out the best in us. How fitting.

How perfect, I thought.

SCOTT

Coach's celebration kicked off at one o'clock sharp. Game time. We didn't have the national anthem or a coin toss, but Natalie did prepare some opening remarks. I made sure I got them on video when she stepped to the podium. As videographer, I was just trying to capture as much of the day as I could so that Mrs. Woods and Mrs. Magenta would have the memories.

"I'm Natalie Kurtsman, your master of ceremonies. I'd like to welcome you to Warrior Field and thank you for coming. In addition, I'd like to make it clear that we are here to have a razzle-dazzle time celebrating the life of this great man, Wesley Woods, whom many of us affectionately knew as Coach."

My filming got bouncy then because I was clapping and cheering after she said that.

"At this point in our program anyone who'd like to say a few words about Coach is invited up to the microphone," Natalie said, and stepped away from the podium.

I was surprised when I saw that Meggie Davids was the

Trevor

I stepped to the podium after everyone had finished saying what they wanted to about Coach. I imagine everyone expected me to get up there and do more of the same, but I didn't. That was my first surprise.

"I'm not up here to talk about Coach," I said, "but I am up here to help us honor him. When I found out that today's ceremony was taking place on Coach's old field, which happens to be our high school football field, otherwise known as Warrior Field, I approached Mr. Allen with an idea."

I turned around and left the podium. I could hear murmurs and whispers. People were confused. What was I doing? They watched as Mark and I walked over to the scoreboard, where two stepladders lay on the ground waiting for us. We stood the ladders upright. Then together we climbed to the tops and each grasped a corner of the sign we had covering the scoreboard. The sign had Coach's name and dates of birth and death written on it, similar to what you'd find on a gravestone. To all attending, the sign was a nice touch for the ceremony, but really it was only a temporary cover. I looked at Mark, and on three we pulled it down, unveiling our surprise.

It took a second, but once everyone realized what they were seeing, they were on their feet and clapping. Painted on the scoreboard were the words "WESLEY WOODS FIELD." Warrior Field had been renamed and dedicated in honor of Coach. It was perfect.

Randi

I didn't talk from the podium, but I did have a talk. It happened after the ceremony when I realized that I had to pass Coach's words on to somebody important.

I asked Mom for the keys and started toward the car.

"Randi, where are you going?" Natalie asked when she saw me leaving.

"Natalie, sometimes a woman's gotta do what a woman's gotta do."

She scowled, and I laughed.

"Relax. I'm not blackmailing anyone," I said. "I'll be right back."

I jogged off. When I got to the car, I grabbed my crutches from the trunk and I went and found Mr. Davids.

"I'm done with these now, Mr. Davids. They served me well, and I don't mean to be superstitious, but I'd like to give them to you for good luck."

"Thank you, Randi, but I don't need them quite yet."

"No, but you will soon. Mr. Davids, I didn't have much

direct interaction with Coach, but the one thing he did tell me was that my recovery after getting injured was all about attitude. And he was right. You've got to stay positive, Mr. Davids. You can do it."

"Thank you," he said, taking the crutches from me. "And, Randi, thank you for being there for Gavin during these hard times. I hope you two always have each other."

"Don't worry, Mr. Davids. I'm not going anywhere."

GAVIN

Coach's celebration was nice, but hard. Real hard. Saying goodbye to someone like that is way tougher than football. But I got through it. And I said the things I wanted to say. I could hear Coach saying, "Of course you got through it. You're a football player." That thought made me smile. I guessed that was a good sign 'cause I hadn't been doing much smiling.

Nicky Holmes and his mom and little brother showing up was something I'll remember. I didn't talk to Nicky, but that didn't matter. His being there was all that needed to be said. I'll remember the different things people said about Coach and I'll remember when Trevor and Mark revealed Coach's name on our scoreboard. Next year I'd be playing on Wesley Woods Field. Coach would be with me every play. That definitely made me smile.

The day was full of special moments like that, but it was later that night, when I was back home leaning against my tire-target tree, just taking a few moments to myself, that the most important thing happened.

"Hi, Gavvy," Megs said, cuddling up next to me.

"Hi, Megs," I said. *So much for time to myself,* I thought.

"Wow, Gavvy, look." She pointed to the sky. "That star is so big and bright."

I smiled. "That's Coach," I said.

"Did the angels help him get up there?"

"That's right."

"He's got the best seat in the house, Gavvy. He can watch you throwing all your passes from up there."

My little sister had just used her superpowers on me. I wiped my eyes. "Yes, he can," I said, smiling more.

There Coach was—the perfect star.

Epilogue

NATALIE KURTSMAN
ASPIRING LAWYER
Kurtsman Law Offices

BRIEF: #23
June: A Final Razzle-Dazzle

Mr. Allen ended the school year in the same fashion he'd started it—with an impromptu assembly. There was, however, one minor difference this time—the Recruits knew about it in advance. The reason being, Mr. Allen wanted our final *Razzle-Dazzle Show* to broadcast live from his event. We jumped at the opportunity.

The six of us and Mrs. Woods met at school even earlier than early on that day so that we had enough time to get our equipment moved and set up in the auditorium. Mr. Allen was also there to help and to make sure we had everything that we needed, which we did. Though a bit of a hassle, we pulled it off and were ready to go. The only thing missing was the audience, and they began filing in right on cue.

I hadn't stopped to consider what broadcasting in front of a group of people would actually look or feel like. It had sounded fun when Mr. Allen had proposed the idea, so I'd jumped without hesitation, but now that the event was here, now that there was a packed house sitting in front of me, I had the jitters.

"Okay," Mr. Allen said to us. "Looks like we've got everyone assembled. It's time. Do your thing."

I took my seat behind the desk, and Mark dimmed the lights.

"In three, two, one," Trevor whispered.

"Good morning, Lake View Middle. I'm Natalie Kurtsman, coming to you live from our school auditorium."

Trevor panned the crowd with his camera, and a roar of cheers went up. My jitters were instantly replaced by goose bumps.

"We have a special show planned for you this morning, with a surprise announcement from Mr. Allen coming up soon, but first, a look at the weather. Let's hear it for our weatherman, Scott Mason."

The auditorium went bonkers as Scott strode out to take his place in front of the camera. That alone made my day—but there was much more to come.

We ran through our normal routine of announcements and recaps, and then I introduced Mr. Allen. He took his spot in front of the camera, and Mrs. Woods and Mrs. Magenta joined him off to the side. I was surprised to see Mrs. Magenta, since technically she was out on maternity leave. I wondered where baby Eric could be, but when I glanced into the audience, I spotted Mr. Magenta standing against the wall, holding his son.

"One of the best things about being principal," Mr. Allen

372

began, "is that I get to be surrounded by passionate people. Teachers striving for excellence in their classrooms, coaches and teams in pursuit of perfection, and students daring to dream big.

"The group sitting up here onstage, known collectively as the Recruits, has made us laugh. They've surprised us, challenged us, and brought out the best in us, time and time again. They've inspired us. They've inspired me to start something new here at Lake View Middle School.

"Today marks the opening of the Lake View Middle School Hall of Fame. And I'd like to introduce our first six inductees."

Clapping and cheering broke out in the back. I looked and saw then that all of our parents were in attendance.

Mr. Allen proceeded to call us up one by one. With Mrs. Woods's and Mrs. Magenta's help, he presented each of us with an engraved plaque bearing our picture and name.

"It's your first Hall of Fame," Randi whispered to Gavin.

"With more to come," Mrs. Woods said, and winked.

"This is awesome!" Scott exclaimed.

Mr. Allen chuckled and gave him a high five. "Following the broadcast we will do a brief photo shoot, and then these plaques will be hung up on the wall outside my office," Mr. Allen announced. "I look forward to inducting another batch of students into the Lake View Middle School Hall of Fame at the end of next year, in what will become our new end-of-the-year tradition.

"I'll now turn things back over to Natalie so that she can wrap up. Thank you."

Mr. Allen, Mrs. Woods, and Mrs. Magenta left the stage under more applause, and we resumed our positions. I sat up straight and readied myself for what would be my final monologue.

"I speak for all of the Recruits when I say we're sad to be leaving but proud of what we've accomplished. We were able to make a difference with your help, Lake View Middle, and for that we extend our biggest thank-you. Of course, a special shout-out goes to Mr. Allen, Mrs. Woods, Mrs. Magenta, and our parents.

"We hope some of you sixth and seventh graders sign on to keep the morning broadcast running. As for us, we'll be taking our show on the road. We fully intend to shake things up at the high school."

The audience laughed at that comment, but the Recruits eyed me wearily. They knew I wasn't bluffing. *What's she got planned now?* I could hear them asking. I didn't know yet, but whatever it was, it would be worth remembering.

"I'm Natalie Kurtsman, saying, 'Have a razzle-dazzle day.'"

ACKNOWLEDGMENTS

Huge thanks to my daughter, Emma, for being my trusted reader. Your name might end up on the front cover yet. To Beth for always helping me make decisions about the hard scenes and sentences. To Lily and Anya for the gymnastics lessons and suggestions—Randi appreciates it. And to my dogs, Jack and Potter, for getting me away from the desk and out on our hikes, where important work in the head takes place.

Thank you to my agent, Paul Fedorko, for sticking with me every step of the way.

A huge thank-you to the entire team at Random House Children's Books for all of your help making another one of my books look *perfect*. Special mention to Leslie Mechanic for a third round of Gavin's sketches. And to Beverly Horowitz—for everything.

Gavin would agree, the relationship between an author and his editor is as critical as that between a quarterback and his coach. When it comes to my editor, Françoise Bui, I'll never be able to fully express my gratitude. I've scored a touchdown. Your comments, patience, keen insights, and friendship are invaluable to me.

And finally, an extra-special shout-out to Anya for giving this book its title!

ABOUT THE AUTHOR

ROB BUYEA taught third and fourth graders for six years; then he taught high school biology and coached wrestling for seven years. Currently, he is a full-time writer and lives in Massachusetts with his wife and daughters. He is the author of *The Perfect Score* and *The Perfect Secret,* companion novels to *The Perfect Star.* His first novel, *Because of Mr. Terupt,* was selected as an E. B. White Read Aloud Honor Book and a Cybils Honor Book. It has also won seven state awards and was named to numerous state reading lists. *Mr. Terupt Falls Again* and *Saving Mr. Terupt* are companion novels to *Because of Mr. Terupt.* Visit him online at robbuyea.com and on Facebook, and follow @Rob Buyea on Twitter.

Seven kids.
Seven voices.
One special teacher
who brings them together.

ROB BUYEA'S beloved
mr. terupt series

Delacorte Press